D0768364

NIGHTSTALKERS: TIME PATROL

May 2015

NEW YORK TIMES BESTSELLING AUTHOR

BOB MAYER

AREA 51

THE NIGHTSTALKERS BOOK 4

NIGHTSTALKERS: TIME PATROL

This is a work of fiction. Names, characters, organizations, places, events, and incidents are either products of the author's imagination or are used fictitiously.

Text copyright © 2015 by Bob Mayer
All rights reserved.

No part of this book may be reproduced, or stored in a retrieval system, or transmitted in any form or by any means, electronic, mechanical, photocopying, recording, or otherwise, without express written permission of the publisher.

Published by 47North, Seattle

www.apub.com

Amazon, the Amazon logo, and 47North are trademarks of Amazon.com, Inc., or its affiliates.

ISBN-13: 9781477821879
ISBN-10: 1477821872

Cover design by Jason Blackburn

Library of Congress Control Number: 2014950613

Printed in the United States of America

To all the Special Operators who have paid the ultimate price.
Particularly those who died on 28 June 2005 during
Operation Red Wings.

Please donate to the Special Operations Warrior Foundation
www.specialops.org, which helps fund education for the children
of these departed comrades in arms.

Or donate to www.warrior2warrior.org, which helps Special
Operations troops deal with traumatic brain injury (TBI) and
post-traumatic stress disorder (PTSD), founded by a widow from
my former unit: 10th Special Forces Group (Airborne).

Thank you.

The long unmeasured pulse of time moves everything. There is nothing hidden that it cannot bring to light, nothing known that may not become unknown. Nothing is impossible.

—Sophocles

Stuff happens; sometimes really bad stuff.

A Nada Yada

WHEN IT CHANGED

When it changed, Roland, stone-cold killer, otherwise nice guy, and weapons man for the Nightstalkers, had the stock of a sniper rifle tucked tight in to his shoulder with a righteous target approaching, and that made him happy. Neeley, a usually stone-cold killer from the Cellar, was in overwatch, with her own sniper rifle, and she was acting wonky. That made Roland unhappy since he liked her, and *like* for Roland was the equivalent of rabid devotion in a well-trained attack dog. However, it all balanced out and mattered little since he was in combat mode, and feelings were of no consequence to him in that mode. There was only the mission.

Roland was a man who could live and flourish in the here and now.

That's a rare, and valuable, trait.

It was going to get a lot more valuable.

It changed for Scout—now eighteen years old and almost two years past her first encounter, run-in, kerfuffle, whatever, involving the Nightstalkers—with a whiff of bacon. She'd only smelled real bacon outside the confines of her home; never inside. Inside it was always fakon, vacon, or one of the other imposters. If you gotta fake it, Scout had always reasoned ever since she was old enough to reason, which had been pretty dang young, then isn't imitation the sincerest form of flattery, and one should go with the original? Her rail-thin mother, who counted each calorie as if it were mortal a sin, did not see things that way.

Thus the mystery of the odor permeating the house.

For a moment Scout lay in bed wondering if perhaps it was wafting in from the old house next door, the one with the barn where she stabled her horse, Comanche. Out of the old stone chimney. People with a barn and a stone chimney had to eat bacon.

But in this relatively new house with its fake gas fireplace, with Scout's mother ruling the kitchen, with the aroma of honest-to-goodness real bacon filling the air, Scout questioned reality.

That's a good trait, one the Nightstalkers had found valuable in the past and would need in the future.

If there was to be one.

It changed for Nada, team sergeant of the Nightstalkers, the most experienced member of the group, a man who'd stared death in the eye and French kissed the Grim Reaper (figuratively, although stranger things have happened on Nightstalker missions), with irritating voices singing "It's a Small World," the whiny tune echoing in his head as his niece Zoey tried to spin their teacup faster and faster.

Definitely down a rabbit hole of dubious merit.

They'd gone from hell to a deeper hell, was Nada's estimation, walking from It's a Small World to The Mad Tea Party. He was not the type of person Disneyland had been designed for, and he was a bit disappointed Zoey was attacking each new ride with such zest. Of course she was just a kid, but still. He expected better of someone who shared his bloodline.

As they spun about, Nada wondered, how small was the world really?

And why did Disneyland bother him so much and on a deeper level than irritating songs?

Little did he know, he was about to find out the answers to both.

And the answers were not good.

<hr>

It changed at Area 51 deep inside the sprawling complex set in the middle of Nowhere, Nevada, because many problems on the cutting edge of science, physics, and the weird and the wonderful started at Area 51. But this time it was not in the labs where scientists tested the outer boundaries of man's knowledge, occasionally traveling from genius to stupid at lightspeed (literally sometimes) and requiring the Nightstalkers to clean up their messes. This time it was in the repository of the results of all those tests and so much more: the Archives. If the Ark of the Covenant was indeed found by some Indiana-Jones-type character, it would have been stored here, and it would have fit right in with many of the other weird and wonderful and frightening items gathered from around the world and hidden away deep under the sort-of-secret-but-definitely-most-secure facility in the continental United States.

Even though the CIA had acknowledged the place existed (it was on Google Earth now for frak's sake), that didn't mean they were holding an open house any time soon.

It changed with Ivar—or rather the sudden lack thereof, of Ivar—which, considering Ivar's recent history and what had happened during the *Fun in North Carolina*, might not be as strange as it seems.

But Ivar and Doc—who was with Ivar, at least initially— were both physicists, and they understood the law of entropy (or thought they did) and knew that when something was taken away, something was returned in kind (or thought they knew).

Or at least they understood a distorted law of entropy, which Doc would come up with later. Sort of.

If there was a later.

━━━━━━━━━

It changed at the Ranch, outside of Area 51 on the other side of Extraterrestrial Highway, but still pretty much Nowhere, Nevada, known to only a few as the headquarters of the Nightstalkers.

It was only because Eagle had a hippocampus twice that of a London cabbie, and the resultant phenomenal memory, that it was noticed at all. Noticing didn't mean awareness though.

Which meant Eagle was going to have to learn something new. If he was given the time.

It changed for Moms by figuratively traveling into her past, both in place and time. She was already in the place, having made the drive of tears back home. She was sitting on the front porch of the abandoned shotgun shack where she'd grown up in the middle of Nowhere, Kansas. Interstate 80 was to the south, across the flat plains, but so far away that no sound traveled from the eighteen-wheelers racing across the middle of the country.

There was no other house in sight, just miles and miles of slightly undulating fields, and despite all the years since she'd left, Moms still had a sick feeling in the pit of her stomach. It had started when she'd entered Kansas and grown stronger every mile she drew closer to "home." The house was empty, long deserted. Her younger brothers never came out here, smarter than she was, understanding some memories only brought pain.

It seemed Moms was a masochist, going back to her roots in order to remember.

But sometimes, going into the past is necessary in order to move forward.

There are variations on that, such as changing the present in order to move forward, which Moms was soon to discover.

It had changed for Foreman, closing in on seventy years of service, in February 1945 in an area called the Devil's Sea, off the coast of Japan, in the waning days of World War II. The event was after he and his pilot were forced to ditch because of engine trouble. Minutes later, the rest of their squadron simply vanished into a strange mist in that enigmatic part of the world. No trace of the other planes or crews were ever found.

Then it was reinforced in December of that same year, the war finally over, on the other side of the world, when he begged off a mission because of the same premonition he'd had before the Devil's Sea flight, and watched Flight 19 disappear from the radar in an area called the Bermuda Triangle.

He'd determined then and there that he had to know the Truth.

So he'd gone from the Marine Corps into the short-lived precursor to the CIA, the Central Intelligence Group, in 1946, then morphed with it into the CIA, where he moved upward, and, much more importantly inward, into the darkness of the most covert parts of various branches whose letters and designations changed over the years. But their missions grew more and more obscure, to the point where he'd outlived and outserved all his contemporaries so no one in the present was quite sure who exactly he worked for anymore or what his mission was.

If he worked for anyone at all.

Not that anyone really cared.

They should.

He was now known as the Crazy Old Man in the covert bowels of the Pentagon and by some other names, associated with bowel movements.

How crazy he was, some people were about to discover.

CHAPTER 1

Cleopatra's Needle pierced the sudden downpour with the relative indifference of granite, having faced the many depredations of time in its 3,500 some-odd years of existence. However, just one hundred years in New York City's weather had done more damage to the hieroglyphics on the four faces of the obelisk, particularly the southwest corner, than over three millennia in Egypt's much drier climate. It wasn't the rain as much as the acid pollution rising from the city, some of which came back down in the rain.

Edith Frobish hated the rain for more than just the damage it did to the Needle. Still, she paused as she always did to look at the ancient Egyptian monument set, strangely, in Central Park in the middle of Manhattan, in the middle of New York City, far from its origin. The fact the obelisk had nothing to do with Cleopatra VII (yes, there were six before *that one*, but none had achieved *her* fame/infamy, so only the historically finicky added the number—count Edith among those who did) was a trick of historical "publicity," more notoriety, that Edith would never understand. Why name something for someone who had had nothing to do with it, other than ruling briefly a thousand years after the Needle was commissioned by the Eighteenth Dynasty Pharaoh, good old Thutmose III? He was considered the "Napoleon of Egypt,"

1

expanding the empire to its widest breadths, but did anyone remember his name? Nope. But they remembered Cleopatra, seventh with that name. Plus, few knew or cared there had been six Cleopatras before the one who'd bedded mighty Caesar, then not-quite-as-mighty Mark Antony, and then had a date with a snake.

Was it just because she'd snagged and shagged two notable Romans? Edith found such an idea misogynistic to the extreme, which showed that despite her brilliance and degrees, there was much she didn't know about the real world.

Edith also couldn't understand that Cleopatra's Needle sounded so much better than Thutmose's Obelisk. To her, the correct history should always win out over popularity.

She was rarely invited to parties.

Towering a surprising seventy feet high, weighing over two hundred and twenty tons, and covered in hieroglyphs, the Needle was part of a set of three, the others located in Paris and London. Technically, though, the structures were not a set, as Edith would tell anyone who bothered to ask.

Few did outside of the Patrol. But those inside cared very much about such things.

The one in London was a twin in size to the one here in New York, also commissioned by Thutmose, and they were both originally from Heliopolis, Egypt.

The one in Paris was commissioned by Ramses II, some time after old Thutmose's two, and was originally in Luxor. He also had the inscriptions carved on Thutmose's two to celebrate his own victories, trying to permanently write his own history.

Edith tried to focus on the inscriptions, but in this thunderstorm, being pelted by rain?

All three obelisks were moved by the Romans under Augustus (who'd taken down Cleopatra's second Roman, Mark Antony) to the Caesareum in Alexandria, a temple begun by Cleopatra to honor her first Roman lover, Julius Caesar, and completed by Augustus, who dedicated the temple to a cause he held dear: himself.

Narcissism seems a trait of emperors, or vice versa.

Thus, Cleopatra entered the path of the Needles tangentially, but not directly, in that she built the temple in front of which they were placed after her death. It all gets rather confusing.

But such distinctions in history can be important.

The New York obelisk was emplaced in Central Park in 1881 and Edith could regale one with tales of how it made its very difficult way from Egypt to New York and why, but that would be important if one day she were walking by and there was suddenly no obelisk.

That would be bad.

She viewed the Needle as a signpost of history that she checked religiously. But today, perhaps it was the downpour that kept her from looking closely enough, or else she might have seen something in the hieroglyphics that would have alerted her. But perhaps, given the vagaries of the variables, the story hadn't even changed yet.

But she had a job to do and was carrying things that shouldn't get wet, primarily lots and lots of documents. One would think in this digital age a thumb drive would do, but for her position, a thumb drive would not do. Documents were the original source and were also more secure. Back and forth to the various museums, the Archives, the Smithsonian, and ranging even further afield, covering the globe, as the situation required, Edith always came back with documents. Sometimes she came back with artwork costing millions of dollars, "borrowed" under the authority of the auspices of the museum, but really for the Patrol to analyze.

She never came back empty-handed.

On this trip she'd been gone only a few hours, having to dive into the stacks at the main branch of the New York Public Library to retrieve information someone in the Patrol had requested. Interestingly (the requests were always interesting, even the time someone had asked about the history of teddy bears), the RFI was about another obelisk, the largest one in the world, the Lateran Obelisk, so named because it was in the square opposite the Archbasilica of St. John Lateran.

In Rome.

Seemed the Egyptians had a hard time holding on to their obelisks.

Edith's head was now full of arcane facts about not only the Lateran Obelisk, but the history that was woven around it. Over thirty-seven meters high, the Lateran had over ten meters on Cleopatra's Needle. Why exactly someone on the Patrol had requested this particular piece of information, she had no clue (she was never given one for any of the many arcane requests), but the research, as always, had been fascinating, leading her from the Obelisk to the as-fascinating history of the Archbasilica. The research had cascaded upon her as she dove deeper and deeper into the stacks until she had accumulated enough for several volumes, which she was now going to have to distill down to a cogent, six-page report.

Always six pages. No more. Less was better; a mantra of the Patrol. But details were important, so they always ended up being six pages. She'd even begun shrinking the font size, until finally the Administrator noticed and told her to stop.

The research was why she loved her job. Boiling the research down to six pages or less; not so much.

And she still hated the rain.

Over the years she'd bought so many umbrellas, including brands that weren't supposed to blow out in the wind, but they eventually did. She'd been excited when she bought the umbrella favored by Queen Elizabeth because it was a clear dome, like a see-through mushroom, over her head. And it was used by a queen. But it still leaked in a downpour. They all eventually leaked and surrendered to the weather, so she'd given up on them.

So now she had a very good waterproof raincoat with big pockets sewn into the interior, like a professional shoplifter. In New York City one could get anything made without question or even a strange look. It had been as if someone came in to the tailor's shop every day and requested such a thing.

Perhaps they did.

She'd debated a long time about whether she could tax-deduct the raincoat.

In the end she didn't.

There were times, though, when the load was too big for the pockets, and she still had to cradle her old leather briefcase, stuffed full, in her arms and run with her burden, bending into the wind and rain in a semblance of a shield as she wound her way across Central Park.

So it really wasn't her fault that in her effort to protect the papers, and her ruminations on another obelisk, she might have missed a few things in the park and on Cleopatra's Needle. Then again, maybe she hadn't. She'd never know. She can be forgiven if she had, because very, very few people had noticed anything yet, and most never would until it was too late.

If it became too late, which was the whole point of what she was part of.

Such is the nature of time and many more variables. The *vagaries of variables*, a phrase the Administrator was fond of using and most of those around him were bored of hearing.

Plus, to be fair, she was also thinking about the art in the building behind her. That was the main reason she had her position. A position wasn't a job, by the way. She'd been told that early on. She had double majors, art and history, at the university, and at first hadn't understood the importance or the relevance of her expertise to the Patrol.

But eventually it made sense. Art is a timeless recorder of history. From the first drawings on the walls of caves, art is fixed. If the art changed—Edith shuddered, fearing where that led.

Because she was an art person, she didn't focus on people, which was another oversight for the day.

Edith shoved open the blank metal door decorated with AUTHORIZED PERSONNEL ONLY written in faded red on a rusting metal sign. The door was on the south side of the Metropolitan Museum of Art. The Met was on Fifth Avenue, but on the west side, in Central Park. The museum was accorded the privilege of being the only substantial building inside the massive rectangle of Central Park, granted the land by the City of New York in 1871, a decade before the Needle arrived.

And who says New Yorkers aren't cultured?

Actually, that was the exact reason why the Met was founded. Edith knew the history of the museum as she knew her art, because the two were intertwined. It was believed back in the nineteenth century that art "elevated" anyone who had access to it, making them better people. While other museums focused on geographic areas (usually the one they were in the middle of) or specific eras, from the very outset the Met strove to be "encyclopedic" in its collection. A visitor to the museum could figuratively cover the globe and the extent of civilization in one visit.

Central Park is the most visited urban park in the United States, with over thirty-five million visitors per year covering 840 acres smack-dab (as Mac, demolitions man for the Nightstalkers, and Texan, would say) in the middle of one of the most densely populated cities in the world. Hiding the Patrol there might seem folly, but it fell under the Purloined Letter theory that the best place to hide something was in plain sight. More importantly, there was the art.

Technically, though, the Patrol was not in plain sight.

Since its founding, the Met grew and grew until some of the original parts of the building were encapsulated inside the current sprawling structure, which was over twenty times the size of the first building. Viewed from above by Google Earth, the museum was a hodgepodge of add-ons, making it clear there had not been a master plan but rather spurts of expansion when the funds were available. The complex stretched for a quarter mile along Museum Mile in Manhattan with a current cumulation of over two million square feet of floor space for exhibits, offices, and, deep below, not officially counted in the square footage, something very, very different.

In sum, the Met represented the art of the world covering over five thousand years. A twitch in the life span of the planet, but covering the critical portion of what we like to call "civilization," as if humans, who've only existed for the blink of an eye in the long saga of the planet, were so important. Such is our hubris. Even more is the belief that we are actually civilized, a point a history major such as Edith Frobish could argue.

Stepping onto the dry marble as the door shut ponderously

behind her, Edith shook her head, spraying water about, even though her locks were cut short. She straightened, gaining several inches. She assumed the five foot eleven inches that God had chosen to fit her with and years of ballet training had refined. She had a long, beautiful neck, the sort of neck only great genes and dance give you. She had captured the hearts of many young men with that neck, men who'd been willing to ignore the equally long nose genetics had also bestowed with such largess.

But they eventually couldn't ignore the obsessiveness for exactness in almost all things in her life.

Edith was a firm believer in proportion. On others less secure, her nose might have led to a quick appointment with the best plastic surgeon in New York. But for her, it worked because it was perfectly in proportion to the rest of her, which was all slim, angled, and long. If any one of her friends—of which there were only two, not being a people person—had been forced into a one-word description of Edith, it would be "long." She was long, her memory was long, and her patience was long.

Even dampened by the rain, she smiled and said hello to Burt, the longtime guard on the employee side door, while she held up her badge, as per Protocol. The Patrol was very big on Protocol, as was the museum. The blank look he gave her and the way he actually squinted at her badge, she chalked up to too much imbibing the night before. Burt was a good man, but he did tend to indulge his off-hours with the soothing nothingness of beer. Technically, she didn't think he was a *guard* guard, really protecting something. That came further in. Like guards in most buildings in Manhattan, he was there to keep the homeless out when they sought a respite from weather. Apparently there were some of the masses the museum could not lift up.

Edith continued down the hallway, and then, where everyone else turned left, she turned right into a narrower, dimly lit corridor. A sign warned: CLOSED FOR CONSTRUCTION.

That sign had been there as long as Edith had been doing her job. It amazed her that no one showed curiosity about what might be taking so long to build. Then again, the Met was full of art people, not building people.

She passed through one of the strange transitions of versions of the building, going from an addition to an older part, where the outside wall of the original structure was now an interior wall of the new building. She was in what had been the workers' entrance back when an informal caste system dictated different entrances. An old elevator awaited, but there was a sign hanging on it that said it was OUT OF ORDER.

Edith had pondered that sign late at night, usually after a daring second glass of wine. It wasn't much of a deterrent (like the construction sign), because the only people it would stop were rule-followers, and rule-followers weren't a problem, were they?

(As a history major she should have known that rule-followers could be a huge problem; for example, Nazi Germany, but her pondering didn't go in that dark direction.)

Edith pushed the down button and waited, as she'd done so many times, and wondered where to have lunch. One of the benefits of working in Manhattan was that there were so many excellent places to eat within walking distance.

While she waited, her mind went in the other direction in time, to the past, to the day at Columbia when her art history professor had suggested she apply for a "special" position. At the time she'd been thrilled and wondered what unique thing he'd seen in her that she wasn't quite aware of, for over the years she'd realized it was not only her memory that was applauded but her patience as well. Not something she herself thought was so special, but evidently it was. She didn't fidget, tap her toes waiting for the slow elevator, and didn't push the button again.

That wasn't who she was.

She didn't get in a rush, and that was important in a job where detail was important.

The other important trait she had, and how her professor had noticed this she had no clue, was that while her curiosity was passionate, she did not feel the same way about needing to share her font of knowledge with others. She was not one who had to tell tales; and, of course, she had some fantastic tales to tell from her time working with the Patrol.

The doors would open when they did, and she was quite comfortable with that as she was with most things. The doors slid apart, revealing a surprisingly large freight elevator. She walked in and stood ramrod straight. She pushed a button that wasn't there, leaving her finger on it long enough for her fingerprint to be checked. Well, the button was there, but it was labeled "Fire Department Use Only" and looked like a key opening. Where she worked wasn't exactly a floor of the museum. She just thought of it as some place below the basement. It was actually six hundred feet below the basement of the Met, buried deep in the bedrock on which Manhattan Island rested. So deep it could survive a direct nuclear strike, but then what would be the point of that? Edith often wondered, which indicated *she* wasn't a narcissist and would not have made a good emperor or pharaoh.

Edith stood tall as the apparently old elevator descended with new elevator speed. While the elevator shaft was surrounded by bedrock, around it in the base of the island was a maze of tunnels, which were the lifeline of Manhattan. While no one knew of the existence of the Patrol beneath the city, most New Yorkers were also unaware of the extent of the network beneath their feet that kept their city functioning. They knew of the subways, of course. In a city where owning a car was as expensive as owning a second apartment, the subways were essential. But there are water tunnels, the largest of which was big enough to drive dump trucks through, as well as sewage lines, cables, steam, access tunnels, and abandoned tunnels whose uses, such as coal transportation, were no longer needed.

This network extended from just below the sidewalks to the deepest part of the city's bedrock (other than the Patrol area): a water aqueduct along the west side of the island that was five hundred feet below the surface, whose contents flowed one hundred and twenty-five miles from the Catskills far north of the city and crossed the Hudson near West Point. There were abandoned rail lines and stations, such as the one at City Hall. There were uncompleted open spaces whose reason had been lost to history. And there were what Con Edison workers called voids, empty spaces in the rock that they came across every now and then, voids that had come into existence when the land came into existence.

There was no map that detailed the entire maze. And if there had been, the deepest place of all, the headquarters of the Patrol, would never have been on it.

It existed because it did not exist, except to the extremely small handful of people who had a need to know. And in fact it wasn't a hand, but a single finger, a single person, outside of the Patrol, who was aware of its existence.

The raincoat with pockets stuffed full of papers was heavy on Edith's shoulders as she plummeted into the bedrock, and the voice of her dance instructor echoed in her head: Stand tall, shoulders back, head held high. The elevator doors finally opened onto an even narrower hallway lined with brick. The lightbulbs were the cost-effective type, which meant they weren't light-effective.

Edith was used to it. She strode purposefully over the hideous tiles only a government contract could manage to lay and turned left.

The brick was an oddity, indicating this tunnel had been here a long time. How long, Edith had no idea, and the Administrator had ignored her the one time she'd asked. She'd then learned she really couldn't ask any direct question of the Administrator. If he wanted her to know something, he would tell her.

He didn't tell her much.

For twenty-two years, Edith Frobish had taken this left and met a man at a guard post, rotating among a half dozen, the entire crew rotating every six weeks and never a repeat, and always wanting the same thing: the badge she wore around her long and elegant neck, and then for her to lean her long form forward, press her face against the detector, and have her eyes scanned. Despite the change in faces, the men all had the same dead look in their eyes; it chilled Edith that those eyes had seen things she didn't want to know about. Each man was dressed in black, wore body armor, and carried an automatic rifle along with a pistol and various other gear that Edith assumed were tools of the trade of combat.

They never made small talk. In fact, they never spoke at all as if they had absolutely no desire to get to know her beyond her badge. Not even a "Good morning" or "How's the coffee?" Perhaps they were mute? Edith sometimes wondered this on her extremely rare third glass of wine. After a string of non-replies and dead-eyed stares from a dozen or so guards, Edith had learned to match their muteness.

If Edith had been as versed in covert operations as she was in art, she might have realized why such a distance was maintained by these *guard* guards. It occurred when the guard had classified orders, that, in extreme circumstances, if the post was about to be taken, to terminate those he guarded rather than have them compromised. That's captured in spy speak. Thus, the Protocol for no personal contact.

It's easier to kill someone you aren't buddy-buddy with.

But today the guard guard wasn't there and for the first time, perhaps too late, Edith felt a sense of alarm.

She tugged the raincoat with the files in the secret compartments closer around her and held her briefcase with both arms in front of her chest. Her first thought was that someone was in trouble, and she was happy it wasn't her. She did notice some flecks of red on the wall to the right above the guard station, as if someone had squirted a can of spray paint at a distance, but her focus was now directly ahead at the ponderous steel door that blocked her way, her anxiety pushing her forward. There was also a strange odor in the air, one she couldn't place.

Taking charge, Edith leaned over and placed her face against the scanner. She was rewarded with a green light, and the steel door at the end of the corridor slid open. Edith walked down to the end and paused. A second steel door awaited. As she stepped past the first, it slid down, enclosing her in a small space, with just a single lightbulb flickering above.

This time she placed her hand over a sensor. There was a slight prick. Her DNA was checked, and approved. The inner door went up, revealing a cavern, a void in the bedrock on which Manhattan rested. Two hundred meters long by a hundred meters wide and over thirty meters high.

Except there was only darkness facing her where there should be a spotlight focused on the HUB.

It was an absolute blackness, one which the scant light coming from above her couldn't penetrate. In fact, like a black hole, the light was sucked in and absorbed completely. Edith swallowed, because there was a palpable sense of evil emanating from the darkness. As soon as she felt it, and then thought it, she felt foolish, because how can one sense evil?

But she could.

Edith reached to her left, fingers fumbling on the wall, searching for the master switch. Maybe they were playing a prank? A surprise party?

As soon as she thought that, she knew it wasn't true. The Patrol didn't do pranks, and it wasn't her birthday. And the sense of dread she was experiencing was unprecedented. While she logically knew one could not "feel" evil, she knew that knowledge was wrong.

The Administrator had told her one time that there were things in the universe the human brain could not comprehend, but the body did.

Trust the body, he'd told her, but for someone like Edith, that wasn't acceptable.

Later she would wonder why she tried several times to turn on lights that didn't exist with a switch that didn't exist into a darkness that she intuitively knew couldn't be breached. And why she stood so long staring into that darkness, mesmerized. She'd always known something like this was a possibility, but after so many years of the HUB being there, the absence didn't quite register. She looked left and right and then back the way she'd come, seeing only the steel door, as if she'd made a wrong turn and missed the place she knew better than anywhere else.

Finally she accepted that the HUB wasn't here. Edith had absolutely no desire to move forward and try to touch or penetrate that darkness. The thought never even occurred to her. She dropped the briefcase from her arms, files tumbling out, and ran her fingers over the stone next to her, trying to ground herself in something real.

She'd been briefed on this, but it was like so many briefings about so many possibilities: It had been endured as part of the process of becoming part of this organization and assuming her position. Edith turned and hit the switch, opening the steel door behind her. It slid up as the one into the cavern slid down; the two could never be open at the same time; another Protocol.

Edith took a step back into the corridor, turned to her left, and saw the "fire" alarm. She'd passed it for so many years, aware of its existence and its real purpose, but never really thinking of it. But it was still there. As per Protocol, she broke the glass and pulled the small lever as she wondered if there was anyone to hear it. For a moment there was nothing, and she felt a surge of pure fear.

Then a light flashed at the top of the alarm, but there was no screech of a siren or klaxon. Apparently this emergency was registering somewhere else.

Then an alarm sounded, undulating up and down, for ten seconds. It pierced into Edith Frobish's brain, and she screamed in concert with it, before collapsing to the floor.

After a minute or so she came to, her head throbbing. She peered about, confused as to where she was. She had no clue at the moment, as if her brain had been covered by a mudslide.

But some things stick with you through the mud.

Edith bent down and picked up the files and rearranged the papers and put them back in the briefcase. She stood straight and tall and waited patiently for the people she knew should come.

She hoped.

She had no idea who they were and could only grab the vaguest of memories as to where she was. Then Edith did remember something. She walked back to the start of the corridor and stood close to the wall. She looked inside the guard station. There was a pile of expended brass on the floor. She realized the odor was from gunfire.

She reached out and tentatively touched her finger to one of the flecks of red.

The blood was still warm.

CHAPTER 2

When it changed, Roland, stone-cold killer, otherwise nice guy, and weapons man for the Nightstalkers, had the stock of a sniper rifle tucked tight in to his shoulder with a righteous target approaching, and that made him happy. Neeley, a usually stone-cold killer from the Cellar, was in overwatch, with her own sniper rifle, and she was acting wonky. That made Roland unhappy since he liked her, and *like* for Roland was the equivalent of rabid devotion in a well-trained attack dog. However, it all balanced out and mattered little since he was in combat mode, and feelings were of no consequence to him in that mode. There was only the mission.

Roland was a man who could live and flourish in the here and now.

That's a rare, and valuable, trait.

It was going to get a lot more valuable.

The problem with hiding off the grid was that sometimes you went off the grid.

Jane Eyre led to Wuthering Heights. The names of the trails comforted Teri Stevens, not her real name, as she settled into her nine-minute-per-mile pace as verified by the GPS program on her iPhone. She wondered who had come up with the names, while noting that she had no cell phone signal in this old-growth forest of the Pacific Northwest. She was very conscious of the pace, a means to use time to push herself. People approach time differently, as if it were something they could control or use.

Teri was running in Putney Woods on the south end of Whidbey Island, Washington, which was in the middle of Puget Sound not far from Seattle. She was dressed for the weather, with long black Gore-Tex pants and a yellow rain jacket. She skirted the puddles as best she could, but mud seemed to be an integral part of negotiating these trails, and after her first week running in the woods, she'd surrendered to that fact.

She was a striking young woman, just past thirty, who cursed those genetic gifts every time she looked in the mirror because she was aware on a fundamental level those had been the first thing that had attracted *him*.

It was something she ruminated on often, going back in her memory, looking at all those choices and non-choices as paths, much like Jane Eyre and Wuthering Heights, with many branches spinning off. She wished she could go back in time and make a decision at times when she'd simply let fate push her down a path, and perhaps change a decision or two or three.

One for certain. And that was the decision to marry him.

But things were as they were, and there was no changing it.

Such is the way most people view time. She had little idea that there were some who viewed it quite differently.

Towering pines and moss-covered trunks lined the trail and her eyes darted into the dark green shadows, on the nervous edge between believing the trees were an enveloping protection or a dark hole for her fear to lurk.

Sixty-two meters down Wuthering Heights from the intersection, Roland wouldn't have liked the word "lurked." He was in what was technically called a hide site and had been in the same position for twenty-eight hours, plus fourteen minutes, give or take some seconds. He'd cut back eating a week ago, so the only calls of nature were a slight roll to the left to urinate. The rain cleansed the mud he lay in, if one could be considered clean in four inches of mud, but Roland had been in worse spots, which tells most of what one needs to know about Roland's past. He was hungry, but that wasn't important. He was covered by a ghillie suit he'd spent three days preparing for just this forest, for just this weather. The outfit made him indistinguishable from the rotting log four feet to his right. Roland, in the flesh, was an imposing figure—six and one-third feet tall, solidly muscled, and sporting a scar along the right side of his head—a scar that was now poorly masked with a barbed wire tattoo.

Neeley hadn't commented on the tattoo when she saw it for a first time and, although Roland would never admit it, that omission hurt his feelings. It also made him wonder if the tattoo had been a mistake. Roland pretended otherwise, but he cared very much what the women around him thought, especially Moms and Neeley.

He had a CamelBak of water tucked under the suit and the nozzle was an inch from the right side of his mouth. He'd been sipping it on a schedule that allowed a one-quarter reserve past the time he planned on being out of the hide site because plans sometimes went wrong and one always planned on that. Anyway, given the damp weather of the Pacific Northwest, dying of dehydration wasn't high on Roland's concerns for this mission. There were so many other likelier possibilities.

It was Protocol and Roland knew Nada, the team sergeant of the Nightstalkers, would have approved. When he had time, and he'd had time on this op, Roland always ran his actions through the Nada filter. It was useful in little things, and little things added up to big things, like staying alive. Roland had every Nada Yada memorized, the rules by which his team sergeant ruled his life and that of the team.

Roland wasn't off the grid from the Nightstalkers on this op working with Neeley, like he'd been on the last one in South America. This was a mutually approved operation, Moms slapping Roland on the shoulder as he headed out for the airstrip at Area 51, wishing him good hunting. Nightstalker and Cellar operative working side by side.

What was the world coming to? Cats and dogs . . .

Even though he liked (perhaps not exactly the right word) Neeley, he missed his team. Most of all, he missed Moms, to whom he owed the deep and abiding allegiance of a blood debt since she saved his life in Iraq years ago.

For a man like Roland, there was no greater bond.

His left cheek rested lightly on the stock of the sniper rifle, but that eye was closed as he used his open right to scan the trail. He had that sixty-two meters' line of fire to the intersection, which made the sniper rifle seem like overkill, but Roland never minded stacking the odds in his favor. Better to over-, rather than under-kill. Roland never understood those movies where the bad guy walked away from the supposedly mortally wounded good guy only to end up on the wrong end of the good guy's gun by the end of the movie. Bad guy deserved to die then, not particularly for being bad, but for being stupid.

Roland's training had kept him alive this long and he'd learned early in combat that there were no rules, no sporting, gentlemanly code of honor. There was alive or dead. An "honorable" death was still dead and Roland considered any dead a sucky dead.

The receiver in his right ear crackled, volume set so low not a sound escaped the inner ear.

"Beta on schedule, on Jane Eyre, heading to Wuthering Heights. On pace. Over." Neeley's voice was subdued, matter-of-fact.

"Roger. Over." Roland's whisper was transmitted by the electronics wrapped around his throat.

Wuthering Heights. It occurred to him that he'd never read the book. Of course, Roland had never read any novel. He'd tried one, a *Conan the Barbarian* novel someone had passed around on a deployment, but it had hurt his head. He'd read lots of weapons manuals, but those had pictures and, for him, a practical purpose. He only knew *Wuthering Heights* was a book because Neeley had remarked on it as they studied the map and satellite imagery of the woods.

"How's it end? Over."

Neeley had been with him long enough that she knew what he was referring to.

"Badly. Guy doesn't get girl. Girl doesn't get guy. No happily ever after. Over."

There never was, Roland thought, which was a very profound thought for Roland.

Teri Stevens wasn't a big believer in happy endings either. The psychiatrist in Coronado had suggested running as a stress reliever, failing to see the irony, which might have made a less desperate person doubt his perception, but Teri had faithfully taken up the regime, and it *did* seem to take the edge off a little bit. She'd started on the beach, the same beach where he'd earned his "Budweiser" insignia when he'd graduated from SEAL training.

He'd made her memorize all the trivia about the insignia, and at first it had been exciting, to be part of this special group. A golden eagle clutching a trident and a flintlock pistol across an anchor. The informal "Budweiser" designation came from the fact current SEAL training had developed out of BUD/S, Basic Underwater Demolition/SEAL training. The anchor represented, of course, the Navy, parent service of the SEALs. The trident represented the ancient god of the sea, Neptune, or Poseidon, depending on which mythology flavor whetted the appetite, Roman or Greek. The pistol, if one looked closely, and she'd been forced to, was cocked, representing the SEAL's ability to always be ready.

To go off, she remembered ironically. To go off. She should have paid more attention to that bit. And the eagle, lastly, represented the ability to parachute in from the air. The last bit of trivia she also found ironic in that the eagle, usually portrayed on flags looking upward, was looking downward on the insignia, to remind the wearer that humility is the true measure of a warrior.

That part hadn't seemed to take hold in her ex.

Of course, he hadn't always been that way. The first couple of years he'd been almost normal, as normal as someone who had made Special Operations their occupation of choice. But in 2005, on a deployment to Afghanistan, bad things had happened to a bunch of his SEAL buddies during Operation Red Wings, and he'd come back dark and bitter. He'd never talked about the greatest loss of life on one operation the SEALs had ever experienced. She'd read the books about it and saw the movie from the Lone Survivor, but still didn't understand her husband's role in it all.

They'd divorced a long, hard year later.

She'd stopped running on that beach when she was warned he was back from wherever it was he'd disappeared to. How "they" knew that, she had no clue, but within five minutes of the call she'd had her stuff in the car and was driving. She went about as north as one can go on the West Coast and still be in the States, then off the coast to an island.

And started running again.

After six months she was up to ten miles a day. She was also thirteen hundred miles away from where she had last seen the man who had begun his love with flowers and ended it with his fists and worse.

She turned from Jane Eyre onto Wuthering Heights. Her right foot slipped on the edge of a puddle and slid out from under her. With a splash she went to her knees in six inches of black water without an expletive or complaint. Years of fear can blunt and silence even the most instinctive reactions.

Teri got to her feet, stepped out of the puddle, and let water drain out of the pant legs.

While she was doing that, Roland moved his head two inches to the right, removing his cheek from the rifle stock. He opened both eyes. The fall was the unexpected, which was to be expected. It would shift the timeline. How much? Roland hated when the timeline got shifted on an op. But he was trained to adjust. As he'd learned in his first infantry assignment as a young private: The best plan works up until you make contact with the enemy.

Neeley chimed in. "Alpha on schedule, on Jane Eyre, heading to Wuthering Heights, moving faster than yesterday. Closing for the kill. Over."

"Roger. Over."

Teri began walking up the trail, letting each footfall squeeze water out of her socks and through her shoes. There was something to be said for a treadmill. But gyms required membership, and she was no longer a joiner. Even with the fake identification the Navy had given her, she kept her new name as tight to her as her skin.

She checked her GPS. The fall had thrown her pace off, and she'd become obsessive about keeping time. She stood still and pushed buttons, updating the setting. Still no cell signal.

It was only because she wasn't moving that she heard the light patter of feet behind her.

She turned and saw her ex-husband, Carl Coyne, come around the curve from Jane Eyre, running on the balls of his feet, his stride long and loose. He wore gray sweats, a hood pulled low over his forehead, almost hiding his eyes. The sweats were soaked from the rain, but she knew his answer to that: The human body was waterproof.

She saw that look on his face, the familiar one, and knew she could never run far enough or fast enough. He was almost floating to her, easily skirting the puddle she'd fallen into. It was all for nothing, all the running, because his promise to destroy her had not been spoken as lightly as he now ran. That threat was a fuel that had kept him searching for the past six months with more ferocious determination than her trembling fear could propel her to hide.

She was surprisingly calm as he closed in on her. Running would only gain her a few futile seconds. Screaming would just startle the wildlife. She realized she was actually *almost* relieved to be done with the constant fear, to have it end in the way she'd always known on a very deep level was inevitable. Death and taxes and here came the former.

The moments were stretching out, the way they did when adrenaline surges and warps time, which should be an indication to all that perhaps time is not absolute, but a variable? Coyne was slowing to a determined walk, a narrow, double-edged knife in his right hand, a cluster of plastic cinches in his left; that last bit caused her to reconsider running.

Those cinches indicated the inevitable would not happen fast. Her previous almost-relieved feeling floated away with a gasp of terror as the realization of torture before death hit Teri, and what little sense of self she'd held on to died.

Carl stopped ten feet away and just stared at Teri, relishing the moment, his excitement palpable. It was getting dark even though it was not late, but daylight was different on this island that she had chosen for its remoteness and lack of a bridge. Teri should have known water would be no barrier to an ex-Navy SEAL. They lived and thrived in the water. Instead of protecting herself with a barrier, she'd enclosed herself in a prison.

The thick trees surrounding them made it even darker. Teri looked up to the sky as if there was an answer, but she saw only leaves and a few specks of cloudy gray. She felt sad, wishing that she could see the sun one more time. The Pacific Northwest was indeed a great place for vampires to make their home, but for a Southern Californian girl, it was oppressively depressing. An eagle flashed by overhead, and she wished fervently she could take wing with that bird, experience that freedom. Be anywhere but here.

Any time but now.

Teri looked back at him. As she gazed into those rage-filled eyes, she saw a speck of red in the left eye. Something she'd never seen in it before.

Carl took a step, closing the distance between them.

Unfortunately, Roland couldn't make one hundred percent positive identification because Teri's head was in the way of most of the target's face, plus the hood was pulled down low. Roland did have a clear line of sight just past her head on the suspect's left eye and could put a 7.62x51mm steel-jacketed NATO round straight through the orbital socket, through the skull, and take a nice chunk of brain matter out the rear. And Roland did have Neeley's positive identification. However, Neeley did not have her finger on the trigger.

There were rules to a Sanction, and they were rules Roland took seriously, because they were the Cellar's version of the Nightstalkers' Protocols. Plus Neeley had insisted he take them seriously.

One could never be wrong on a Sanction because they were what Neeley had called a "No-Do-Over."

Dead was not reversible.

Of course, it didn't occur to Roland: Who the hell else would be out here trying to kill this woman?

Neeley had insisted, and Roland was a team player.

Roland shifted the rifle ever so slightly and his finger curved over the thin sliver of metal.

Roland had been following the rhythm of his heart ever since the woman turned the corner. Now he synchronized it with his shallow breathing as Carl stopped once more, five feet short. Blinking, as if the red in his left eye were a bug, distracting him.

For a moment, Carl seemed to flicker. Most would have attributed the anomaly to an overactive imagination.

Except Roland didn't have one.

He noted it, knew the flicker was real, but kept his eye on the target.

"What is—" Carl began in a slightly puzzled tone, staring past her, but there was a breeze by Teri's right cheek, as if a very fast hummingbird had flitted by. A crimson streak appeared just above and outside of Carl's left eye along the skin on the edge of his skull, extending back over his ear. The gray hood was torn back, as if an invisible hand had grabbed it and jerked.

Roland shed the ghillie suit with one smooth movement as he got to his feet, leaving the rifle lying on the log. Coinciding with his first step onto the trail, he drew his MK23 MOD-O Special

Operation pistol, a bulky suppressor on the end of the barrel marring the gun's smooth lines. He brought it up to the ready as he strode down the trail, in a proper two-handed grip as he'd been taught on the ranges and in the Killing House at Fort Bragg so many years ago.

"Going in to confirm," he informed Neeley, still in a whisper. "Over."

"Coming in to back up," Neeley replied. "Over."

Carl dropped the cinches, his left hand pressing against the side of his face, blood flowing over the fingers. "What the hell?" he yelled.

He lurched toward Teri, the point of the commando knife leading.

Teri heard a soft pop from behind and saw the splash of blood in Carl's right elbow as a .45 caliber bullet hit the joint. Such were the vagaries of bullet trajectory on impact with the human body that the round hit the base of the humerus, changed course, traveled up the arm parallel to the bone, and then punched out Carl's right shoulder with a pretty red spurt.

Pretty to someone like Roland, that is.

The impact of the heavy bullet spun Carl around and ripped tendons in his arm as they strained to keep it attached to his body. The tendons succeeded, barely. With a splash, Carl dropped to his knees in a puddle from the shock, a few drops of water hitting Teri on the cheek along with some specks of blood from her ex. She numbly reached up and wiped them off.

She finally looked over her shoulder and saw Roland, a massive figure dressed in black, wearing a black watch cap, his face smeared with camouflage paint, striding down the trail at a fast, but not hurried, walk, a large gun extended in his left hand, right hand cupped under left, weapon held steady and on line with his left eye. He didn't even seem to register her, his focus was on Carl.

This sudden appearance—his casual approach—frightened her more in a much different way than the danger she had experienced just moments before. There was no anger, no rage, no passion emanating from Roland. Just cold efficiency.

He was nothing like Carl at all, she sensed.

But then again, he was.

Carl roared, sheer rage echoing through the forest, and Teri spun back to face the monster she knew. Carl flipped the knife from ruined arm to good hand and got to his feet. "You bitch!"

He lurched forward and Roland pulled the trigger. The bullet punched into Carl's other shoulder, staggering him back several feet.

Dimly, Teri realized that Carl had yet to get close enough to her to reach her flesh with the blade. It was as if he were a puppet, being controlled by strings of lead. Carl dropped the knife and pressed his left hand against his head once more.

"Keep running," Roland said to Teri as he passed her.

She didn't move.

"Go run home," Roland added, after passing Teri. He looked at Carl's rage-filled face and knew he had a confirmed Sanction, the face matching the previous visuals, matching the file. The attack on the ex-wife had been the slamming of the gavel, proving Carl was not reformed as he had sworn so earnestly to the government shrink during the sessions before he went rogue; tapes Roland and Neeley had watched over and over.

"She's scared, Roland." Neeley's voice was in his ear. "Be nice. Running is a bad word choice."

"Nice is not something I'm good at," Roland said to Neeley in another moment of profound (for Roland) insight, confusing Teri, who was not part of the other end of the conversation.

"Who the hell are you?" Carl managed to mutter, as blood dripped over his left hand on the side of his head, while his right dangled uselessly. He had a large hole in his shoulder, through and through, that hadn't seemed to register in his consciousness yet.

"The Cellar," Roland said, and something blossomed on Carl's face. Something Teri had never seen there: fear.

"No!" Carl screamed. "I'm secure. I'm reformed. They need me."

"Not really," Roland said with simple Roland logic. "Or else I wouldn't be here."

"They need my information!" Carl's voice dropped from scream to beg. "It's important. They need to know about the Ratnik! About the Patrol! About Sin Fen."

Roland paused at this unexpected tactic. "He says he has important information," Roland said over the radio.

Neeley's reply was cold and dry in Roland's ear. "They always do. It's too late for that."

Carl took a step back.

Teri had never seen Carl take a step back.

"I'll be gone. No one will ever hear about me again. I'll disappear. I'll do my duty."

"You can't change," Roland said. "You can't stop. It's your sentence." Roland knew Neeley could hear his words and his brain searched for something brilliant. "It's inevitable."

"I've got friends among the Ratnik," Carl said. "I can get you in contact with them. They can make you rich. You've got no clue what's happening."

Roland was getting bored. "I usually don't, but it usually doesn't matter."

Carl's shoulders slumped in the face of Roland's implacability. "Red Wings," Carl said. "Operation Red Wings."

That got Roland's attention, because he knew about that. Everyone in Special Ops did. "What about it?"

Carl dipped his head and did the second thing Teri had never experienced: apologized. "I'm sorry. I wanted to go back and change it. Change what happened. Make amends. It's too late. They won't let me take it back. They won't let me change it. I can't take it back." He looked up. "Do what you gotta do."

"Later, dude." Roland pulled the trigger. A dark hole appeared in the center of Carl's forehead, right between his eyes. His head snapped back, and he abruptly collapsed, legs bending awkwardly beneath, dropping like a bag of sand, the way all suddenly dead people do. Nothing graceful about his death at all. Not movie dead, real dead. Sucky dead.

Roland fired a second time, the bullet entering the left eye, through the orbital socket (less bone in the way) and shredding the already dead brain.

Always double-tap.

A *Nada Yada*.

Roland finally turned to Teri. "You're safe, Ms. Stevens. I'll take care of all of this. Go home. You don't have to be scared anymore."

Teri couldn't form words.

Neither could Roland any longer, having exhausted his meager supply of sympathy.

But then Neeley was standing there, tall and slim in her black pants and turtleneck underneath a black jacket. Her short black hair, with a tinge of gray, was plastered to her scalp by the rain. She smiled at Teri, much more reassuring than Roland with his gun and barbed wire tattoo.

"You have your life back, Teri," Neeley said. "He's been on your trail for seven days, ever since he learned you were up here. But we've been trailing him for eight days. He would have never gotten to you ahead of us. You've been safe. It's over."

"Eight days?" Teri managed.

Roland slid the pistol into a holster, the end cut open to allow the suppressor to pass through, waiting for the women to be done with the chitchat. The asshole was dead. What more did she want? A band to play? Balloons to fall out of the trees?

"We had to be certain," Neeley said. "I'm sorry he scared you, but we had to be exactly right about this. A little scared is worth a lifetime of safety, isn't it?"

For a moment Roland wondered who the "he" was that Neeley was referring to. Certainly not him?

Teri laughed, a manic edge to it. "A lifetime of safety?"

Neeley reached out and touched her shoulder gently. Teri started; no one had touched her in years.

"You're safe," Neeley repeated. "It's our job to make people like you safe. Forget all this and live your life. Go home. No one is coming for you ever again. Go. *Now.*"

Something in the way she said that last word finally evoked a response. Teri believed Neeley in a way she'd never believed Carl.

Teri took a step. Then another.

Wuthering Heights.

Teri began to run, mud splattering her rain pants. Just before she reached the turnoff for Oliver Twist, she looked over her shoulder. She saw Neeley watching her; Roland was kneeling next to Carl's body. Neeley nodded. Then Teri was gone behind the trees.

Roland was confirming Carl was dead, not that the double-tap in the head left any doubts.

Another *Nada Yada.*

Roland then walked back along the trail, picking up the pistol shell casings along the way. He jammed the ghillie suit in a stuff sack and grabbed the rifle, retrieving its single expended casing.

By the time he got back to the corpse, Neeley had the body bag laid out next to Carl.

"Why did you lie to her?" he asked. "This was a Sanction. Not family court."

"I was being nice," Neeley said. "Might want to try it some time."

Roland was referring to the fact that it wasn't the Cellar's job to go after wifebeaters. Carl's fatal transgression had been free-lancing for the enemies of the country after having been in the formal employ of the United States government. He'd sworn an oath and he'd violated it, much as he'd violated his marriage vows to honor and love his wife. Roland supposed if you broke one oath, it wasn't hard to break others.

Another profound thought for the big man. He was on a roll.

"I can be nice," Roland muttered, his feelings hurt.

Neeley paused and looked at him. "I'm sorry. That was rude of me."

Roland flushed bright red, unseen underneath the camou-flage paint.

"I'm hungry," Roland said, for lack of anything else.

"You should be," Neeley agreed.

Neeley knelt, putting her hand on Carl's legs. Roland took the shoulders and they rolled the dead weight, always heavier for some reason from living weight, into the bag. Neeley zipped it shut.

The rain came down harder, mixing the blood deeper into the mud.

Neeley grabbed the handles on her end. "Telling her she was bait and a test for a Sanction probably wouldn't have gone over well."

"Probably not," Roland agreed as he took his handles.

"Thanks."

Roland paused, puzzled. "For?"

"Being nice in your own way." She was looking up at him and for a second Roland could have sworn her entire figure flickered, just like Carl's had, but it was over before he could be sure.

And then she shocked the unshockable Roland by letting go of the body bag, standing up, reaching out, grabbing his short hair in her fingers, and pulling him close. Roland let go of the bag, surrendering easily to her clutches. She kissed him, hard, and Roland was too surprised to resist; not that he wanted to.

Neeley held on to him for several long seconds, and then let go. She blinked in confusion. "What just happened?"

And then it got even weirder as the body bag slowly deflated.

"What the frak?" Roland muttered as he reluctantly let go of Neeley, very reluctantly, and knelt next to the bag. He unzipped it.

There was no body inside.

CHAPTER 3

It changed for Scout—now eighteen years old and almost two years past her first encounter, run-in, kerfuffle, whatever, involving the Nightstalkers—with a whiff of bacon. She'd only smelled real bacon outside the confines of her home; never inside. Inside it was always fakon, vacon, or one of the other imposters. If you gotta fake it, Scout had always reasoned ever since she was old enough to reason, which had been pretty dang young, then isn't imitation the sincerest form of flattery, and one should go with the original? Her rail-thin mother, who counted each calorie as if they were mortal sins, did not see things that way.

Thus the mystery of the odor permeating the house.

For a moment Scout lie in bed, wondering if perhaps it was wafting in from the old house next door, the one with the barn where she stabled her horse, Comanche. Out of the old stone chimney. People with a barn and a stone chimney had to eat bacon.

But in this relatively new house with its fake gas fireplace, with Scout's mother ruling the kitchen, with the aroma of honest-to-goodness real bacon filling the air, Scout questioned reality.

That's a good trait, one the Nightstalkers had found valuable in the past and would need in the future.

If there was to be one.

But this was a new house, well insulated and sealed. She looked at the window in her bedroom over the pretty bench seat, and it was shut tight. It was late in the morning, actually past noon, so technically *early* in the afternoon, which made her feel a little better. Which further deepened the bacon mystery.

Scout had spent the evening and well into the night texting her sort-of boyfriend, Jake, a nice guy who she was sure Nada would not approve of. She wasn't sure there was a guy Nada would approve of, but he wasn't here in Tennessee and Jake was, so that ended that train of thought.

Bacon. How strange.

Scout got out of bed. Jake was sweet and nice and seemed to care about her and wasn't pushing for sex, something she equated with a particularly long and troublesome root canal. They liked the same books and the same films and sometimes they wore the same T-shirts. They were as close as two people could get, Scout thought. But she'd awoken to the smell of bacon and her iPhone was still in her hand and, checking it, her last text to Jake had been *I think you're my Heathcliff, Cathy*, and now she stared in surprise at his response: *Hu T Fk Is This????*

She didn't remember that from last night, and it puzzled her and disturbed her. Not at all like Jake. But then again she'd been gone for three months. And she'd lied to him about where she'd been, and she knew she wasn't experienced enough in the Nightstalker world to carry off the lie to someone she was close to.

Foreign exchange had sounded good, but Jake had asked too many questions last night. She couldn't tell him, ever tell him, where she'd really been. Training. Training. Training. Fort Bragg, Quantico, Langley, the Hangar at Lakehurst, and other places. A bewildering journey through the shadow world where instructors who knew her only as a number taught her skills, some of which she'd never known existed, never mind thought she needed.

It had been exhausting, and she'd only returned home yesterday.

The bacon worried her.

Scout carefully opened her door. It swung easily on hinges she kept oiled. She padded lightly down the hall to the stairs. She descended carefully, avoiding the one where the metal rod that went up the handrail was loose and rattled slightly every time someone hit the stair. A great early warning device up or down, but it made her question her father's focus to not have fixed it since moving in almost a year ago.

There was, of course, the possibility that a marauding gang of breakfast makers had found their way out here to this thumb of land outside Knoxville, Tennessee, surrounded on three sides by the river of the same name.

Stranger things have happened, and Scout had personally witnessed some of them from the invasion of the Fireflies into her gated community back when they lived in North Carolina, aka *the Fun in North Carolina*, to the Portal opening just twenty miles downriver from her new home here in Tennessee at Loud-oun Dam, aka *the Zombie at the Dam*.

She didn't understand a lot of it, and Googling the events had turned up no answers. The Nightstalkers had good Cleaners coming after them, spinning cover stories, which, no matter how far-fetched, worked because they were more believable than the truth. They were much better at lying than she was, but she imagined if she had a few more years' experience in that world, she'd become pretty good herself.

Scout paused just before the bottom of the stairs as she heard a noise, a sound she'd never heard before.

Her mother was singing. So much for the breakfast-making hooligans. Her mother was singing something about blackbirds singing in the dead of night, which seemed a bit redundant to Scout. She was sure Eagle could tell her about the song and the band and all of that, but right now it wasn't important. This morning, check, this afternoon, was going weird in a major way.

Scout peered around the corner of the hallway into the kitchen. Her mother was at the stove. She was using tongs to pull long strips of bacon out of a frying pan and lay them on a plate covered with a paper towel. She seemed very happy, which was as odd as the bacon and the singing.

Scout put a hand over her mouth to squelch her surprise. She remained still, bathing herself in the aroma of the bacon and the surprisingly nice sound of her mother's voice, but more than anything, enjoying the warmth of happiness emanating from her mother.

"Greer, darling," her mother called out, surprising her. "Grab a plate."

For once, use of her real name didn't bother Scout in the least. How had her mother known she was watching? Another mystery to pile on the others. Scout walked into the kitchen. "Bacon, Mother? 'A moment on the lips—'"

"Hush, dear," her mother said. "Your Nana was the best cook ever. She taught me so much."

Then why have I never had any of it? Scout thought. *Before now,* she amended, looking at the crisp strips of bacon. Her mother hadn't been any different when Scout was dropped off at the front door last night. A perfunctory "How was Europe?" and that was that.

Her mother was expertly breaking eggs into a bowl with one hand while retrieving the last of the bacon with her other. Scout did not recall working at a Waffle House listed on her mother's résumé.

Scout sat at the counter, on the opposite side from where her mother was working. She had her iPhone out, hidden underneath the marble ledge, and began writing a text, her fingers flying over the tiny keyboard with the experience of an eighteen-year-old. It didn't take long to write, but she paused with her finger over the key.

She wasn't texting Jake.

"What's the deal, Mother?" Scout asked.

Her mother turned from the stove, looking truly puzzled. "Why food is love, Greer. And I love you so much and I am *so* glad you're home!"

That caused Scout to hit the send button on the text.

The Loop on which she'd sent the last message to Nada after the *Clusterfrak at the Gateway* was no longer working, having been compromised during the *Zombie at the Dam* incident. With the blessing of Moms, Nada had given Scout his private cell phone number so they could communicate directly if something out of the ordinary happened, if need be.

The need be now.

And then Scout got a plate. Just because reality had taken a bit of a lurch didn't mean she was going to miss the first real breakfast her mother had ever made.

———

It changed for Nada, team sergeant of the Nightstalkers, the most experienced member of the group, a man who'd stared death in the eyes and French kissed the Grim Reaper (figuratively, although stranger things have happened on Nightstalker missions), with irritating voices singing "It's a Small World," the whiny tune echoing in his head as his niece Zoey tried to spin their teacup faster and faster.

Definitely down a rabbit hole of dubious merit.

They'd gone from hell to a deeper hell, was Nada's estimation, walking from It's a Small World to The Mad Tea Party. He was not the type of person Disneyland had been designed for, and he was a bit disappointed Zoey was attacking each new ride with such zest. Of course she was just a kid, but still. He expected better of someone who shared his bloodline.

As they spun about, Nada wondered, how small was the world really?

And why did Disneyland bother him so much and on a deeper level than irritating songs?

Little did he know, he was about to find out the answers to both.

And the answers were not good.

But he was trying to pretend. *Fake it until you make it*, Eagle had advised when Nada was due two days off and was going to use it to visit his niece and mentioned that a trek to Disneyland was part of the festivities. The team had begun taking bets on how long it would be until Nada pulled his MK23 Special Ops pistol and shot Mickey and Minnie. Roland had put his money on Goofy going down first with a double-tap right between his big eyes, but had added he would be very upset if Nada shot Goofy. Mac had asked he not shoot Snow White, since Mac had a thing for her, but then again Mac apparently had a thing for anyone in a skirt.

The team didn't seem to have much faith in Nada's ability to suffer.

But there are many different kinds of suffering, and everyone has a vulnerable spot. Nada should have remembered that from SERE (Survival, Evasion, Resistance & Escape) Training, where participants learned everyone had a breaking point. It was just a matter of time.

But isn't everything?

The teacup twirled about, Zoey putting all her energy into spinning the wheel, but they stayed relative to all the other cups twirling about.

Nada didn't get it. Bumper cars he could understand. But there were no crashes here, no movement other than the spin, which wasn't dictated by the person on the ride. And most of the other adults had their phones and cameras out, recording the event. That was beyond comprehension to Nada: It was bad enough being here. Who'd want to watch a recording of being here? And if you were recording it, perhaps you weren't altogether here to start with? A sort of remembered present?

Nada glanced at his younger brother, dutifully recording the teacup adventure from the safety of the fence with his cell phone. His brother, Zoey's dad, was smiling, either at Zoey having fun or Nada's misery. If he'd been a betting man, Nada would have put his money on the latter.

But then he noticed the woman in the next teacup. She didn't have her hands on the center wheel. She held a baby in her arms. She had long, dark hair, flowing over the baby whom she was staring down at. Her skin was dark, exactly like Nada's, except while his face was pockmarked, hers was smooth. And when she glanced up and saw Nada staring at her, he felt a lurch deep inside, as if a hand had clenched his heart and given it a tough squeeze. He quickly averted his gaze, but not before everything seemed to flicker for a second, as if the power that drove the universe had suffered a momentary short.

A volcano erupted in Nada's mind. It was the only way he

could describe it. Memories poured forth, hot and scalding with the utter desolation of the awareness of the loss.

He remembered a wife and a child.

Here. Years ago.

His wife and child.

Nada cried out, the sound masked by the music piped in via speakers overhead and unnoticed in Zoey's determination to spin their teacup ever faster. His breath was gone, and he forgot how to breathe.

Discipline was a cornerstone of Nada's life and he gathered himself, especially as his phone began ringing, a distinctive tone, Warren Zevon singing about "Keep Me in Your Heart," a song the performer had written after being diagnosed with terminal cancer. Nada had always thought his whole Warren Zevon thing had centered around "Roland The Headless Thompson Gunner" because it had been the unofficial dirge of the 10th Special Forces Group (Airborne) when he was a member, but now he knew how special and personal that other Zevon song had been to him.

How could he have forgotten? How could he have no memories of them?

Nada reached for the phone, glanced at the screen, and something passed over his face, a look Zoey caught and had never seen on it before but wasn't too young to place: sadness, overriding the deepest kind of pain.

The ride slowed and stopped. Zoey got up, but Nada remained seated. He put the phone away and fumbled in his pocket for something, pulling out a pack of cigarettes, trying to comprehend the memories flooding his brain.

"What are you doing?" Zoey demanded.

Nada pulled out a lighter and fired up the cigarette, staring out at the teacups as everyone else made for the exit.

"We need to leave," Zoey said.

One of the pimple-faced attendants was herding everyone toward the exit so the next wave of youngsters and camera-toting parents could have their spin. He saw Nada smoking; his mouth opened to say something. Then a primeval sense of survival snapped his mouth shut, and he turned his head away.

Smart kid.

"Come on, Uncle," Zoey said, grabbing his free hand and giving a tug.

Nada got to his feet and numbly followed his niece. He walked over to a wooden bench and sat down on it as if suddenly exhausted. Nada finally pulled out his phone and glanced at the screen once more, actually reading the message. He gave a wistful smile. "You'd like Scout," he said to Zoey as he put the phone back in his pocket.

"You called me Scout at the park," Zoey reminded him.

"Sorry about that," Nada said, apologizing for the umpteenth time for abandoning her during the call of duty in their last outing together.

"What's wrong?" Zoey asked with the innocence of an eight-year-old able to cut to the heart of the matter. Her father came over, concern on his face. He placed a protective hand on his daughter's shoulder.

"You okay, brother?"

"That song," Nada said. "The ring tone. I shouldn't have picked it. Reminds me of someone." As had the woman and baby in the next teacup.

"What song?" his brother asked, but he was looking about anxiously, stoking Nada's dark fear.

"Warren Zevon. 'Keep Me in Your Heart.'"

A shadow passed over his brother's face.

Nada stared at his brother, having to ask, dreading the answer. "What did they do to me? They told you never to tell me, didn't they? You had to be in on it. It's why you've tolerated me so long, even after I had to leave Zoey at the tar pits."

His brother's face crumpled in sadness also, and that confirmed it for Nada. "They said you'd be better off. Not knowing. I'm sorry."

Nada got to his feet and stepped close to his brother, gripping his collar tight. He whispered harshly: "They were real? What I remember is real?"

His brother nodded.

Nada let go of his brother and slumped back down on the bench. Then he reached under his jacket for his pistol. His brother anticipated the move and jumped on him, fighting him.

"No!" his brother urged. "Stop!"

Nada was a trained killer and could have tossed his brother aside and drawn the gun and ended it, ended his life as he now knew he'd contemplated many times in the past.

The only thing that stopped him wasn't his brother's arms or even Zoey's scared look, but the message on his phone. Someone needed him.

Nada quit trying to go for the gun and his brother snatched it and tucked it into his belt, hiding it under his jacket.

Nada slumped down onto the bench once more. "Why? Why? Why take them from me?"

His brother sat close by his side and lowered his voice so Zoey wouldn't hear. "They were gone. Nothing you could do to bring them back. You were crazy, man. Drinking, having all your guns around. You'd call in the middle of the night ranting. I was afraid you were going to kill yourself. Or kill someone else. They were too. Those people you work for. They said it was for the best. They asked me, and then they threatened me. Some guy with a fake eye in a black suit. He was scary, man. Really scary. But he said it was in your best interests. That it would give you peace. And it did, man."

And then Zoey got scared because her uncle began to cry. Not heaving sobs, but tiny little tears at the corners of his eyes and a brief hitch in his breath. As a trickle of dampness rolled down his pocked skin on each cheek, Zoey reached out and took his free hand in her tiny one.

"Why are you so sad?" Zoey asked.

Nada mustered a reply. "I miss some people."

"Who?" Zoey asked.

Nada looked up at his brother and lied. "I promised your father never to speak of it."

"It'll be all right," Zoey said. "You're my favorite uncle!"

"I'm your only uncle," Nada said, forcing a smile.

Zoey threw her tiny arms around him, almost around, because they weren't long enough.

But Nada knew it wouldn't be all right because there was a hole in his heart that could never be filled, and he couldn't figure out why the blackness that had hidden that part of his past in his mind was gone and the searing, unbearable memories were back.

And he didn't have to wonder too hard who had taken the memories away. A man with a fake eye might have done the dirty work, but there was always someone pulling the strings.

His brother sat next to him and put an arm around his shoulder. "You can't change the past, bro."

If only that were so.

It changed at Area 51 deep inside the sprawling complex set in the middle of Nowhere, Nevada, because many problems on the cutting edge of science, physics, and the weird and the wonderful started at Area 51. But this time it was not in the labs where scientists tested the outer boundaries of man's knowledge, occasionally traveling from genius to stupid at lightspeed (literally sometimes) and requiring the Nightstalkers to clean up their messes. This time it was in the repository of the results of all those tests and so much more: the Archives. If the Ark of the Covenant was indeed found by some Indiana-Jones-type character, it would have been stored here and it would have fit right in with many of the other weird and wonderful and frightening items gathered from around the world and hidden away deep under the sort-of-secret-but-definitely-most-secure facility in the continental United States.

Even though the CIA had acknowledged the place existed (it was on Google Earth now for frak's sake), that didn't mean they were holding an open house any time soon.

It changed with Ivar—or rather the sudden lack thereof, of Ivar—which, considering Ivar's recent history and what had happened during the *Fun in North Carolina*, might not be as strange as it seems.

But Ivar and Doc—who was with Ivar, at least initially—were both physicists, and they understood the law of entropy (or thought they did) and knew that when something was taken away, something was returned in kind (or thought they knew).

Or at least they understood a distorted law of entropy, which Doc would come up with later. Sort of.

If there was a later.

But that's getting ahead of the occurrence.

Doc stood on the top rung of a ladder inside the Archives and yelled for Ivar to get ready to give him a push. It shouldn't be that hard since it was a big walking ladder with four large wheels, all well lubricated and balanced. Plus Doc didn't weigh much. His parents had come to the States from India when he was young, both well educated and on the academic fast track, and they'd imparted a burning desire for knowledge in their only son. Doc was slight of build, with dark hair and thick glasses—the typical science nerd, except he was the scientist for the Nightstalkers and that elevated him far out of nerddom.

Doc was grabbing for the last box in this upper stack. It was covered in dust the way most of the boxes in this part of the Archives were covered in dust, especially those on the highest shelves, because in any stack, boxes were layered in term of inquiries. Those easy to grab, on the ground-level shelves, had been looked in, for whatever reason. Those that remained high up had most likely never been looked in or moved since being put in place.

It gave Doc a slight thrill each time he checked one of these old boxes, shoved up here over half a century ago without anyone giving them a second thought. Doc considered each box as having the potential to reveal great insights, although most yielded boring reports of mundane activities. Regardless, he used the scanner to take a snapshot of the faded lettering on the form taped to the side, took the bar code label it printed out, and stuck the label on the side of the box.

Information that couldn't be accessed was useless, a Nada Yada of particular insight. So Doc and Ivar had been detailed to work on inventorying the information in the Archives in order to make it into something that could be put in a database and then the box accessed if needed. The fact they would probably never finish the job, given the size of the Archives, didn't stanch Doc's enthusiasm for it. He approached it as an old-time prospector might regard a mountain streamed, hoping to sift through tons of sand, trying to find a few nuggets.

The faded writing on the sides of the old boxes had turned from a bright black to a withering, barely legible gray. Doc often thought about the men—and women—who'd written those notations on the boxes, years before he was born. Had they wondered who'd open the box next? If the box would ever be opened? Could they conceive how big the Archives would grow, from the single building deep inside this cavern in the early days, to the largest building in the world, even bigger than the Boeing factory in Seattle that builds jumbo jets?

Yet the building was inside a cavern deep under Groom Mountain, in the midst of Area 51, and unknown to everyone except those who had the proper clearance and a need to know. Would those who had placed these books here decades ago understand that it was only Doc and his driving need to understand truth that caused him to be up here on the ladder, undertaking an inventory no one believed would ever be completed?

Ready to move on, no nugget uncovered in this section, Doc signaled for Ivar to nudge him over to the next stack.

"Push the damn ladder, Ivar!" Doc finally shouted, reaching for the next row and his fingers falling short of the new, old boxes. "Sleep on your own time," he added, having noticed a bit of sluggishness in the newest member of the Nightstalkers when they'd entered the Archives this morning.

"Ivar!" Doc yelled once more, looking down to—nothing.

He'd been there just a few seconds ago. Had he wandered off to one of the porta potties stationed throughout the massive Archives? Surely he would have said something. Doc shivered as a wave of static electricity passed over his body. Somewhere in the distance a lightbulb exploded with a sharp pop. A rhythmic thumping that constantly rumbled through the Archives was no longer thumping.

Utter silence.

Doc swallowed hard. He looked back at the boxes he'd just tagged. On some the writing was no longer faded, but bright, as if done just the other day. Doc took a deep breath to steady himself. He swore he could smell fresh ink from the markings. He closed his eyes because for the moment he didn't want to see, didn't want to accept.

He took another deep breath.

Most unusual, Doc thought with the predominant rational part of his mind, as he pulled out his phone. He dialed Ivar's cell phone number.

Why was he not surprised when he was informed that the number had never existed?

Ivar was *gone* in the deepest sense of the word.

It changed at the Ranch, outside of Area 51 on the other side of the Extraterrestrial Highway, but still pretty much Nowhere, Nevada, known to only a few as the headquarters of the Nightstalkers.

It was only because Eagle had a hippocampus twice that of a London cabbie, and the resultant phenomenal memory, that it was noticed at all. Noticing didn't mean awareness though.

Which meant Eagle was going to have to learn something new.

If he was given the time.

Technically, Eagle, Kirk, and Mac were not in, but close by the Ranch, in an abandoned mine. Eagle stood at the bottom of a mineshaft so deep that the surface was a distant blue spot far overhead. He was not happy.

He watched as Mac and Kirk tried to knock each other off the wall of the shaft, coming perilously close to achieving their goal several times. They weren't using ropes because that would be cheating (in their opinion, not Eagle's, who had a climbing harness on and a rope ready for belay) and take away from the adrenaline rush.

Eagle didn't believe in adrenaline rushes anymore. He was older than the two young men clinging to the wall and everyone would agree he was smarter. They were all combat veterans, but Eagle had a scroll of scars on the left side of his head, marring his chocolate skin, and he liked to think he'd had some common sense burned into him when that IED had gone off in Iraq years ago.

The truth was deeper than that though. Eagle was one of those people who'd been born old, with wisdom and common sense always far ahead of his physical age. He'd learned to read by age two, and accelerated from there. So trying to kick your buddy off the wall of a mineshaft for shits and giggles struck him as just plain dumb. He didn't rate the actual climb itself much higher on the common sense scale, but the climb was a quarterly requirement. Who knows when they'd have to climb some rocky, vertical surface in order to achieve their goal? Eagle had pointed out, every time the test came up, that he flew their transport, the Snake. He could put them at the top of any cliff or wall they desired with no sweat.

Such logic held little sway with Nada and Moms, neither of whom, Eagle noted, were currently with them. He filed that away because he would make damn sure they did their quarterly evaluation climb when they got back.

Eagle hated the climb. It reminded him of the rope he couldn't climb in ninth grade for his Presidential Merit certificate. Perfect academic scores hadn't been enough. But maybe there had been a purpose to the requirement, because when he failed on his first attempt, Eagle worked out for six months, ate his first salads, and practiced technique until he could climb the rope in under thirty seconds and touch the ceiling of the high school gym.

Except that he did it alone, with no one to certify the effort. That's when he realized he sought no approval but his own. He never climbed it in front of others, even when he "failed" during gym classes and some of his fellow students called him names. He was content with his secret knowledge of his own achievement. It gave him a thrill he was sure Frasier, the Nightstalker shrink, could put some DSM-IV tag on, but Eagle had never shared that memory with Frasier, or anyone else.

Which was why he thought Mac and Kirk were a pair of idiots trying to outdo each other just because he was there, even though he was pointedly not watching. They were both expert climbers, the ones who Nada would turn to if he needed someone to "lead" the team up a tough pitch in case they had to take down some mad scientist who set up his lair at the top of, say, Mount Everest, or more likely, a volcano. Mad scientists always seemed to put their lairs in volcanoes in the movies. Particularly active ones, which just seemed dumb to Eagle. Still, Eagle smiled as he recalled Doctor Evil's monologue about his childhood from his volcanic lair. Word for word it ran through his brain.

Eagle waited patiently, trying to ignore the two idiots above and trying to read a book on his phone. He loved his print books, but he'd been converted to the eBook a few years ago mainly by the convenience: His books were literally at hand as long as he had his phone with him and, as a Nightstalker, he always had his special phone at hand.

Eagle frowned as the screen flickered for a moment, the digital letters becoming hazy, then re-forming. He'd have to take the phone in to IT for a checkup. He'd never had to take a *book* book in to IT to get fixed, he thought with the grouchiness of the techno leery.

"Rock!" Kirk called out, and Eagle did as he'd been trained, tucking his chin in to his chest. Proper training, he thought as he waited for a boulder to splat him into oblivion. Most people very wrongly looked up at the alert.

Mac's climbing shoe bounced off Eagle's helmet.

"What the frak?" Eagle yelled. "Would you two idiots cut it out?"

Frak was still a buzzword on the team, even though the *Battlestar Galactica* marathon was long in the past. Moms frowned on cussing, so the team had picked up the word, and it had stuck for some of them.

"Sorry," Kirk said as he tapped the worn wooden plank that indicated the top of the climb. Mac shoved in and also tapped the plank, and then they tried to beat each other back down.

"Be faster if you just let go and let gravity do the work," Eagle observed before going back to his book, a history of ancient Rome.

"Funny guy," Mac yelled out. He was the team engineer, more commonly referred to as the demo man, although he had built some things on occasion. He was movie-star handsome if one considered a young Tom Cruise handsome, and his humor was always on the edge of painful irony, masking some inner darkness, which did not make him unique on the Nightstalkers. One usually did not go into Special Operations and then the covert world of black ops unless you were outside the bell curve.

And one was not selected for the Nightstalkers unless you were "special," and special didn't necessarily mean on the plus side of the bell curve, as Eagle tried to point out to the other members of the team enough times that they didn't listen to him anymore about it.

Kirk partially took Eagle's advice and leapt off the rock face of the mineshaft for the safety line both had heretofore ignored. He grabbed it and slid down as fast as he could without burning the skin off his palms. He reached the bottom a couple of seconds before Mac.

"Pay up," Kirk said. He was the Nightstalkers' commo sergeant (although the Nightstalkers didn't do rank, some things associated with the Special Forces A-Team stuck): a narrow man, all bones and lean muscle stretched over the skeleton. Hailing from Parthenon, Arkansas, zip code 72666, he was a former Army Ranger whose expertise at cheating and willingness to do anything for a cause he believed in had caught Ms. Jones's attention and brought him eventual assignment to the team. He was serious about money because he sent practically all of it back home to his younger siblings to "keep them on the farm," according to Mac. Actually he was helping them keep the farm, since their father had blown himself up cooking meth.

"What's wrong?" Kirk asked as Mac forked over the bills.

Eagle hadn't been aware he was frowning as he looked at his phone's screen. "Strange. Here it's stating that the Lateran Obelisk is still in Egypt."

"Oh, that's bad," Mac said with the sarcasm of the ignorant.

"But it's in Rome," Eagle said. He was sliding his finger on the screen, trying to find out why this mistake was in the text. "This author is very reliable on his history."

"History is written by the winners," Kirk said, nudging Mac.

"Funny guy," Mac said.

"History is important," Eagle said, looking up from the phone. "It's the absolute of our past leading into the possibilities of our future. You can't mess with history."

"Right," Mac said. "Your turn to climb, oh wise one."

With a sigh, Eagle put the phone in his pocket. He moved to the rock wall and looked up. He was rescued from starting as his cell phone belted out a Warren Zevon tune: Nada's personal one. Mac's and Kirk's phones joined the chorus.

"This isn't good," Eagle said.

Whether he meant the call or the burp in history or both remained to be seen.

It changed for Moms by figuratively traveling into her past, both in place and time. She was already in the place, having made the drive of tears back home. She was sitting on the front porch of the abandoned shotgun shack where she'd grown up in the middle of Nowhere, Kansas. Interstate 80 was to the south, across the flat plains, but so far away that no sound traveled from the eighteen-wheelers racing across the middle of the country.

There was no other house in sight, just miles and miles of slightly undulating fields, and despite all the years since she'd left, Moms still had a sick feeling in the pit of her stomach. It had started when she'd entered Kansas and grown stronger every mile she drew closer to "home." The house was empty, long deserted. Her younger brothers never came out here, smarter than she was, understanding some memories only brought pain.

It seemed Moms was a masochist, going back to her roots in order to remember.

But sometimes, going into the past is necessary in order to move forward.

There are variations on that, such as changing the present in order to move forward, which Moms was soon to discover.

She was not only back here in Kansas, she was back at the place where she'd begun. She dared not enter the house. Bad things had happened here. Sometimes, alone and off duty, with a half-empty bottle on the table next to her bunk, Moms had allowed herself to remember.

Moms had a cheap picture album on her knees, made of imitation leather, with gold lettering on the cover: OUR WEDDING.

This was her way of traveling back in time, but avoiding the one time and person she couldn't face.

Moms's mother had purchased the album with her employee discount at the Dollar Store in town. Things were so bad here in this part of the country, even that store had gone under during the last fiscal crunch.

With a deep sigh, Moms went back, flipping open to the last page of the album.

It was not about a wedding. It was a recording of futility, lost dreams, and broken lives. How Doctor Golden from the Cellar had tracked it down, Moms had no idea. The Cellar's reach was long and deep and never stopped at personal boundaries.

The latter part of the book was filled with travel postcards. The last two were from Istanbul, and just before that terrible visit. Moms sighed, now seeing how futile and naïve it had been of her to send them to her mother. She'd picked them up on a layover, en route to a clandestine deployment to Afghanistan.

Moms flipped back in time, noting the postcards her mother had carefully pasted in the book, all from places Moms had traveled through en route.

Moms paused. Maybe that was the story of her own life: en

route. Always to places where there was bad. She never sent the actual destinations. And all she'd ever done in the en route places was get the postcards because she'd been going to a destination to do a job, and there was no time for anything else.

Postcards from the edge, Hannah, the head of the Cellar, had called them.

Then Moms reached the part of the album where the post-cards ended and there were the earlier pictures cut out by her mother from *National Geographic* magazines. Places her mother had dreams of visiting.

But never did.

Moms went further back, recognizing some of the places from when her mother had first cut them out and pinned them to the old, wheezing fridge with magnets boasting grain company emblems.

Then she got to the dreams her mother had had of a fancy wedding. Fancy by poor Kansas standards. Cut out from maga-zines: A white dress. A church. Most importantly, a groom.

None of it had come true.

Moms looked up from the album. A half-finished dollhouse, three feet high by six long, big enough for a child to crawl into, rotted on the end of the porch. Her father had started it for Moms one Christmas day, and then disappeared (the proverbial leaving to get a pack of cigarettes), never coming back, making the doll-house a testament to abandonment.

At first Moms had thought it was some kind of forlorn monu-ment to the failed marriage, but later in life, with the wisdom of age, she'd realized that her mother simply hadn't cared enough to do anything about the dollhouse.

Which was worse.

What if he had stayed? Would things have turned out differently? Moms had no idea, because she really didn't understand how her mother had turned out the way she had.

Moms flipped the page to the first one, the only one that featured something other than dreams of an event and places never traveled to.

Moms shook her head and sniffled, wondering for a moment if she were catching a cold.

The picture was of the family. Her mother standing in the center with both hands on a five-year-old version of Moms standing in front of her and the younger brothers flanking both of them.

The picture was blurry and, for a moment, Moms thought it was because her eyes were full of tears from the trip down a memory cul-de-sac.

It was all wrong. Moms wiped a sleeve across her eyes and squinted, not believing what she was seeing. The Polaroid picture was faded, more faded than she remembered, but it had been years since she'd last thumbed through it. But that wasn't the issue.

Because now there was a man standing next to her mother where there had been no man before. A man she vaguely remembered from childhood but was certain had never been in this picture. And her mother was in a white dress, the dream wedding dress on the next page. And she was smiling.

Moms tried to remember her mother smiling, but all she could conjure up was her mother in a drunken stupor, face slack. That was the most peaceful she'd ever looked. The rest of the time her face had been full of rage and pain and darkness.

Moms flipped the pages.

The rest of the book was as she remembered.

Moms went back to the first page. The picture wasn't as faded, as if the Polaroid film was slowly developing after more than thirty years.

Then her phone phone began to ring, a tone she'd only heard once before when Nada had played it for the team. His personal cry for help. *Keep me in your heart . . .*

Nada had never made such an appeal before.

Moms looked at the picture, at the happy family, and then slowly closed the album with a shaking hand.

████████████████

It had changed for Foreman, closing in on seventy years of service, in February 1945 in an area called the Devil's Sea, off the coast of Japan, in the waning days of World War II. The event was after he and his pilot were forced to ditch because of engine trouble. Minutes later, the rest of their squadron simply vanished into a strange mist in that enigmatic part of the world. No trace of the other planes or crews were ever found.

Then it was reinforced in December of that same year, the war finally over, on the other side of the world, when he begged off a mission because of the same premonition he'd had before the Devil's Sea flight, and watched Flight 19 disappear from the radar in an area called the Bermuda Triangle.

He'd determined then and there that he had to know the Truth.

So he'd gone from the Marine Corps into the short-lived precursor to the CIA, the Central Intelligence Group, in 1946, then morphed with it into the CIA, where he moved upward, and, much more importantly inward, into the darkness of the most covert parts of various branches whose letters and designations changed over the years. But their missions grew more and more obscure, to the point where he'd outlived and outserved all his contemporaries so no one in the present was quite sure who exactly he worked for anymore or what his mission was.

If he worked for anyone at all.

Not that anyone really cared.

They should.

He was now known as the Crazy Old Man in the covert bowels of the Pentagon and by some other names, associated with bowel movements.

How crazy he was, some people were about to discover.

Foreman had to use a cane, a concession he'd made most reluctantly a year ago. He had to give the cane up at every security checkpoint he went through at the Pentagon as he worked his way further and further into the belly of the beast. He was dressed in a suit, only a decade out of fashion and, strangely, wore a small black porkpie hat, à la *Breaking Bad*. He'd enjoyed that show and had taken up wearing a hat similar to Walt's because he liked it, he identified with Walt, and because it made him look crazier than usual. Besides, the fedora he'd worn for several decades had become passé with *Mad Men*. The changing of fashion with time was something that amused Foreman. What was old is new again and vice versa.

He'd found *crazy* kept people away, and Foreman didn't particularly care for people.

World War II was history to the people in this building, ground having been broken on the building just a few months prior to Pearl Harbor. It was completed in the beginning of 1943, in time to see service during the conflict. Foreman's first visit had been in 1946, at the beginning of his career in covert operations.

He felt his age as he limped up to a desk manned by two military police. It blocked the corridor on the supposed lowest level of the Pentagon. With a sigh, he pulled out his identification card and showed it to them.

It was one of those strange identification cards, designed for the handful of people who had the highest security level possible but were not formally affiliated with any agency that these guards would be aware of. Both MPs snapped to attention. One of them scanned the QR code on the ID and got a green light. Then he took another scanner.

"Your glasses, sir?"

Foreman removed his thick spectacles, another concession to age.

The guard checked both retinas and got two more green lights.

"Good to go, sir."

Foreman put his glasses back on, retrieved his card and his cane. He walked past, aware that cameras were tracking him. With another sigh, this caused by the pain in his replaced knees, he took the stairs down to a sublevel of the Pentagon that wasn't supposed to exist.

In stark contrast to the hustle and bustle of the corridors above, this level was eerily quiet. At the end of the corridor was an old metal desk. An old man, young to Foreman, sat behind it, doing a crossword puzzle. He peered up over his reading glasses.

"Good day, young fella," he greeted Foreman.

"Same to you, old man."

"Here to see anyone in particular or stopping by your office?"

"I need to chat with Mrs. Sanchez. Then go to my office and clean out the inbox. Perhaps nap for a bit."

The last guard laughed. He didn't pull out a folder with personal, obscure questions to ask Foreman as he did with everyone else who approached his desk, questions only someone who had lived the answers could correctly reply to. He was facing the only person who predated his position as the last check before entry into the covert world attached to, or, more accurately, underneath the Pentagon. While there were rules, there was also the reality that Foreman was an institution. Or at least he was to another human institution, of which there weren't many left in an increasingly technical world.

"How are the knees?" the guard asked, looking down at something behind his desk.

"You tell me," Foreman said.

The man looked up from the scanner. "They look good." He reached underneath his desktop and hit a button. A door behind him swung open, revealing a telephone-booth-sized room.

Foreman got in and sat down in the chair, grateful for the relief of pressure off his knees. He'd had them replaced decades ago and the doctors had told him the replacements needed to be replaced; he'd worn out the metal and plastic.

But Foreman was realistic enough to know he didn't have the energy, strength, or patience to go through two more surgeries. Plus he didn't have the future.

Reality sucks.

The door shut and with a slight jolt, the box moved sideways. It halted abruptly and then moved backwards, riding along a unique rail system, the only means by which someone could get to the buried offices of the denizens of the darkness underneath the Pentagon.

Foreman also understood another reality of the rail/booth system. Once seated inside one of the booths, the occupant was at the mercy of the system. Foreman had no doubt that there was a detour that ended with some grim folk on the other end who made sure the occupant was never seen again.

The booth came to another abrupt halt and the door opened, not at some executioners' post, but at the comptroller's office. Foreman slowly got to his feet, using his cane as a prop. He walked up to a chest-high counter, reached into his pocket, and pulled out a leather sack.

"Are you trying to get my agent killed?" Foreman demanded of Mrs. Sanchez. He held up the leather bag of coins and shook one out. "This is Amin-Zeus!" he exclaimed, shoving it in her face. He flipped it. "This says *Ptolemy* in Greek!"

The two might have been in the DMV. Mrs. Sanchez was on one side of the counter, and Foreman was on the other. She never allowed him on her side, as she did many other visitors who were more amiable and less apparently demented. And her daughter was at her desk, not pretending to be focused on her work as she usually was, but watching warily, one hand underneath the desktop on the alarm, which would bring a dozen heavily armed guards to the room.

She really wanted to press the button.

Mrs. Sanchez was the comptroller for the Black Budget, currently estimated to be 52.8 billion dollars. But it was so highly classified, who knew exactly how much it was?

Mrs. Sanchez did. She knew to which person/agency/entity every single dollar went, all overseen from this tiny office on a level of the Pentagon that wasn't listed on any official description of the Pentagon.

That was because it had been built using funds from the Black Budget. There's a synchronicity to it all.

Mrs. Sanchez checked her clipboard. "You requested two dozen ancient Egyptian bronze coins, Amin-Zeus stamped." She dropped the clipboard. "Two dozen. Egyptian. Original. Amin-Zeus stamped."

"You fool!" Foreman shouted. "But Ptolemy? That's third century BC. *After* the time period I need them for."

Mrs. Sanchez shrugged. "You didn't say anything about the flip side, Mister Foreman. Every coin has a flip side, you know." It was not a question. And like someone behind the counter at the DMV, she proceeded to give him the same lecture she gave him almost every time he came in. "You have to be very, very specific when you fill out the form. It's not our job to interpret your requests."

Mrs. Sanchez was in Southwestern apparel, with flowing white hair, dark skin, and an angular face. Silver and turquoise jewelry adorned her fingers, wrists, and neck. Colorful rugs decorated the walls along with etchings of the desert. She was in her late sixties and retirement wasn't even on the horizon for her, although she had no doubt when she did retire, her daughter would fill her shoes quite nicely, thank you, just as Mrs. Sanchez had filled her own mother's so many years ago. The Sanchezes had carved out their own unique place here in the bowels of the Pentagon.

Foreman had done the same, except in a quite different direction. He was muttering to himself as he put the coins and leather sack down on the counter.

"Do you have the new order?" Foreman asked.

Mrs. Sanchez put a briefcase on the counter and opened it, turning it so Foreman could inspect it. He searched through the objects in the briefcase with shaking hands. They represented currency across the spectrum of history, from BC to current day.

"I'll need the older Amin-Zeus coins," Foreman said. His old, once-thick white hair was beginning to give way to a liver-spotted scalp. His face was like a hatchet, no softness in it at all. His eyes, once like steel, had softened over the years with cataracts, and he wore a pair of thick spectacles that were smudged with fingerprints.

"What's the special word?" Mrs. Sanchez asked, as if speaking to a child.

"Please," Foreman said.

"I'll work on it," Mrs. Sanchez said. "Is the rest in order?"

"It appears to be," Foreman grudgingly said.

"You're welcome," Mrs. Sanchez said as she slapped the top of the case shut. She placed her hand over a sensor and a red light flashed. "I'll have it shipped to New York by courier, as per Protocol."

"Yes, yes," Foreman muttered. "But the Egyptian currency. It's important."

"It will be here when it gets here," Mrs. Sanchez said. "There are some things that take time. Finding the original currency, especially such rare and valuable coins, isn't easy."

"*Time?*" Foreman gave a snort. "You know nothing of time!"

"I believe we're done here," Mrs. Sanchez said. She hit a button under her side of the counter and the door behind Foreman slid open, revealing his transportation.

"Yes, yes." Foreman turned around and went into the room, taking the chair that awaited. The door hissed shut.

"Have a nice day." Mrs. Sanchez sighed as she took the briefcase to a glass door, which she opened, and then slid the case in. It was gone in a second, whisked away by some hidden mechanism.

"That crazy old man scares me," Mrs. Sanchez's daughter said.

"His budget last year was one hundred forty-six million, two hundred and twelve thousand, five hundred and forty-five dollars," Mrs. Sanchez said. "He doesn't file a breakdown on how it's spent. But it's appropriated every year, grandfathered in."

"What exactly does he do?" the daughter asked. "Who does he work for?"

"I don't know," Mrs. Sanchez said, and that was the scariest thing her daughter had ever heard her mother say.

In the box, Foreman was moved horizontally and vertically along tracks, one box among several underneath the Pentagon. It wasn't the smoothest ride, with some starts and stops and the occasional backwards movement. In a sense, the covert world that was literally underneath the Pentagon had mastered the concept of cubicles.

The box came to a halt and the door opened—once more where it was supposed to and not at the "final destination." Foreman stood up as the box door opened, and then a door beyond it slid aside. Before stepping out, Foreman reached around the doors to the left and blindly flipped off an infrared sensor. Then he entered the windowless cube that had been his Pentagon office for over fifty years.

It made Mulder's fictional basement room underneath FBI headquarters look chic, clean, and modern. Files were stacked everywhere. The walls were lined with tin foil, which might make a visitor wonder, but there hadn't been a visitor here to wonder in a quarter century. Foreman was buried deep, literally and figuratively.

He'd put the foil up one day in a fit of frustration at his lack of knowledge, not because he thought it did anything to protect him, but because it had given him something to do. He figured if anyone did bother to visit him, it would rattle them, make them think he was nuts, and they'd be anxious to leave. All good things in his opinion.

On top of the foil on one wall was a large-scale map of the entire world. It was covered in writing and post-its. Several highlighted areas seemed to be the focus of a lot of attention: the Bermuda Triangle; an area in Cambodia near the location of the ancient, abandoned city of Kol Ker, also known as Koh Ker, depending on who one spoke to; Lake Baikal and the Chernobyl areas in Russia; and some others, including the Devil's Sea off of Japan. In all those places, written in red marker was: *Here There Be Monsters.*

Seventy years earlier in the vicinity of the Devil's Sea, Foreman's squadron hadn't contacted the enemy and been lost to combat. He would have heard that over the radio. His own pilot had been forced to ditch their plane due to engine problems, and they'd bobbed in the ocean for almost an hour before being forced to take to their life raft. Eventually they were picked up by a destroyer.

In reality, the rest of the squadron had simply gone silent a few minutes after Foreman's plane went down, heading in the direction of a strange cloud formation. Gone. Disappeared. Never heard from again. No sign of them ever found.

Foreman had done research and learned that the location where his fellow Marines disappeared was called the Devil's Sea. Then, after the war, he'd been reassigned to Naval Air Station Fort Lauderdale. Just before a routine training mission, Foreman had been overwhelmed with a feeling of dread. He'd begged off the mission, instead spending the time in the tower. When all five planes of Flight 19 disappeared, and a PBM Mariner Flying Boat sent to search for them exploded with all hands lost, it initiated a lifetime of obsession.

Also on the map were thumbtacks with different colored string stretching between them, arcing across the globe from point to point. There was almost a pattern to the lines.

Almost, but not quite. Another frustrating thing for Foreman. It seemed the motto of his seventy years of research: Almost, but not quite.

There was no "The Truth Is Out There" poster hanging on the wall. He'd hated that show, because he believed it trivialized matters that were critically important. And it had never revealed its fictional *truth*. Foreman had yet to find his real truth, but he was going to try every day until he died.

He got along okay with Edith Frobish.

There were a couple of posters, though. One had a famous saying from Shakespeare, more a quote since it was longer than a saying:

> Tomorrow, and tomorrow, and tomorrow,
> Creeps in this petty pace from day to day,
> To the last syllable of recorded time;
> And all our yesterdays have lighted fools
> The way to dusty death!

Not exactly the most cheery words, but it had kept Foreman sane all these long decades, because while he believed one hundred percent that his mission was critical, he also accepted that in the big scheme of things it was all going to end in death.

For everyone.

Thinking of death, Foreman opened a folder and pulled out an MRI image of a head. He walked over to the saying and tacked the image at the bottom of Shakespeare's famous lines. He stared at it for a few minutes, and then reached out and ran his finger over a dark mass at the base of the brain.

So small in the big scheme of things.

Which reminded him. He reached into a pocket and pulled out a handkerchief. He carefully unfolded it in the palm of his hand. He counted six pills of varying sizes and hues. Carefully, fingers shaking, he put each one in his mouth one by one, until he had them all. He grabbed a bottle of water and took a swig and swallowed with a grimace.

Another day.

With a sigh, Foreman walked away and sat behind the gray metal, government-issue (circa 1978) desk. He retrieved his keyboard from underneath several folders. The software on the computer was up to date because every year Foreman unplugged the whole thing and hauled it out to the security post and turned it over to IT for service.

A series of emails from the National Security Agency were piled up in his inbox, all part of the results of his daily requests for information. That no one in the NSA apparently cared that somebody in the Pentagon (or technically underneath the Pentagon) was interested in subjects as diverse as the Bermuda Triangle, ley lines, unexplained disappearances of ships, planes, Amelia Earhart, Atlantis, strange cloud formations, and a couple dozen other topics spoke to a level of bureaucratic apathy. The kind that led to events like 9/11. And Foreman being left alone.

Foreman clicked on the first one to begin his reading when he suddenly looked up from the smudged computer screen. He cocked his head as he closed his eyes, as if listening. He opened his eyes as the computer screen went blank and then began flashing bright red, bathing his haggard, lean face with the blood light.

He reached into a drawer in the desk and took out an ancient Egyptian coin. One with Amin-Zeus on one side, but no Ptolemy on the other. He expertly flipped it through his fingers, calming the shake that was normally in them.

"So it begins," he whispered as he got to his feet and picked up his cane.

He actually seemed kind of happy.

███████████████████████

"Where is the American?" the Russian asked.

"Not here," the woman replied.

"I can see that," the Russian replied. "Get him."

"I do not fetch like a dog," the woman said. She was seated behind a desk in the corner of a quiet warehouse, not far from the airport on Grand Cayman Island in the Caribbean. Across from her was the Russian, a cadaverous man, whom she knew to be former Spetsnaz. He had two comrades flanking him, both also emaciated. They were not openly brandishing weapons, but Sin Fen knew men like that didn't go to the bathroom without at least a gun and a knife and a hair trigger of anger. Strange for the warm clime, all three men wore slacks and long-sleeve shirts. Both of the flanking men wore hats with wide brims, pulled down low over their faces. They also wore gloves. Strange indeed.

The Russian smiled, which obviously required a lot of effort. His face was stretched tight as if it were a mask, the skin pale and unmarked. "No. You do not look like someone who would fetch." The oddest thing about the man was that his eyes were different colors: one blue, one brown.

Sin Fen was six feet even, slender, dressed in tight black slacks and a red, loose blouse. Her face was exotic, a mixture of various cultures: Chinese, Cambodian, Thai, French, and traces of others were mixed in her genes. She had high cheekbones and almond-shaped dark eyes. Black hair, cut short and efficient, framed her face. Her skin was smooth, making it impossible to determine her age; anywhere from twenty-five to fifty and one could still be wrong.

The Russian, his face weathered from time spent out in the vagaries of weather, from the steaming desert of southwest Asia to the icy blast of the Siberian tundra, gave a half bow. The left side of his already-worn face was seared with burn lines, just outside his eye socket, running down to his jaw.

"I am Serge. May I have the honor of your name?"

"I am Sin Fen," she replied. "Are you named after Saint Sergius of Radonezh?"

Serge slowly straightened, and there was no trace of the smile. "So you are an educated as well as a beautiful woman. A dangerous combination. But assumptions about assumptions can be dangerous. Where is the American?"

"He's gone."

"Where?"

"Back to the United States."

Serge looked over his shoulder at the man to his right, who shrugged. Then back at Sin Fen. "That is a problem. We have some merchandise that was commissioned by the American. We require payment."

It was Sin Fen's turn to shrug. "I cannot help you with that. The American is gone. And he will not be coming back."

"How do you know that?" Serge asked.

Sin Fen stood and the Russian looked her up and down, impressed with her height. "I know."

"You are sitting at his desk," Serge said. "Perhaps we can deal with you?"

"It is my desk. It always was my desk."

Serge frowned. "Then—"

Sin Fen held up her left hand, one slender finger extended. "I do not like having weapons pointed at me."

Serge held up both his hands, empty palms exposed. "There are no—"

"I like lying even less," Sin Fen said.

The Russian to Serge's right finally spoke, his voice hoarse. "Let's cut this bitch's throat and find someone with money."

Sin Fen's extended finger slowly went from vertical to angled, pointing out the open warehouse doors to the building across the street. "If I raise my other hand, your man on the second floor, who has been holding a sniper rifle aimed at me, will be dead. Then all three of you will be dead."

"There are more of us," Serge said.

"I know. That's why your man, and the three of you, are not dead already."

"You are a fool," Serge said.

"You are ignorant," Sin Fen returned.

"Not as ignorant as you are," Serge said. "After all, my comrades and I are here, when we should not be."

"You threaten the entire world for *money*?" Sin Fen shook her head in disgust. "You will be tracked down and destroyed. In fact, that process has already begun."

Serge smiled. "You can lower your hands. You have this situation under control. *This* situation. But the larger situation? We have it under control." He looked at his watch. "And as far as being tracked down? We've already dealt with that. What we've come out of, your threats mean nothing to us."

"But it's not really money you're after, is it?" Sin Fen asked.

Serge glanced over his shoulder. "What we need is none of your business."

"You use the money to get what you want," Sin Fen said. "People."

A nerve on the side of Serge's face spasmed, but he said nothing.

"You're reaping," Sin Fen continued.

Serge was startled for the first time. "I don't know of what you speak."

"You lie poorly. Most Russians do."

"Who are you?" Serge demanded.

"Your comrades look like extras in a television show," Sin Fen said. "*Walking Dead.*"

The side of Serge's face twitched. "We can still kill you."

"You could try," Sin Fen said.

Sin Fen's cell phone urgently buzzed, the sound echoing in the warehouse.

"I suggest you deal with *your* problem," Serge said. He turned and left the warehouse, his two comrades following.

Sin Fen turned the phone on. "The Russians were just here. I could stop them before—" She was cut off.

She listened and then grimaced. "This is dangerous." She spoke quickly, stopping a reply from the other end. "I know it's necessary. But it's still dangerous." She looked at her watch. "The clock has begun. Let us hope all works as planned."

On the top floor of the White House, in a tiny office with no number or name on the door, the Keep was meeting with the new president. It was their third meeting this year since the first female president had taken office, which was about the norm, since there was usually only the inbrief, then the outbrief, and a few incident briefings. No previous president had wanted to spend any more time around the Keep, except for those essential briefings as they arose.

A need had arisen.

This desire for distance was not because the Keep was unpleasant in appearance or demeanor. She was a relatively young woman, in her mid-thirties. She had short dark hair, cut close to her skull, and pale skin. She was petite, barely crossing five feet in height. Her name badge simply said Elle, but the President knew her as *the* Keep.

As if there were only one.

The problem the President had with the Keep was the information she held in her brain and in a leather-bound book she kept close by her side. The first month in office, the President had received a private briefing from the Keep, who'd shown her the Book of Truths. It was a compilation from every president starting with Thomas Jefferson forward, consisting of the top ten lessons learned in office, written down by the Keep and then passed on to the incumbent.

A way of preserving institutional knowledge. In the book were truths presidents would never put in their memoirs or have in the archives of their libraries. Here were listed the brutal realities of the office and the secrets that had to stay within the confines of the White House and the Oval Office.

The briefing had been a shock, as it was for every new president. Entering office they were expecting secrets, of course. But the harsh truth about the way the world really worked was more than any had nightmared about. The Keep had briefed the President on the Cellar, the Nightstalkers, and various other secret organizations and what it was they fought against. Some of it ventured into the realm of science fiction, such as Rifts and Fireflies. Some of it was brutal, such as Cellar Sanctions.

The current President had protested, naturally, given her platform and background, about Sanctions. That one woman, the head of the Cellar, held the power of life and death over American citizens, the President found immoral, illegal, and repugnant. The Keep had shown her the presidential decree founding and authorizing the Cellar and its actions, and explained the necessity of such an organization, so the President had only been left with immorality and repugnance.

And the Cellar.

The rest of the White House, beyond the President, thought the Keep worked for someone else's staff. She was bland, tiny, and didn't make a fuss. Some even thought she worked for housekeeping.

In a way she did.

Just at a very high level.

"I was in an important meeting," the President said, more out of frustration than making any impact on the Keep.

"There's been an incident, Madam President," the Keep said. She was sliding back an old framed print of the White House hanging on her wall, revealing a safe. The President recognized it as a twin to the one in the Oval Office. Top of the line and it could be opened only by authorized personnel, or else everything inside would be destroyed. The one in the Oval Office could only be opened by the President.

"And the incident is?" the President asked.

"We're about to find out," the Keep said. She went through the retina scan, the fingerprint scan, the voice analysis, and the rapid DNA check in thirty seconds. The red light on the screen remained on. "Your turn, Madam President."

"Dual safeties?" the President said as she walked around the desk. "How did you get my data?"

"We copied your safe, Madam President," the Keep said.

"Of course." The President went through all the checks and the red light went out, replaced by green, and there was a distinct click. "By the way," the President said, "who is 'we'?"

The Keep ignored the question and opened the door. She pulled out a thin red envelope. It wasn't stenciled with the usual Top Secret Or We Kill You markings like most of the manila envelopes the President handled on a daily basis. It had, archaically, a wax seal on the flap. The Keep sat down and the President resumed her seat across from her. Two Secret Service agents were outside the door, but no one sat in on a meeting between the Keep and the President.

Using an ancient opener shaped like a saber—"Andrew Jackson's," the Keep informed the President—the Keep slid the blade under the flap and cut the wax. She opened the envelope and slid out a thin sheaf of papers. She scanned the top page while the President waited impatiently, a woman not used to waiting.

The Keep pursed her lips. If the President had spent more time around her, she would have known that as a sign of extreme agitation, the equivalent of someone of lesser self-control running around in circles and screaming, "We're all going to die!"

"What is it?" the President asked, her mind racing ahead to having to go down to the Emergency Operations Center, open nuclear launch codes, start World War III, battle zombies, and who knew what else, given this was the Keep. After reading the Book of Truths, her imagination was open to anything.

Or so she thought. She'd already forgotten that she'd thought she was ready for anything when she took office.

"There's been a breach of a facility," the Keep said. "Actually"—she paused, a frown crossing her face as she flipped a couple of pages—"it appears a facility has disappeared. More importantly, the organization that was housed in the facility has disappeared."

"What organization?" the President asked.

The Keep looked up from the papers. "The Time Patrol."

CHAPTER 4

"Doctor Golden," Hannah, the head of the Cellar, said. "Meet Frasier, the psychiatrist for Area 51 and the Nightstalkers."

Doctor Golden was not pleased that there was another person, a psychiatrist at that, in Hannah's office. Not quite an affront to her professional integrity, but it threw her off. Then again, the man, Frasier, tended to throw everyone off when they first met him.

"Pleased to meet you," Frasier said in a tone that indicated neither pleasure nor any other emotion. A stating of a convention. He stuck out his right hand and Golden noticed that his left hand was covered with a black glove.

"Pleased to meet you," she lied in return, shaking his one live hand.

Frasier was dressed in a black suit, black tie, and white shirt. He wore sunglasses, which was incongruous since they were three hundred feet underneath the crystal palace of the National Security Agency at Fort Meade.

Forced pleasantries over, they both sat down in hard plastic seats facing Hannah's desk. Unlike Moms, who went by the name the Nightstalkers gave her, or Ms. Jones, who'd been a bit more formal, Hannah was simply known as that. No last name, since it had been her husband's and he was years dead after having betrayed her. Not a title, because how do you give a title to someone who ran an organization that no one was supposed to talk about?

Hannah sat behind a wide desk that was devoid of any personal items. In fact, it was currently devoid of anything except a small stack of folders. Hannah was in her forties, fit and trim, but the line between the gray hair sprouting from her scalp and the blonde ends indicated she'd made a command decision to give up on coloring her hair anymore sometime in the past year. There are many reasons women make this decision, if they ever make it, and even Doctor Golden with her degrees would be hard-pressed to delve into Hannah's psyche to determine hers.

And there was no way Hannah would ever allow Golden, or anyone else for that matter, entry into her psyche. Her predecessor, Nero, had done that quite effectively, which is why he had chosen her to be his replacement.

"I've asked Mister Frasier here," Hannah said, "because there are some decisions that I need to make and I desire input." She placed her hand on the stack of personnel folders to emphasize her point.

The office was, naturally, windowless. There was a door behind Hannah, which led to her personal space where she spent her off-duty time.

There wasn't much of that.

The Cellar was founded in the dark days after Pearl Harbor, while smoke still poured out of damaged ships and desperate, trapped sailors pounded on armored hulls that had been designed to protect them but that became their prison instead. As those taps faded out over the days that followed, the sleeping giant that was the peacetime United States awoke and was filled with a terrible resolve. Which is exactly what Admiral Yamamoto, who'd planned the attack, had cautioned would be the ultimate result.

The last three sailors trapped in the USS *West Virginia* survived sixteen days.

One of Sun Tzu's maxims was that: *"Secret operations are essential in war; upon them the army relies to make its every move."* Someone had been wise enough to realize that once organizations became secret, they became dangerous not only to the enemy but also to the country that had founded them, with the potential particularly for rogue individuals to cause harm. It was much like the armor hull that was supposed to protect those Pearl Harbor sailors, which instead ended up dooming them.

So the Cellar was founded. The secret police arm for the secret agencies.

The Cellar battled through World War II, riding herd on organizations such as the OSS, aka the Office of Strategic Services, later to become the CIA, and a cluster of other supersecret groups, which sprouted like the snakes on Medusa's head in the burning exigencies of world war. But it was after the hot war ended with the ashes of Hiroshima and Nagasaki and the Cold War began that the need for the Cellar blossomed because, paradoxically, the number of secret organizations increased dramatically.

In 1947, President Truman formed a top-secret committee code-named Majestic-12 and headquartered it at Area 51. It dealt with things, well, things that go bump, slither, explode, infect, etc., in the night. Sometimes in the daytime too. And the committee also dealt with the screwups, intentional or not, of scientists, which were growing exponentially. That was much more common, especially now that the atom had been split. With scientists pushing the edge of our knowledge, often venturing past that edge, the world was a more dangerous place than it had ever been.

So units had been founded, such as the Nightstalkers, which Ms. Jones had commanded.

All these secret *if-I-tell-you-about-them-I-have-to-kill-you-and-cut-your-head-off-and-stick-it-in-a-safe* organizations fell under the domain of the Cellar as far as discipline was concerned. Which meant Hannah held the life of every single person in the covert world in her hands. Well, her head actually, which was much better than any safe.

Once a housewife in St. Louis, she'd been chosen, recruited, and tested by her predecessor, Nero, through a crucible of near death, with Neeley at her side.

Like Nero, she could order a Sanction on anyone, which meant the field operative whom she dispatched, much like Neeley was doing in the Pacific Northwest with Roland, was judge, jury, and executioner. There was to be no formal trial, no lawyers, no mercy.

The Cellar had been founded by Presidential Decree in order to legally do the illegal.

"So." Hannah said it as a statement and an inducement for input. "Moms is out. Who do we replace Ms. Jones with to command the Nightstalkers?"

"Why is Moms out?" Frasier asked.

Golden answered, "She's too close to the members of the team."

Frasier smiled, without managing to convey any warmth. "She's not as close to the team as you might think she is. Or she thinks she is." And then Frasier pulled his patented move, removing his sunglasses and revealing his one solid black artificial eye, surrounded by scar tissue.

Golden was ready for it. "Reading me, Mister Frasier?" She was referring to the eye's ability to pick up changes in her body temperature and other data and feed it into his brain. A crude, but effective lie detector.

"No, Ms. Golden."

"It's Doctor Golden."

"Is there a need for me to read you?" Frasier asked, and it was unclear whether the question was directed to her or Hannah.

"We're all on the same side here," Hannah said.

"Right," Frasier said. "By the way, *Doctor* Golden, I have a doctorate too, but I'll go with Mister Frasier. On the team they just called me Frasier. But you're not on the team," he added, "so Mister will do just fine."

"And why did you get that name?" Golden asked. "The Nightstalkers christen each new member with a single moniker based on first impressions, don't they?"

Frasier smiled. "Guess they thought I was a bit like the character from that old TV show."

"Fussy, stuck-up, narcissistic?"

"Maybe," Frasier said. "Then again, maybe it was for my wonderful sense of humor and keen observation of the traits of others." He shrugged. "The Nightstalkers make snap suggestions during the naming ceremony, working off first impressions, and we both know how misleading those can be." He shifted his attention to Hannah. "And then Ms. Jones makes the final determination of each team member's new name, and you're stuck with it whether apropos or not."

"Sort of how we were burned by Burns?" Golden asked, referring to a not-too-long-ago mission.

"Nice play on words," Frasier allowed.

"Did you handle his psychological vetting?" Golden asked.

"I did," Frasier said. "As they say in the artillery, looked good when he left me."

Hannah interrupted, getting them back on track. "We have been without Ms. Jones's services for a bit too long now."

"Pitr has been doing an adequate job," Frasier said. "Why not leave him in place? He knows the missions, he knows the history of the Nightstalkers, he knows the team."

"Adequate isn't good enough," Hannah said of Ms. Jones's long-time assistant. She nodded at Golden, who spoke up.

"The team will always see Pitr as a shadow of Ms. Jones since he was her attendant. Subconsciously they will not give him the respect he needs to command the team."

"So Pitr is out just like that?" Frasier said. "I assume his folder is not in that pile." He nodded toward the desk. "Although, I'm not sure I agree with Doctor Golden's reasoning about either Moms or Pitr. The team members are professionals, and they've had no complaints about Pitr. Or his shadow."

Golden shrugged. "We wouldn't be sitting here if Pitr was acceptable to Hannah."

Frasier reluctantly accepted that reasoning.

"Outside of Pitr," Hannah asked Frasier, "do you have a suggestion?"

Frasier turned to Golden. "How is Neeley's therapy going?"

"She's killing someone as we speak. She and your man Roland."

"That's not answering the question," Frasier said. "Although the fact she's working in concert with another operative is a change for her."

"It is," Golden said, and her tone indicated displeasure, but whether it was at someone being killed (doubtful), Neeley working with someone else (possible), or just Frasier in general (likely) wasn't clear.

Hannah spoke up. "Neeley is an excellent field operative, but she isn't managerial material."

"You don't want to let her go," Frasier said.

"My desires play no role in field decisions," Hannah said in a voice that dripped ice.

Frasier backtracked slightly. "Certainly." He gestured at the folders. "It's obvious you have candidates," Frasier said. "If we knew who they were, we could—"

Further words were forestalled as a strip of red light all around the edge of the ceiling began flashing, accompanied by a klaxon. For the first time in the presence of others since taking this position, Hannah was rattled. She stared at the light, mouth slightly open, eyes blinking. Then she shook her head, gathering herself, and opened the top, right-hand drawer of her desk. She pulled out a leather-bound file secured with a red ribbon, which was sealed with, of all things, wax. Hannah ran a finger under the ribbon and broke the wax seal. She flipped the file open.

Frasier and Golden exchanged glances, the klaxon resounding in their ears, but Hannah was focused on reading.

Hannah stood up abruptly and walked across the office. She slid aside a panel that had appeared to simply be part of the drab gray metal wall, exposing a switch. Hannah pulled the switch and the klaxon stopped. The red light stopped flashing but it stayed lit, tainting the room with its glow. Another panel slid down just above the switch and an old red bulb display appeared; a countdown apparently from the time of Dr. No.

12:00

As they watched, the first second counted off.

11:59:59

Hannah stared at the timer for five seconds and then returned to her desk. She sat down, and the look on her face dissuaded either of the two psychiatrists from asking any questions. She read some more from the file, slowly, steadily, before putting it on the desk and raising her eyes to her guests.

"What is it?" Doctor Golden asked, having never seen her normally somber boss so grave. It was as if a statue had frozen into diamond. "What happens in twelve hours?"

"Unless we stop it," Hannah said, "the end of our existence."

CHAPTER 5

Eleven Hours

Scout was riding Comanche through the neighborhood, glad that the construction boom that had started this housing enclave over two years ago had ground to a standstill along with the economy. When her family had moved in, the latest construction, five empty lots down, had been proceeding furiously, even on Thanksgiving, but then it had suddenly ceased and the house remained almost complete. This gave Scout quite a few empty lots to race her horse across when she was home.

And fewer neighbors to give her grief.

She was still mightily puzzled and disturbed by her late breakfast. More accurately, her mother's cooking of the late breakfast: the food and the singing. And then there was the strange text from Jake who'd ignored her calls this afternoon. She hoped Nada would give her a ring and she could run it all by him. He was always a voice of reason and reassurance.

She heard a helicopter in the distance, but that was nothing unusual. A unit of Army Air National Guard was based at Knoxville Airport and OH-58 observation helicopters flew over all the time.

Scout knew what kind of aviation they were because she'd flown in enough copters during her training to be able to differentiate. Scout halted Comanche and cocked her head to the side to hear more clearly. There was something different about this helicopter. A different thrum to the rotors and engines. A UH-60 Black Hawk, and it was coming closer.

Comanche was startled as the Black Hawk helicopter raced in, just above the treetops, and banked hard barely thirty feet overhead. Scout got the horse under control with great difficulty as the chopper landed in the field in front of her. A side door slid open and a man in camouflage fatigues hopped off. He jogged toward her with the gait of a man who wasn't used to jogging. He had a small camouflage bag in one hand.

His face was flushed red when he reached her. "Scout, I'm Colonel Orlando. I'm here from the Nightstalkers."

Scout slid off her horse. She looked past Orlando at the chopper. There was a door gunner, weapon at the ready, and Scout had no doubt there were real bullets in the machine gun. "Where's Nada?"

"He's en route to the rally point," Orlando said. He gestured toward the chopper. "We need to go now."

"What about Comanche?"

Orlando put a hand on her elbow. "I've got Acme support coming. They'll find your horse and stable it. You can count on it."

"But—" Orlando cut her off.

"Scout, I'm sorry, but we don't have time to discuss this. We have to move now." He reached into the bag and pulled out a piggy bank. "Nada said to give you this."

Scout reluctantly let go of the reins and took the bank. She allowed Orlando to lead her to the chopper.

"Really sorry to be in such a rush," Orlando repeated, and she sensed he was. "Normally I do a test on a new recruit. Harvey, or the suicide bomber, or something like that, but Nada vouches for you and that's good enough. You've had three months of training, which is barely enough to get you in the Army, never mind the Nightstalkers. But you've already worked with the team. And you're still alive, so that's a pretty good test that you've passed. Twice."

They reached the helicopter and Scout hopped aboard, placing the piggy bank on her lap. Orlando had a little more trouble getting on board, but the second he was inside, the chopper lifted.

The import of what Orlando had said struck her suddenly. She had to shout to be heard above the blade and engine noise. "Does that mean I'm a Nightstalker now?"

"Not up to me," Orlando said.

"Are we going to Area 51?"

"Nope."

"Is this in regard to my text?"

"No idea."

"My training?

"No clue."

"Well, okay." Scout saw Comanche standing calmly where she'd left him, peering up at the receding helicopter. The horse didn't seem that upset, but then again, it was a horse. Then she shifted her gaze. Scout could already see the Knoxville Airport directly ahead. "Where are we going?"

"New York City."

"Cool beans," Scout said. "I've never been to the Big Apple."

An F-14 Tomcat was waiting for Roland at Naval Air Station Whidbey Island, engines throttled back, pilot at the ready.

Roland got out of the truck, still dressed all in black, his face covered with camouflage paint, his field pack over one shoulder, his other hand holding the case for his sniper rifle. Neeley got out also and stood next to him. They waited awkwardly, side by side, neither certain what to say. Roland's stomach rumbled since he still hadn't gotten a chance to eat since the shooting.

Roland settled on mission, which is what he always did when nervous. "That guy said some weird stuff."

"What weird stuff?" Neeley asked.

Roland relayed Carl Coyne's last words verbatim.

"People say strange things facing death," was all Neeley could say. They were both still rattled by the body disappearing. "Any idea what he meant by the Patrol?"

"Nope."

"Ratnik is interesting," Neeley said. "Russian, I think. We'll have to check into it."

"Okay." It was obvious Roland could care less what Coyne had said.

"And Sin Fen," Neeley said. "A name perhaps?"

"Perhaps."

"That was a strange anomaly," Neeley added about the disappearing body, for lack of anything else to say.

"It was."

Of course, they were also rattled by the kiss.

"Well . . ." Neeley cleared her throat. "You best be going. Be careful with that"—she nodded at the case of the sniper rifle. "Don't hit anything important in the cockpit."

"Yeah." Roland took a step toward the waiting jet, and then

turned back to her. He stuck a big paw out. "It was an honor to serve with you."

Neeley shook his hand.

Roland flushed red once more underneath the green and black camouflage. Then he turned abruptly for the fighter.

As the jet roared down the runway and disappeared into the clouds overhead, Neeley's cell phone began to ring.

There was only one person who had that number: Hannah.

SEE ALL THE POISINUS SNAKES 75CENTS

The sign was punched full of bullet holes and rusting so badly it was difficult to read the letters. Eagle was driving the Humvee (Eagle always drove), Mac was in the passenger seat listening to Pitr give him an update (not much information other than to get to New York City ASAP), and Kirk was in the center turret manning the .50 caliber machine gun (because someone always manned the .50). Doc was in the backseat, still complaining about the lack of Ivar.

No one was singing Warren Zevon's "Lawyers, Guns and Money."

Eagle slammed on the brakes in irritation as two guards popped up out of hide holes, their laser sights sending red dots dancing on Eagle's and Kirk's foreheads. Eagle also knew a Hellfire missile had been targeted on the Humvee as soon as they got in range. Its firing mechanism was slaved to the guards' triggers and also their body monitors: If they either fired their weapons and/or died, the Humvee would be blasted.

Sometimes the intense security at the Ranch got on his nerves.

One of the contractors came forward and flashed the retina scanner into Eagle's eyes.

"Are any of us who we really think we are?" Eagle asked the contractor, because Eagle always liked jangling their psyches.

The guard ignored him, as they all learned to do. The guard waved them through, although Eagle picked up a glint in the man's eyes that indicated he'd like nothing better than to pull his trigger, or even die, just to have that Hellfire let loose.

Eagle accelerated toward the barn. Which is what it looked like. Old wood planking, sagging roof, paint faded away by desert storms. Certainly long abandoned, the casual observer would assume.

He aimed for the doors that appeared to be drooping on rusting hinges. The doors were actually reinforced concrete that could take an RPG hit and shrug it off. Mac reached up and hit a button on the top of the windshield. The sophisticated garage door opener sent the correct signal (the wrong signal got the Hellfire up the ass of the approaching vehicle), and the two doors swung smoothly open, hydraulic arms handling the heavy loads.

Eagle raced through the doors while they were still opening (the engineer who designed them hadn't accounted for Eagle's skill and speed) with barely an inch of clearance on either side. He slammed the brakes and twisted the wheel, bringing the Humvee to an abrupt halt right next to the Snake.

The prototype aircraft was a couple of generations beyond the tilt-wing Osprey. The most prominent differences were jet engines instead of turboprops and angled black surfaces on the outside, indicating stealth technology. A refueling probe poked out the front underneath the cockpit where a powerful chain gun was housed in an interior well. The craft took up most of the space inside the Barn.

The four men scrambled out of the Humvee. "Checklists, people," Eagle said, the senior man taking charge. "Protocol saves lives."

He grabbed the acetated Nightstalker Protocol that was usually Nada's province and an alcohol pen and began checking off each preflight task as it was accomplished.

"The only information Pitr gave me," Mac said, "is we might have to do some breaching."

"Load for that," Eagle ordered.

Mac, Doc, and Kirk began loading pre-packed gear to supplement the standard load already in the cargo bay of the Snake. A team box was tied down in the center holding everything from climbing ropes to arctic clothing to chemical/biological protection suits, parachutes, dry suits, spare radio batteries, two million in gold coins for barter, etc., etc.; someone with an extremely paranoid and inventive mind had packed it. Aka Nada.

Eagle did his quick preflight pilot check, walking around the aircraft (even though he'd done one yesterday as part of his own Protocol), and then walked inside and climbed into the pilot's seat. He hit power and the dual engines began to whine.

"Kirk, cut me loose," Eagle ordered over the team net.

Kirk removed the power cord underneath the nose of the aircraft. Then he ran up the ramp and took a seat next to Doc on the ubiquitous red web cargo seats along the outside of the cargo bay that all military aircraft seemed to have.

Doc had his laptop open and was trying to access data about the potential mission.

There wasn't any.

"Mac, open her up."

Mac went to one of the numerous dirty glass cases set on tables along the edge of the Barn and reached into one that warned DANGER: EXTREMELY POISINUS. He hit the open button and then joined Kirk inside the cargo bay. The ramp was closing as soon as he was clear.

The sagging roof of the barn, which was anything but, split apart, powerful hydraulic arms opening up the heavy steel.

The Snake lifted while the doors were still opening, and once more, Eagle cleared the portal with inches to spare.

Eagle banked the hybrid aircraft hard and accelerated as the wings rotated from vertical to horizontal. Less than thirty feet above the ground, Eagle headed east. He pulled back on the controls and the Snake headed up at a steep angle. Eagle kicked in the afterburners.

"Yo, Eagle," Mac said over the net.

"Yes?"

"Got a round in the chamber?"

Eagle's jaw was tight, most of his mind focused on flying, while another part was still on the anomaly in the book he'd been reading and the bigger anomaly of no Ivar.

"Actually," Eagle said, "I do."

In the cargo bay of the Snake, this unexpected development caused the other three Nightstalkers to all share a concerned look. Eagle making sure his pistol was ready for action was almost as disturbing as the other anomalies they'd encountered so far.

THE SPACE BETWEEN

It smelled bad. That was Ivar's first conscious thought. The air was thicker than normal, with an oily quality. And he sort of recognized the smell, similar to the lab in North Carolina when the Rift had opened there, and the mirror Ivars had come through. He'd been so confused then he'd begun to lose track of which Ivar he really was, which actually didn't make sense.

Unless you'd been there.

Ivar didn't want to open his eyes because he knew by the smell it was likely he would not be seeing anything good. Like a child hiding under a blanket, there was a part of him that wanted to believe not seeing meant there was nothing out there.

His last memory was of being in the Archives and Doc yelling at him to move the ladder. Then blackness, as abrupt as being put under before surgery.

He hadn't even had a chance to count back.

The sense of touch wormed into his brain after smell. He was on his back. He twitched his hand and could feel a coarse, larger-than-sand material running through his fingers.

A beach?

A beach would be good, Ivar thought, so he knew he wasn't on a real beach.

With resignation and a sense of dread, Ivar opened his eyes. It was dim, not dark. But not light. And the light wasn't coming from the sun, he knew that right away. It was diffuse, coming from all around. And there weren't clouds up above. Just a gray, mixed with black, misty haze. And he knew, without being able to see it, that there was something solid above there, a roof. Very far up.

Ivar moved only his eyes, shifting left, right, up, and down. Nothing but the haze. He sat up.

He *was* on a beach. Sort of. There was water to his right. Dark, black water, perfectly smooth. Which made sense since the air was perfectly still. The water looked thicker than water should be.

Perfect was the wrong adjective, Ivar thought as he got to his feet. There was nothing perfect about this place.

The black water stretched as far as he could see into the haze, a distance that was hard to determine. Anywhere from a hundred yards to four hundred or more. He had nothing to scale a distance reference against. It was peculiarly uninviting.

Blinking and focusing, Ivar could barely make out what appeared to be several black columns extending up out of the water and disappearing into the haze above. They didn't appear to be solid. They were of varying diameters, their dark surfaces shimmering.

Strange, Ivar thought.

The "sand" was a black, coarse granular material. The "beach" stretched along the shore in a very gentle (another poor adjective he realized as soon as he thought it) curve in either direction.

And it was littered with vessels. Some large rafts consisting of logs tied together with vines were about ten meters away. Each had a long rudder sweeping back, dug into the sand. Each also had a tattered sail, which drooped, windless, from a mast in the center.

Just past the rafts was a freighter, an old one from as much as Ivar knew about freighters. He walked past the rafts to a point where he could see the name painted on the bow: *Cyclops*. That tingled something in Ivar's memory, but he couldn't grab onto it.

But even as he pondered that, he saw what lay on the other side of the freighter: five Spanish galleons, stranded on the sand as if evenly parked by some massive hand. Scattered on the black sand around them were ransacked chests and supplies.

"Hello!" Ivar called out, knowing as he did so there would be no answer. It was all so still and quiet. And if there were people here, Ivar wasn't sure he wanted to meet them. He was drawn forward, curiosity overwhelming his confusion about this place.

"Whoa," Ivar whispered as he saw what was beyond the galleons. An old ship. Very old. Something he must have seen on the History Channel or some similar show. A single-masted ship with holes on the sides for a bank of oars. The ship was old in design, but the vessel looked relatively new, definitely not a thing for the museum.

A replica, Ivar wondered, but he knew that wasn't the case. It was the real thing.

He climbed up a ladder attached to the side of the ship with wooden pegs. As he came up over the bulwark, he saw something on the other side of the ship that caused him to halt: five military propeller aircraft, lined up wingtip to wingtip.

"Flight Nineteen," Ivar whispered, remembering the opening of *Close Encounters of the Third Kind* and knowing it had something to do with a formation of planes that had disappeared with no trace.

The five TBM Avengers were in mint condition, no sign of accident or foul play.

"Okeydokey." Ivar climbed down the ladder to the "sand." He went over to the planes. There was no sign of the pilots, not that he expected to see any.

He turned away from the water. Ivar took several deep breaths, then looked "landward."

In that direction, the land rose up to a dune about fifty yards away, which blocked any further view. Besides the black sand and the vessels, there was no vegetation, no rocks, nothing. Ivar took a step landward. The sand gave way slightly, but was firm enough to walk on. He moved toward the dune, to gain some altitude and try to get some sense of the terrain.

Ivar crested the dune and wasn't surprised to see similar dunes rippling away into the haze.

"Great," Ivar muttered. He wondered if this was another one of Orlando's tests to see how he would react to this unique environment.

Even Orlando couldn't come up with something this complex and vast.

"Aliens," Ivar muttered to himself, which he knew wasn't a good sign, but there was no one to notice. Maybe a big spaceship with a lot of lights flashing and organ sounds. People coming out of it. The pilots of the Avengers. Except he wasn't on top of Devil's Tower but deep inside some sort of place. "No spaceship," Ivar said.

Ivar made his way down this dune and up another, no idea what he was in search of, but with a feeling that moving was better than staying still. He had to have gotten here some way, so there had to be a way back.

It was the way a scientist would think.

Of course, the ships and planes had gotten here some way too: They'd disappeared off the face of the planet.

And they were still here. In what looked like the exact same condition as when they'd disappeared.

Ivar looked over his shoulder and saw his footprints. As he watched, the black "sand" slowly shifted back into place, making it look as if he had never walked by. Ivar shivered at the deeper implications of that.

He crested another dune and paused. There was really no way to tell direction here, and if his footprints faded away, he wouldn't be able to retrace his steps back to where he'd started.

Belatedly, Ivar pulled out his phone. He wasn't surprised to see no bars: He doubted any of the cell companies had made it this far, however far this was. Still he tried to make a call and got nothing. He shoved the phone back in his pocket.

Ivar puzzled over this predicament for a few moments. He was so lost in thought, he failed to realize he was being surrounded. When he tuned back in to his environment, he had to blink several times to make sure what he was seeing was real: Four men had materialized with no sound, as if sprouting from the ground itself. They were dressed in black lacquered armor and wore ornate helmets. What Ivar focused on, though, were the swords they held in their hands and the spears slung over their backs.

He'd only seen their like in movies: samurai. Or maybe ronin. He wasn't quite sure what the difference between the two was.

One of them gestured, the intent unmistakable. The man took a few steps and disappeared from sight, and Ivar realized the undulating terrain explained their sudden appearance. If he'd been a student of military history, he'd have realized this geography was much the same as that at Little Big Horn, which allowed Custer to be taken so quickly by surprise.

But he wasn't. And he wouldn't have liked the connection.

Bowing to the inevitable, and respecting the sharpness of the blades, Ivar followed. The other three moved in around him without a sound. They walked along the draws, avoiding the crests. After a few minutes, Ivar noticed a change. There were pockets of brown soil here and there. Plants were struggling to grow. As they passed through the junction of two gullies, a small trickle of water cut a path.

"Whoa!" Ivar paused as he saw a stone wall loom directly ahead, arcing up through the haze. One of the trailing warriors gave him a nudge and Ivar continued. They came around a bend in the gully and the pitted wall was two hundred meters in front of them, rising up overhead and disappearing into the haze. Etched into the wall were shallow caves.

More importantly, there were people. Dozens of them. All dressed in a dizzying array of clothes and accouterments, ranging from the samurai/ronin, to medieval garb, to a Roman legionnaire, to more than Ivar could process at the moment.

His attention focused on a woman who came striding toward him, wearing what he recognized as a flight suit. She had curly brown hair and there was something about her striking features that flickered a lightbulb in Ivar's memory but didn't turn it on.

"Do you speak English?" she asked.

Ivar felt a surge of relief. "Yes!"

The woman smiled. "American?"

"Yes!"

"Excellent." The woman extended her hand. "Welcome to the Space Between. I'm Amelia Earhart."

CHAPTER 6

Nine Hours

The Nightstalkers came into New York City hard, and as fast as they could, from their dispersed positions. The word had come down from the top of the National Command Authority, aka the President, and the NYPD had already cleared out the Metropolitan Museum of Art and set up a perimeter around it, including a landing zone for helicopters directly behind the building in the one nearby open space that could take a chopper.

Still, given the Nightstalkers' original displacement, it took several precious hours. But the Keep, first on the scene from DC, had insisted that everyone gather first, which went against Nightstalker Protocol to hit a target quickly. But the Keep had her reasons, actually, reason, dictated by the papers she'd taken out of the safe in her office.

Moms, the second on scene after the Keep, coming out of Kansas, waited impatiently on the south side of the Met. She'd met the Keep once before, during the incident at the White House the Christmas before last involving the Cherry Tree truth serum.

As she'd been then, the Keep was anything but a font of information, telling Moms she only wanted to brief this once.

But with the locals having containment (a terrorism threat was working as cover for the moment, one of the few things New Yorkers actually paid attention to), the focus was on figuring out exactly what the problem was. No one was quite sure. A steel door shuttered the corridor at the bottom of the old elevator. The guard inside the first door was overwhelmed by all the activity, and the only piece of information he could give was that some woman had gone inside and never come back out. Beyond that, it seemed his memory was Swiss cheese.

NYPD SWAT was covering the top of the elevator for the moment, but the moment was stretching out too long in Moms's opinion.

Scout landed after a thrilling fighter jet ride from Knoxville to LaGuardia and a transfer to a military helicopter. She hopped off and looked around. Moms waved for her to come over to the large, modern van the NYPD had given up as the command post, parked on the southwest corner of the museum.

"What's going on?" Scout asked as they entered the CP. "Cool digs," she added, noting the cluster of communication gear, weapons, briefing boards, and maps along the walls, and all the other high-speed gizmos required to run an operation in the City That Never Sleeps. "They got donuts in here somewhere?"

"She on your team?" the Keep asked. "I don't have her on your roster."

"We need her," Moms said, not completely sure why Nada had called Scout in, but implicitly trusting her team sergeant's wishes. "She's been in training for a while now," Moms fudged.

The Keep shrugged. "All right. Your team, your call, your responsibility. But we need the rest of the team here ASAP."

"Nice to meet you too," Scout muttered.

Moms made a brief introduction. "Scout, the Keep. Keep, Scout."

"Charmed," Scout said.

The Keep picked up a phone and ignored her.

"So what's going on?" Scout repeated. "A rift? Fireflies? Zombies?"

Moms stood next to Scout. "We're not sure yet. As she noted, we're waiting on the whole team."

"Okeydokey," Scout said. "Who exactly is she?" she added with a nod at the Keep.

"She works in the White House," Moms said. "For the President. Although it might be the other way around."

"Ah," Scout said, as if she understood something. But it sounded good.

The Keep put down the phone and Moms took the opportunity. "We should move, even without the rest of my team. Containment is the priority."

"NYPD has containment." The Keep looked at Moms. "We're not just waiting on your team. There are others on this list who are en route and need to be here before we attempt to breach whatever is down there." She held up a manila envelope. "Plus, besides NYPD, that steel door at the bottom has containment."

"Says who?" Moms asked.

"According to the information I have," the Keep said, "the facility is six hundred feet underground, surrounded by solid granite bedrock. The only way in or out is via that elevator and a tunnel at the bottom. That door blocks the tunnel in case of an emergency."

"As long as the door isn't breached from the inside," Moms said. "Whoever is in there, if someone is in there, might want to come out. Someone or something sounded the alarm."

To that, the Keep didn't have an answer.

"Who are we waiting on?" Moms asked.

The Keep sighed. "I could pretend to know more than I know. I see it all the time in the White House. But that gets people killed and screws things up." She shook the envelope. "This is how much more I know than you do and there's not much in here. Containment is not the priority here at the moment. Proper reaction is. At least that's what my instructions read." The Keep glanced at her watch. "The clock is ticking and I like it even less than you. We're down to nine hours."

"Until?" Scout asked.

The Keep was expressionless. "Something bad happens."

"Right," Scout said, as if she completely understood. "Bad."

Further conversation was interrupted by the Snake coming in, engines rotating to allow it to descend vertically. The vehicle settled down, the back ramp opened, and most of the rest of the team (minus Roland and Nada—and Ivar) exited, geared up for combat. Scout ran out of the trailer to them and hugged Eagle, then Doc, then Kirk, and finally Mac, not the meeting they were used to at a rally point. They all entered the command post and gathered round Moms, who gave them the same non-news she'd given Scout.

"How much longer until the rest of your team gets here?" the Keep asked, and it was obvious she too was beginning to question the need for the entire team, and whoever else, to be present. She didn't wait for an answer. "Can you have your demo man prepare to blow the steel door at the base of the elevator?" she added. She opened the folder and quickly transcribed some numbers. "Here's the code to activate the elevator."

Moms gestured, handed the code over, and Mac and Kirk left the CP and ran into the Met with their gear to prep charges.

Moms had her head canted, listening to the radio traffic from Pitr at the Ranch, catching up to the Keep's first question. "Roland is coming in by chopper as we speak. He was already en route back east when the alert came. Ten minutes ETA."

Doc was almost bouncing on his toes. "Moms. Ivar is gone."

That got Moms's attention. "What do you mean *gone*?"

"We were in the Archives and he was pushing me on the ladder. And then I looked down and he was no longer there."

"AWOL?"

Doc shook his head. "No. It appears he just disappeared. And his cell phone. When you call, it says the number never existed. It doesn't make sense."

Moms sighed. "You have any idea what happened to him? I want—" She paused as more information came through her headset. "Roland reports there was an anomaly on the Sanction."

"Does he even know what an anomaly is?" Eagle asked.

"He was with Neeley," Moms said.

"Ah," Eagle said, the explanation of Roland's sudden vocabulary expansion now clear. "What kind of anomaly?"

"He didn't say," Moms reported. "We'll get that when he gets here."

"A Sanction's not important right now," the Keep said.

"What about one of our people missing?" Moms asked. "Something isn't right."

"Something isn't," the Keep agreed. "But let's deal with the immediate problem." She held up a hand to forestall further conversation and pressed her other hand on her earpiece, listening. She checked a piece of paper in the envelope. "Bring him through," she finally said. She had a frown, a major indication of puzzlement, as she turned to the team. "I didn't think Foreman really existed. More an urban legend in the black world. The Crazy Old Man."

"Who are you talking about?" Moms asked.

The Keep pointed as an NYPD patrol car pulled up and an officer hopped out. He opened the back door and an old man gingerly exited. He put on a black porkpie hat and adjusted it, edging it down toward his thick glasses.

"Oh, please," Scout said. "Is this guy for real? Trying to *Break Bad*?"

"I don't think he has to try," the Keep said.

Foreman was leaning hard on a cane as he slowly made his way toward the large van. The Keep opened the door to the CP and Scout quickly reached out and offered him a hand.

"Thank you, young lady," Foreman said as he made his way up the steps into the command post. Once inside, he peered around through his thick glasses as he took off the hat. "Which one of you is the current iteration of the Keep?"

"I am."

"Hmm," Foreman said. "A bit young, aren't you?"

"Bit old, aren't you," Scout whispered to Moms, who hushed her.

The Keep didn't respond. Foreman sat down in one of the bucket seats. "What do you have from below?"

"Nothing," the Keep said. "There's a steel door just outside the bottom level. We're rigging charges to blow it right now."

"Yes," Foreman said. "Be careful though. The doors are there as much to keep something in as keep something out."

"Keep what in?" Scout asked.

Foreman grinned, not exactly from pleasure but from a foreboding sense of satisfaction. "Down there be Monsters. Perhaps," he added.

"What exactly was in there?" Moms asked.

Foreman nodded. "If it's still there, the Time Patrol."

"Cool," Scout said.

The Keep turned to Foreman. "When you say Time Patrol, what exactly are you talking about down there?"

"The HUB," Foreman said.

"What's the HUB?" Doc asked.

"How they travel in time, of course," Foreman said. "A form of a gate."

"And how—" Doc began, but Foreman held up a hand.

"You'll know more once we go in and the rest of your team arrives." And with that he folded his arms over his chest.

The Keep turned to Moms. "Where is your team sergeant, Nada?"

"Nada is—" Moms paused, listening on her own earpiece— "parachuting in. Thirty seconds out."

Nada wasn't exactly parachuting in. Not yet. He was in a pod, tucked tightly inside where the surveillance gear on the Blackswift spy plane was supposed to be. He was breathing oxygen from a small canister and couldn't wait to get the hell out of there.

The Blackswift was the latest version of spy plane, capable of Mach 3, and, most importantly, unmanned. It was a drone, but a very fast drone. Nada had been picked up from Disneyland by a military helicopter and flown to Edwards Air Force Base in the high desert where the Blackswift awaited. It was the fastest way to get him to NY, and they were going to try something experimental.

Nada had still been in enough shock from his memory opening up that he'd acquiesced, not that they were going to give him any choice. They'd shoved him in the pod and assured him he'd be ejected 35,000 feet above New York City, a drogue chute would open and slow the pod to a survivable speed, the pod would split and then he could HALO parachute the rest of the way to the ground.

Seriously.

Sounded good in theory.

Often theories are postulated by those who don't have to end up being the test dummy. Nada had his own theory, not quite a Nada Yada yet, that it should be a rule that whoever came up with something should have to test it personally.

The Blackswift looked like a flying dart, most of the space given over to the ramjet engines. The pod fit in underneath the nose, taking up space that would have been a cockpit in a regular plane. There was usually a surveillance pod in this place, not a people pod.

The hour-and-a-half flight had given Nada time to get through his shock and realize this wasn't the brightest idea, being a pod-test dummy. But it was a bit too late for that.

Actually, he didn't care much one way or the other. If he splatted in, so be it. Because now he could remember, and he kept going back to the Nightstalkers' team leader, the one before Moms, pulling him aside during an op, and telling him the news. Actually, the longer the flight went on, the more the thought of splatting in appealed to him.

A voice came over the small earpiece, interrupting his morbid thoughts. The "pilot," who was still sitting back at Edwards at the controls of the drone, said, "Ten seconds until pod drop."

Nada took a breath and prepared as best he could for the unexpected.

He wasn't exactly dropped from the Blackswift. He was ejected. The pod tumbled crazily, and for the first time Nada was grateful for both how tightly he was jammed inside and the cold weather gear he was swaddled in. This went on for about five seconds, and then the pod abruptly jerked into one orientation and Nada assumed that was the drogue chute slowing it down. Twenty seconds later, the pod split apart with a flash of exploding bolts, and Nada was freefalling in the thin and freezing air at altitude.

This, at least, was familiar. Nada spread his arms and legs and got stable. He also got oriented, looking downward. It was a clear day and he could see all of Manhattan, indeed most of New York City and the surrounding metropolitan area, below him. He checked his altimeter.

Thirty-one thousand feet.

It occurred to Nada that the airspace above the city was full of all sorts of aircraft, particularly civilian airliners given the three major airports that served the area, plus all the ones transiting at about this altitude along the northeastern corridor. He could see contrails all about the sky around him.

What were the odds he'd hit a plane? Nada imagined Eagle could have given him those, but he immediately focused on directing his fall. Central Park was easy to pick out, the rectangle of green in the center of the island of Manhattan. So was Jacqueline Kennedy Onassis Reservoir. He knew the destination was to the south of that and on the east side.

He'd had a chance to check the imagery of the target, so he directed himself toward that side of the park. As he passed below ten thousand feet at terminal velocity, Nada spotted the bulk of the Metropolitan Museum, the only large building inside the perimeter of the park.

At five thousand feet, Nada pulled his ripcord and was rewarded with the opening shock. He grabbed the toggles and began steering toward the command post parked behind the museum. At four thousand feet he reversed his spiral down, because Protocol said to reverse direction.

Nada was a big believer in following Protocol.

As he passed through one thousand feet, something flickered to his left and he twisted his head, thinking perhaps it had been a flash of light off the tens of thousands of windows on the cliffs of stone and steel surrounding the oasis of green he was descending into.

But there was nothing of note there.

Nada reached up and flipped open the covers on his quick releases. He stuck his thumbs through the metal loops and began to apply pressure. Glancing down he saw police cars with lights flashing along with other emergency vehicles. Looked like a clusterfrak.

Nada pulled his thumbs out of the loops.

He focused on the ground just as a Black Hawk helicopter came racing up Fifth Avenue. Nada was above it and realized they didn't see him. The irony almost made him laugh—deciding not to commit suicide and then getting sliced and diced by a chopper anyway.

The chopper banked and headed toward a VS-17 panel staked down in the grass in the only open spot directly behind the museum. Nada did a quick check. There was a huge open area with a bunch of ballfields to the west, but he instinctively knew he didn't have the altitude to make it.

As the chopper landed, Nada jerked his toggles and flared, touching down in the road adjacent to the landing zone. The downblast from the helicopter's blades caught his chute and it knocked him over, dragging him. Nada grabbed the cutaways and pulled them. The chute flew off down the road as Nada did the paratrooper's moment of grace, lying perfectly still in contact with Mother Earth, thankful that all his pieces and parts were still attached.

"Nice entrance," Scout said, slightly out of breath from running over.

Nada got to his knees and then stood. "You're bigger."

"I'm older."

"That too," Nada said. He was surprised at the strength of feelings that washed through him, and he repressed the desire to rush up to her and give her a hug. Fortunately for him, Scout had no such reservations. She wrapped her arms around him, longer than Zoey's and thus fully embracing, even though Nada had on a combat vest loaded with the various tools of his deadly trade.

"Good to see you, old man," Scout said.

"You too, young woman."

Scout stepped back and looked at him in a curious way. "You all right?"

"I'm fine," Nada lied, and as he did so, he knew she knew he was lying. And then he realized her curiosity was infused with concern.

"Why aren't you in college?" Nada asked.

"I'm trying to decide what to do with my life," Scout said. "Right now I'm thinking the Peace Corps."

Nada gave a wan smile. "Right. How was the training?"

"Army training, sir," Scout said in her best Bill Murray voice. "Come on." She tugged at his hand, reminding him of an older Zoey, which reminded him of someone else, and he masked the pain of the fractured memory as best he could.

"Let's move, people!" Moms was standing in the doorway of the CP. Nada glanced over and saw Roland's unmistakable bulk coming from the chopper. Nada followed Scout, and the Nightstalkers were finally assembled. Except, of course, for the disappeared Ivar. And Mac and Kirk, who were rigging charges.

Scout noted that Foreman was checking his watch and making some notes in a small pad, which he slipped back into his breast pocket.

"Who's that?" Nada asked, nodding toward the old man seated near the front.

"Good question," Moms said. "Someone who wants to keep his information close to his chest. Named Foreman."

"Where's Ivar?" Nada asked.

"Gone," Moms said.

"Gone?" Nada repeated. "Gone where?"

"We don't know."

The Keep spoke. "This is Mister Foreman," she said. "He—" She paused. "What exactly is your job, Mister Foreman?"

"That's a little hard to define," Foreman said.

"Right," Scout said.

"You could try," Nada said.

"I could," Foreman agreed, but didn't say anything more.

"Are you in charge of the Patrol?" the Keep asked.

"I was instrumental in their"—he searched for a word and when he chose it, it seemed he wasn't exactly happy with it— "formation. But I am not in charge of them."

"When did they begin traveling?" Doc asked.

Foreman chuckled. "A rather naïve question, especially from someone with so many doctorates. You do understand the paradox involved in the question?"

"Everything has a start point," Doc said.

"I suppose," Foreman said in a way that indicated he didn't suppose at all.

"You know who we are," Moms said, not a question.

"I've read your files," Foreman said. He reached inside his coat pocket and retrieved a manila folder matching the one the Keep had. "We all have our rules and orders and our information."

The Keep made a belated, and apparently unnecessary, introduction. "Mister Foreman, these are the Nightstalkers. As you seem to know, they are a special team designed to deal with special problems."

"Certainly," Foreman said. "The best of the best and all that. I'm certain. You often deal with Rifts, correct?"

"We shut the last one down," Moms said.

"*You* shut it down?" Foreman seemed amused. "I thought it was the other way around. And are you sure it's the last? Willing to bet your life on it?"

Nada took Moms's side, as he always did. "There hasn't been another one since the *Zombie at the Dam*."

"Yes," Foreman said, "when the other side, whoever they are, sent back those from our world who opened Rifts and survived going through. Colonel Thorn, who you might consider one of the first Nightstalkers, took care of the Japanese and Nazi physicists who were, so to speak, spit back to us."

"You say his name like he was someone you knew," Moms said.

"I did know Thorn," Foreman said. "He was a good man. A tough soldier. As evidenced by his last act."

"What exactly are we dealing with here and now, Mister Foreman?" Moms asked.

"I don't know what we're dealing with. That's why you're here." Foreman clasped his hands together to keep them from shaking.

"We're above the Time Patrol. The alarm would only be sounded and the outer door closed if one of two things happened. One. There was an uncontrolled reverse breach via the HUB. Someone or something from another time or timeline coming into our time. Or two. The HUB is no longer down there." He looked at Scout. "In the former, then there might well be monsters down there. So to speak. At least things we would call monsters, which is what we tend to call that which we do not understand. Or in the latter case, there will be just nothing; no Patrol and no HUB. In that instance, we've got a bigger problem because we need the Patrol to protect our timeline."

Doc was focused, as always, on the scientific angle. "So are you talking time travel *and* travel across to parallel timelines?"

"The Patrol only travels in our timeline," Foreman said, evading the import of the question. "That's what makes it different than going through Rifts."

"Who do they guard us against?" Moms asked.

Foreman responded. "Against those who try to attack our past in order to change our present and our future."

"And who exactly are these attackers?" Moms asked.

"People and things that open gates into our timeline," Foreman said. "While we can travel back in our timeline, we do not yet have the controlled ability to travel across timelines like others do. Rifts were aberrations and, as you know, uncontrolled on our side."

There was a short silence as everyone absorbed this.

"So," Moms said slowly, "you're saying the Patrol might have been attacked by another timeline?"

"Yes. If so, I suspect a two-pronged assault. One is to incapacitate the Patrol, while at the same time, our past is being assaulted in order to alter our timeline."

"What are gates?" Doc asked. "Are they a form of Rifts?"

Foreman shrugged. "I've followed all the reports from the very first Rift back in 1947 to your encounter in Tennessee this past year. Quite remarkable, and I applaud the way you've handled them. Rifts have been the result of us, our timeline, our scientists, trying to punch through to parallel worlds. We're probably very far behind some of the other timelines in that regard."

"Clock's ticking," the Keep said. "We can deal with theory after we find out some facts." She focused on Foreman. "So whatever is down there is a threat to our world?"

"It could be," Foreman allowed.

"Who else do we need," Moms asked the Keep, bypassing Foreman, "according to your instructions?"

"We have enough," Foreman said.

"I don't take orders from you," the Keep replied.

Foreman spread his hands and sat down in one of the bucket seats. "Whatever. But if you check the third page of your instructions you will see that you do indeed have enough, even though you are missing one of the Nightstalkers, a Mister Ivar. But it appears we have an addition to the team which balances that out," he added, looking at Scout. "Sometimes it's all in the fine print. Equalization by subtraction and addition."

"We've waited long enough," the Keep said, trying to regain command. "The last addition will get here when he gets here. Charges ready?" she asked Mac, who was standing by the door of the command post, having come back up with Kirk.

"Roger that," Mac said. "Enough to take out the door. Beyond that, I don't know what's down there. I could try cutting a hole and putting a probe—"

The Keep cut him off. "We don't know what's down there but we're going to find out."

"Then let's blow the door," Roland said, cutting to the chase as he always did. "But you know there was this really weird thing that happened on the Sanction Neeley and I just did and—"

"Let's go," the Keep said, heading out the door. She paused as Foreman tried to get up to follow. "Why don't you wait here, sir?"

Foreman spread his hands once more, seemingly unconcerned. "Sure."

The rest of the team followed, except for Scout. She grabbed Roland's arm as they trailed the team.

"What happened?" Scout asked.

The team didn't see the irony in the OUT OF ORDER sign on the old elevator. They stood patiently, waiting, as the Keep checked her folder and then opened a panel exposing a keyboard, entering the long, complicated code that she'd given to Mac and Kirk. With a lurch, the elevator began dropping.

At least there was none of that elevator music.

"Nada," Scout said.

"Yeah?"

"He's lying." No one seemed surprised at Scout's announcement about Foreman.

"He's a spook," Nada said. "They lie every time they open their mouths, even if it's just to breathe."

"She's right," Kirk said. "I don't like this."

"All right," Moms said, casting an uneasy glance at the Keep and knowing Scout was still green. "Keep it tight, team." What she really meant was shut up in front of the outsider.

They reached the bottom in silence and the elevator opened up. "Whoa," Scout said. "Bad vibes."

Everyone hesitated for a moment, and then Nada indicated for Mac to proceed.

The team waited in the questionable safety of the elevator, looking down the narrow brick-lined corridor to the steel door Mac and Kirk had covered with a shaped line of explosives.

Mac held up the remote detonator. "Fire in the hole." He pushed the button and there was a surprisingly disappointing small crack of explosion. The shaped charges cut through the steel, and the door fell outward.

Nada was first through, his old standby, the MP5 submachine gun, tight to his shoulder. He went low. Moms was right behind him, going high, carrying heavier firepower in the form of the MK-17 SCAR (Special operations Combat Assault Rifle) chambered with 7.62 NATO rounds that carried a punch.

"Freeze!" Nada yelled, centering the muzzle of his submachine gun on the tall figure standing under the cheap lighting.

"Please!" the woman called.

The Keep pushed her way through the armed Nightstalkers. "Edith Frobish?"

"Yes! Yes! That's my name!"

The Keep indicated for the team to lower their weapons.

Nada and Moms ignored her and pushed past Edith, checking out the rest of the corridor. They paused at the guard station.

"Someone made contact," Moms reported. "There's blood and a bunch of expended brass."

Nada was staring down the corridor at the black opening at the end. "Someone put up a fight. And lost. No body, though."

"What can you tell us?" the Keep asked Edith.

"We're not clear yet," Moms said, gesturing with the muzzle

of her automatic rifle toward the steel door guarding the other end of the corridor. "Can you open that?" she asked Edith.

"Hold on," Mac said, pointing. "We've got another door that isn't sealed right here." He pointed at a slit in the ceiling. "I'm willing to bet Eagle's Prius that it slides down when that door opens, keeping containment."

"Keep it from sliding down," Moms ordered.

"Roger that." Mac pulled some gear out of his pack and, with Kirk's help, got to work. After a minute of drilling and hammering into the side wall, Mac gave a thumbs-up. "Should be shorted out."

"'Should be'?" Scout muttered.

Moms turned back to Edith and repeated her question. "Can you open it?"

"I don't know."

Mac was looking at the sensor. He whistled. "Never seen nothing like it except in mock-ups. A DNA sensor." He pointed at Edith. "If she belongs here, her DNA can open it." He hooked his finger. "Come here, darling."

Edith came forward and Mac gently took her hand and placed it over the sensor. The light flickered and the door slid up.

The rest of the Nightstalkers pushed past Edith Frobish. They gathered, weapons at the ready, at the entrance to the cavern.

"Give me some light, Kirk," Nada ordered.

Kirk pulled a flare gun out of his pack. He fired one, reloaded, and fired two more as quickly as possible.

They arced up into the cavern and promptly were sucked into a dark wall twenty meters in.

"Whoa!" Roland said. "What the frak is that?"

Kirk fired a flare at an angle, bouncing it off the walls of the cavern and avoiding the pitch-black entity.

The rough rock walls and ceiling and the smooth floor were illuminated in the flickering red light, casting dark shadows on the crevices and being absorbed into the darkness. The Nightstalkers moved in, spreading out, eyeballs scanning, muzzles of weapons following each person's gaze. They were all avoiding the darkness.

"It's shrinking," Doc said. "A meter at least since we entered." He had a handheld scanner up and was peering at the readings.

"What was in here?" Moms asked. "Or in there," she added, with a gesture of the muzzle of her assault rifle toward the darkness.

Kirk fired another flare as the last one sputtered out.

"I don't know," Edith said from behind them, standing at the entrance, but not taking a step in. She had a hand pressed against the side of her head, her eyes screwed shut in concentration.

"This feels bad," Scout said.

"Roger that," Kirk said. "We need to get out of here."

"Ditto," Nada muttered.

"All right." Moms indicated for the team to back up out of the cavern. "Let's get an idea of what we're going into before stepping into it. It looks like that thing is going away, so that's good. I guess."

Nada gestured. "Kirk. Mac. Maintain overwatch that way." He indicated the cavern.

The two Nightstalkers had their weapons at the ready, pointed in.

The rest gathered in a circle around Edith and the Keep.

Scout was back by the cavern entrance between Kirk and Mac and the rest of the team, part of the group, but separate. She wasn't sure of her role, so she figured she'd do what they had recruited her for in the first place: Scout. Which right now meant watch and observe.

"What do you remember?" the Keep asked Edith.

She shook her head. "I know my name. But I don't really know where I am right now."

"The Time Patrol," the Keep nudged.

"Sounds vaguely familiar."

"And?" the Keep asked.

Edith shrugged. "That's it. I did what I was told to do in case something happened, and so I pulled the alarm. Beyond that, I'm having a hard time remembering clearly." Edith struggled, working her jaw, but she remained frustrated. She pressed both hands against the sides of her head. "I know it! I know I know something about this place. But I can't remember what!"

Moms put a hand on her shoulder. "Calm down. Let's back up. Why here? Why are you here underneath the Met?"

Edith blinked and nodded vigorously, touching on something she could access. "I track the art."

"Why?" Moms asked.

"I don't know. But I went to Columbia and majored in art and history."

"Art *is* history," Eagle contributed. "A record of it."

Nada took half a step forward as if to say something, but stopped. Behind him, Scout felt a chill touch her back, sliding up her spine and lifting the hairs on the back of her neck. She looked over her shoulder into the darkness of the cavern, but could detect nothing. Of course it was dark in there. Darker than anything Scout had ever seen. The black wall sucked in what scant light there was. But it was further away, receding and shrinking, so she wondered why she felt worse. Sick to her stomach. Kirk and Mac were sweeping their weapons back and forth, quartering the floor of the cavern with the high-powered lights on the guardrails of their artillery.

"Hey guys," Scout said. "Why don't we discuss this upstairs?"

No one paid attention to her, except for Nada, who frowned and moved out of the circle close around Edith and stood next to Scout.

"And if the art or history changes?" the Keep asked.

"That's called a . . ." Edith stopped short of the answer. She closed her eyes, trying to remember.

"Nada," Scout whispered.

Nada leaned close. "Yes?"

"We need to get out of here." Scout looked over her shoulder into the cavern. "There's something bad in there. Something bad coming this way."

"'Coming'?" Nada repeated. He turned around. He flicked on the light underneath the barrel of his submachine gun and aimed into the darkness. The thin finger of light was sucked into the black wall, but it was still shrinking. "Anything?" he asked the overwatch team.

"Negative," Mac said.

"What kind of bad?" Nada asked Scout.

"Bad bad," Scout said. "Stay Puft Marshmallow Man bad. Do I get a gun?"

"Surprised you didn't ask earlier," Nada said.

"Surprised no one gave me one earlier," Scout said. "I qualified on everything they handed me in training."

But then a look crossed Nada's face and he hesitated. He swallowed hard. "All right. Take my pistol. But be damn careful with it, Scout. It's not a toy."

Scout stared at him for a moment. "I know it's not a toy." She grabbed the pistol out of the cross hand holster on Nada's combat vest. She pulled the slide back slightly, confirming, as she expected, that there was a round in the chamber. The safety was off. "My finger is my safety," Scout whispered.

"Always," Nada said.

"Excuse me," the Keep called out, interrupting the dead-end questioning of Edith Frobish. "What are you two doing?" The Keep was closest to the guard station, having let the operatives take the lead entering the facility.

"Scout says there's something bad in there," Nada said. "Kirk. Get me some more light."

Kirk took a step forward and fired a flare upward into the cavern.

It hit something less than five feet in front of and above him and bounced back, missing Kirk's head by a fraction of an inch, and skittering ablaze down the corridor.

A moment later a spear darted forward, piercing through Kirk's body armor and impaling him. He was lifted up, his body sliding down the haft of the spear. A clawed hand reached down from above, grabbing the top of Kirk's head as he disappeared upward.

Nada and Scout fired at the same moment. A tall figure was swooping up, holding Kirk in one claw, twenty feet above the cavern floor, while the other held the spear. It was over seven feet in height, encased in white armor, with a red cloak swirling about. Blood red hair crested over shoulders. Two red bulging bulbs instead of eyes. No mouth.

It was hovering about five feet over the ground.

Kirk was screaming, while both hands were on the claw, trying to keep his head from being ripped off his body.

Nada and Scout kept firing, bullets flashing close by Kirk. The creature emitted what could only be described as a scream, a sound that cut into everyone's core and caused even the stoutest Nightstalker to take a step back.

The thing let go of the spear and sliced with its other claw, passing right through Kirk's body armor and body, cutting him in two. The separate parts of what had once been the Nightstalkers' commo man fell to the floor.

With a deafening roar to match the scream, the rest of the Nightstalkers opened fire. Their bullets slammed into the creature, having little apparent effect. The Keep hung back in the hallway, weaponless and with no experience in this type of event.

Mac fired the 40 mm HE grenade loaded in his launcher and hit the thing right in the chest. The round exploded, dangerously close (arming distance having been modified by Roland), and the thing was finally knocked back, the team momentarily stunned.

Momentarily, and then the fusillade began again.

The thing hovered, motionless, bullets bouncing off the hard white.

Without Moms or Nada issuing an order, the team was moving forward, vengeance for Kirk drawing them into the cavern. Magazines ran out and new ones were slammed home.

"Eyes," Nada yelled, as he pulled the trigger of his sub, 9 mm bullets hitting the red bulges. Moms followed suit and her larger and more powerful 7.62 rifle rounds punched home. A spark of red exploded from the right bulge and the thing screamed once more, abruptly accelerating backward into the blackness of the cavern, heading for the shrinking patch of absolute darkness near the top.

"No, you don't!" Nada shouted.

Again without an order, training and vengeance the driving forces, the team quickly moved forward as Doc knelt next to Kirk's remains. Mac picked up the flare gun and fired another one ahead of them.

The creature was racing away now, toward the darkness. The team began to run as they fired, maintaining a semblance of discipline, fanning out to ensure they kept each other's field of fire clear. Their rounds were beginning to chip off pieces of white and the creature was turned away, protecting its eyes.

Finally just before it reached the blackness, it turned once more. One eye was completely shattered and, within seconds, so was the second.

"Pour it on!" Nada yelled, and the team did just that. "Mac!" Nada ordered. "Thermobaric!"

Mac grabbed the correct grenade round on his vest by instinct, developed through many hours on the range in live fire exercises, and slammed it home into the breach of the launcher. Developed for combat in Afghanistan, upon detonation the round used oxygen to initiate an intense, high-temp explosion, which was more powerful and lasted longer than a conventional round. Mac loaded and fired.

The round exploded and blew off the thing's right arm.

It remained perfectly still for a moment, and then the thing simply dropped and slammed to the floor.

The team ceased fire.

And the darkness stopped shrinking.

Nada had the light underneath his smoking barrel pointed at the blackness. It was now about ten feet high and six feet wide, fifteen feet above the floor of the cavern.

"It was trying to go through that," Scout said.

"'Through'?" Moms said.

"Like a Rift," Scout said.

"Doc," Moms ordered, emotions shut down and in combat mode. "Check it out. Nothing you can do for Kirk now."

"Secure the rest of the cavern," Nada ordered. He moved forward with Scout on one side and Moms on the other. The rest of the Nightstalkers moved out, checking every crevice in the place while Doc opened up his laptop underneath the dark rectangle and plugged in his handheld scanner.

"I need a bigger gun," Scout said, a tremor in her voice as she and Nada reached the thing and stood over it.

"We all need bigger guns or bigger bullets." Nada fired two rounds into the hole where one of the red bulges had been, a double-tap. "I think it's dead."

"What *is* it?" Scout asked.

"Doc?" Moms asked. "Is that a Rift?"

Doc was looking from his laptop screen and up to the black rectangle, and then back to the screen. "I don't know. Something like a Rift, but not like any I've ever seen. Nor is it giving off any of the usual indicators other than a low-level muonic emission. Surprised the Can back at Area 51 didn't pick it up. Very localized, as if the power is under tight control. I'd have to send a probe into it to learn more."

"Negative," the Keep said. "Not until we know everything we can about it from our sources here."

"We fall back for now," Moms ordered. "Send in a Support team to pick this thing up and analyze it. Secure the chamber and that gate as best we can until we get an idea what the hell we're dealing with."

"Roger that," Nada agreed.

The team pulled back, several with anxious glances up at the dark rectangle. Roland had unrolled a poncho and tenderly placed both halves of Kirk in it. He wrapped it closed. Without a word Mac took Roland's weapons. Roland picked up the body, cradling it in his arms.

Carrying their dead, the Nightstalkers, along with the Keep and Edith Frobish, packed up the elevator and began the ride to the surface in silence.

It was a defeat and a retreat, and they all knew it. They'd lost one of their own and that reality was pouring into each one as the adrenaline drained out.

"Here there be Monsters," Scout whispered, and everyone in the elevator heard her.

Nobody disagreed.

CHAPTER 7

Eight Hours

"Who the hell was Carl Coyne?" Neeley asked.

Hannah steepled her fingers together and considered her old friend and trusted assassin across the empty space of her desktop. "A rogue Navy SEAL. You saw the dossier. You watched the interviews of his shrink sessions. He should have been flagged, but wasn't."

Neeley shook her head. "It's obvious the file we had for the Sanction wasn't complete. And if it wasn't complete, that's a big problem."

Doctor Golden was seated to the left of Neeley, a folder in her lap. Inside the headquarters of the Cellar it was eerily quiet, just the slight sound of air being forced into the bunker as background noise. The positive overpressure the room was kept in and the extensive filters on the pumps that provided the oxygen meant the space would stay safe even if a nuclear, chemical, or biological attack took out the facility above them. Neeley sometimes had visions of Hannah quietly working away while the world above was desolate and destroyed. She wondered how much the isolation from the real world had affected her friend over the years since she'd taken over this position.

Neeley had arrived less than two minutes earlier, taking the seat that Frasier had occupied. He'd been alerted and was racing off to New York City to join the Nightstalkers. Neeley was still focused on the odd ending to the Sanction on Whidbey Island, while Golden and Hannah had spent the time trying to find out more about the Time Patrol.

Neeley shook her head. "I've never had a completed Sanction disappear out of the body bag. You'll admit that's different. And Roland got a strange alert from the Nightstalkers. Not the standard 'Lawyers, Guns and Money.' He was out of Whidbey on an Air Force jet just before I was. I don't believe in coincidence."

Neeley had been flown by the Air Force from Whidbey to Andrews Air Force Base, then shuttled to Fort Meade by helicopter. She was still dressed in the black clothes she'd worn on the Sanction. They were dry, but they were dirty; mud from the Pacific Northwest still encrusted the fabric. Her short hair was sticking out in all angles, a polar opposite from the composed Hannah sitting across from her and Golden by her side.

Neeley didn't notice or care, just as Hannah didn't notice the oddness of having an office three hundred feet below the NSA.

"I've had Doctor Golden do some digging while you were coming here," Hannah said. "Roland was alerted because the Nightstalkers are dealing with a major incident in New York City. One with global implications."

"And is that connected to the Sanction?" Neeley asked. "A body disappearing seems right up the Nightstalkers' mission profile."

"It's bigger than the Nightstalkers," Hannah said. "It deals with the Time Patrol."

Neeley absorbed that without blinking an eye. "Explain, please."

"The Patrol has disappeared," Hannah said. "Their base of operations underneath New York City has simply vanished. That's what the Nightstalkers are dealing with. And the Keep."

"The Keep?" Neeley considered that. "Then it's top level."

"Apparently our world, as we know it, might end if they fail."

Neeley leaned back in her chair. "Okay. That's above top level." She took a deep breath. "I've never heard of this Patrol."

"Neither have I," Hannah said. "One assumes they either travel in time or deal with time travelers infiltrating our world. Or both."

"Well." Which was all Neeley had to say about that.

"I checked with Mrs. Sanchez," Hannah said. "Based on the process of elimination, we believe there's a man in the warren under the Pentagon who controls the budget for the Patrol. A fellow named Foreman. I've never met him and rarely heard of him. He's been running some sort of program since not long after the end of World War Two."

"World War Two?" Neeley shook her head. "How old is he?"

"There's no file on him," Hannah said.

"The Cellar has nothing on him?" Neeley asked.

"Negative."

"Great," Neeley said. "What kind of program is he running?"

"I'm assuming it's the Patrol," Hannah said. "Mrs. Sanchez says he's the only person drawing a significant amount from the Black Budget for a purpose she has no clue about, has a dead drop delivery address in Manhattan, and is weird enough to be in charge of it."

Neeley considered that. "But you'd never heard of it before."

"No."

"And Mrs. Sanchez doesn't have a detailed accounting of his funding," Neeley said.

"No."

"So how does Carl Coyne fit into this?"

"That's the next piece of the puzzle," Hannah said. "Carl Coyne did go rogue. But now we know that wasn't the real reason behind the Sanction." Hannah nodded at Golden.

The psychiatrist opened the folder. "Carl Coyne was a Navy SEAL in good standing for eight years. Well, except for the suspicion of domestic abuse, but there was never a formal report and, as you note, the psychologists assigned to the team didn't flag him. That's because—"

Neeley finished for her. "With the combat requirements for someone with Coyne's training and skill level, it was never fully investigated. We figured that out during mission planning."

Golden continued without comment. "He had constant rotations in and out of Afghanistan and other active areas of operation. He was selected and moved from Team Three to Seal Team Six. Then he was selected for a temporary duty, special work, TDSW, for an operation code named HUB. All capitals—H. U. B. in New York City. Six weeks."

"The Time Patrol," Neeley said.

Golden nodded. "We know that now. Located underneath the Metropolitan Museum of Art in New York City. Coyne was part of a rotating crew of six men, assigned for six weeks, TDSW each, all from elite units, with Top Secret clearances. One man was on duty at all times at the HUB facility's guard post."

Neeley frowned. "One man? That wouldn't be sufficient." Then she nodded. "He wasn't a guard. The concern wasn't people coming in. It was making sure no one got out of there alive if there was a security breach."

"Correct," Hannah said. "But the facility is gone now; just vanished."

"Just like Coyne," Neeley said. "And? What did Coyne do?"

A phone buzzed somewhere and Hannah reached down and came up with a receiver. She listened for a few moments. "All right." She put the receiver down.

"The Nightstalkers lost one of their people in the cavern. They were attacked by what Moms could only describe as a floating, armored humanoid creature wielding claws and a spear. They're awaiting an autopsy on the thing."

"Which Nightstalker?" Neeley asked, with a bit more urgency than was normal for her.

"Kirk," Hannah answered, staring at her assassin a little more closely.

"The team's next move?" Golden asked, covering for Neeley.

"They're regrouping as we speak," Hannah said. "And Foreman is there, in New York."

"Interesting. Tell me more on Coyne," Neeley said, having done her own regrouping.

"He went AWOL a little after that TDSW tour," Golden said. "Then he showed up in Southeast Asia doing various nefarious activities, including arms, drugs, and ancient artifact smuggling."

"Where specifically in Southeast Asia?" Neeley asked.

"Cambodia. From there, he went to the Cayman Islands, we assume to deposit some of his ill-gotten gains. All of this is what we thought was the real reason for the Sanction."

"Who initiated the RFS?" Neeley asked. "It was redacted, as it usually is, in the packet."

Golden held up the folder. "The Request for Sanction came from a cut out in the Pentagon."

Neeley sat up straight. "A cut out?" They all knew that meant someone in the middle who passed messages and knew both sides, but neither side ever knew who the other was. "A cut out could say anything, target anyone. How was this cut out vetted? Who is it?"

"We have to assume it was Foreman," Hannah said.

"All right," Neeley said. "I can do the timeline. Coyne works at a top-secret facility. Not long afterward it's compromised. Disappears, whatever. So Coyne gave up the location. To who? And when and where?"

"Those are the questions we have to answer," Hannah said.

Neeley nodded. "But it's safe for us to assume that the RFS initiated with Foreman?"

Hannah smiled at Golden's surprise. The psychiatrist was good at what she did, but the world of covert operations often baffled her.

"Most likely," Hannah agreed.

"The real question," Neeley said, "is whether Foreman sent the RFS in order to stop Coyne from giving up the location or to cover his tracks because he told Coyne to give up the location."

Mac had piled enough explosive on board the elevator to take out a good portion of the south end of the Museum of Modern Art just in case someone or something tried attacking. They'd swept the cavern and come up with nothing else, except for the black, two-dimensional rectangle. Mac handed the detonator over to the first Support personnel on scene, which consisted of a company of Rangers hastily flown in from Hunter Army Airfield, fully armed and ready for anything. Besides focusing inward, they were setting up a close perimeter, inside the one already established by the New York Police who were now facing outward, maintaining the cover story of a terrorism training exercise.

Nada briefed the Ranger company commander on what had happened. The captain took it all in, and then snapped to attention, not troubled at all by the white creature with spear, claws, and red bulbs for eyes, and what they were now calling *the gate*. "Yes, sir. We'll keep it secure."

And that was why the "N" in Ranger stood for knowledge. But it also made them the best light infantry in the world.

Preservation of culture was the least of the worries right now. Preservation of life was, and the Keep was more than willing to level the Museum if need be. Although the team had found nothing else in the cavern, Moms was taking no chances. She'd alerted Pitr, who had a local Acme forensic team assembling to go down into the cavern and recover whatever it was they had just killed. And then figure out what it was.

Since New Yorkers were particular about low-flying airplanes, the Specter gunship that normally would circle overhead on a racetrack to provide fire support was being held out to sea, a non-threatening distance away from the city.

Pitr also had their FPF en route. Final Protective Fire. To be used as a last resort. And it wasn't just to save the Nightstalkers if need be, but the rest of New York City and mankind as a whole. A B-52 out of Minot Air Force Base in North Dakota had taken off and was winging its way east at maximum speed. The plane, which was older than any of the crewmembers inside, had pods of AGM-129A cruise missiles on each wing. Of the twelve missiles, ten had conventional warheads.

Two were nuclear tipped.

Which meant, if push came to shove, the Nightstalkers were ready to give up a portion of Manhattan to save the rest of the world. They considered it a form of species amputation, to save the core by sacrificing a part.

Nada had also put in a special request for more weapons with grenade launchers, along with plenty of thermobaric XM1060 40mm rounds. While regular bullets had had little effect other than on the creature's eyes, they knew that grenade round had worked. As Scout had pointed out: they all needed bigger guns.

But none of that mattered at the moment.

The team was gathered in the NYPD command post trailer, shaken by Kirk's death and the unexpected assault. While the Keep was on a secure line to whomever the Keep had to be on a secure line to, presumably the President, the team gathered round Kirk's body, wrapped tightly in Roland's poncho.

"What about his family?" Scout asked.

"We take care of our own, and we will take care of his family," Nada said. "But first we must give honors to—" He faltered to a stop, lowering his head and putting a hand over his face, earning him curious and worried glances from the rest of the team. None had ever seen Nada falter before.

Moms stepped into the breach. "It is Protocol for us to acknowledge the death of a Nightstalker because no one else will. We must pay our respect and give honors." She reached out with her hands, and those on either side took hold. Nada pulled his hand away from his eyes and joined the circle around Kirk's remains.

"He was named Kirk by the team," Moms said, "but in death he regains his name and his past. Staff Sergeant Winthrop Carter, US Army Ranger, has made the ultimate sacrifice for his country, for his world, and for mankind. We all speak his rank and his name as it was."

The team spoke together. "Staff Sergeant Winthrop Carter."

This caused even the Keep to pause in her conversation. She lowered the phone out of respect and stood still. Edith Frobish watched with wide eyes. Foreman was in one of the bucket seats, watching silently. Roland was looking down at his hands, stained with Kirk's blood, averting his eyes from everyone else.

"We, the Nightstalkers," Moms continued, "have seen many things and been many places. We don't know the limits of science, and we don't know the limits of the soul. If there is some life after this, or some existence on a plane we can't even conceive of, then we know our teammate is there, in a good place. Because that is what he deserves for performing his duty without any acknowledgement and for making the ultimate sacrifice. If there is nothingness in death, then he is in his final peace and will not be troubled anymore by the nightmares of this world."

There was a moment of silence before Moms continued.

"There will be no medals, no service at Arlington. Staff Sergeant Carter will be returned home to Parthenon, Arkansas, to be buried on his family farm as per his wishes. As Nada noted, we take care of our own. His family will not do without."

This made a few of the Nightstalkers look up at Moms, wondering if she knew their final resting place, and then accepting it was Moms. Of course she did. She also remembered their real names.

"All we can do—" and Moms's voice broke for a second and she glanced at Nada, who nodded and finished for her, teamwork trumping all else.

"All we can do," Nada said, "is keep him in our hearts."

"In our hearts," the rest of the team murmured.

There was a lingering silence inside the command post. Sirens wailed outside, people were shouting, a couple of phones in the front of the large vehicle were ringing, but there was absolute silence around the team and the body.

Moms broke it, releasing the hands of those on either side.

The Keep went back to her hushed phone conversation. Foreman had remained silent, head bowed, listening.

Moms looked around, meeting the eyes of every member of the Nightstalkers, and then settled her gaze on Scout. "Why are we here? Because someone has to man the walls in the middle of the night. The walls between the innocents who go to sleep each night with only the troubles they see in their lives. Normal troubles. Who know little, if anything, of the dangers, the nightmares, surrounding our world. Who need people like us to stand watch over them. To protect them from—" Moms paused, looking down briefly at the body, "things like what we just encountered. Things most people can't dream of, even in their worst nightmare. That is why we, the Nightstalkers, exist. We protect people from the bad." She nodded at Scout. "Do you understand?"

Scout swallowed. "Yes."

"We are here," Moms said, "because the best of intentions can go horribly awry, and the worst of intentions can achieve exactly what it sets out to do. It is often the noblest scientific inquiry that can produce the end of us all. We are here because we are the last defense when the desire to do right turns into a wrong. We are here because mankind advances through trial and error. Because nothing man does is ever perfect. And we are ultimately here because there are things out there, beyond mankind's current knowledge level, which man must be guarded against until we can understand those things. We must remember this." Moms took a deep breath. "Can you live with that?" she asked Scout.

Scout didn't hesitate. "Yes."

Moms nodded. "We normally have a ceremony, a naming ceremony, for new members. But you received your name almost two years ago when we worked together in North Carolina." She looked around at the team. "I assume there are no objections to Scout?"

There were none.

"All right then." Moms pointed at Kirk's body. "Roland and Mac. Please convey Sergeant Carter to Support. And we keep him in our hearts."

CHAPTER 8

Seven-Plus Hours

"We tracked Coyne," Golden said, reading off one of the papers in her folder. "As part of the research for the Sanction. And then we backtracked along his trail."

"But nothing on New York City and the TDSW," Neeley said.

"Of course not," Hannah said. "This HUB is—" She faltered for words. "I've never heard of it or the Time Patrol before."

Neeley had never seen her old friend so disturbed since they first joined forces a long time ago. It had been a desperate race for survival that had turned out to be Nero's way of testing them and finding his own replacement—Hannah. They'd succeeded in the test, and in the process learned some bitter realities about the way of the world, especially covert environments.

Golden nodded. "We knew we couldn't account for six weeks in the trail prior to his leaving active duty. Unusual, but not unheard of for a Sanction target. There are quite a few compartmentalized agencies and operations that even we can't get a light into, including this Foreman's. There's not even a name for it as far as we can tell. As if he himself is the agency."

"But even if we can't get details, I've heard of all of them," Hannah said. "Foreman was just a rumor."

Hannah's job as head of the Cellar was based on knowledge. If there was a hole in that knowledge, she could not adequately analyze the situation. And when the Cellar wasn't on top of a situation, bad things tended to happen.

"Let's think this through," Neeley said. "We do know now where he was in those missing six weeks. Working security for this HUB. And we assume he gave up the location later on. But he probably gave up the site after he left the security detail and after he left active duty. So let's start from his time after the tour."

Doctor Golden opened the file. "He went right back to SEAL Team Six. That's when he put in his paperwork to leave the military since his end of enlistment was coming up and he declined to enlist despite the offer of a rather generous bonus. While the request was being processed, he was deployed to Africa."

"They were going to wring him dry of every op they could run him on before his ETS," Neeley said. "He must have been a little pissed."

That earned her a sharp glance from Hannah.

Doctor Golden pushed on. "He did some ops in the Horn of Africa, pirate interdiction, but was never alone. Always with his team and always on board ship. His paperwork went through and he was discharged. He returned to the States and out-processed." Golden nodded. "He signed out of Little Creek, Virginia.

"Then he went directly to the Far East where he engaged in the activities for which the Sanction was ostensibly for," Golden concluded. "Particularly in Cambodia. He went from Cambodia to the Caymans. The assumption was to deposit money in an account there."

"Perhaps the assumption is wrong," Neeley said.

"Perhaps," Hannah agreed. "We don't have much in the file on the days he spent in the islands. Then he came directly back to the States to Coronado and began searching for his wife. That's when you and Roland began your surveillance."

"The drugs and weapons smuggling I get," Neeley said. "But the antiquities. That's outside of a SEAL's experience. It might be a stretch, but if we're talking the Time Patrol and antiquities, there might be more to what he was doing in Cambodia than we thought. I think the Caymans are key too. I don't think a SEAL is going to just suddenly set up offshore banking on his own. He met someone there."

"Likely," Hannah agreed.

"When did you get the RFS?" Neeley asked.

"When Coyne was in the Caymans," Hannah said.

"Then he did something there," Neeley said. "Something Foreman found out about and didn't approve of, since he allowed all that time to pass until the Caymans without putting in for the Sanction."

"That would be logical," Hannah said.

"Or," Neeley said, "he did something in Cambodia or the Caymans that Foreman wanted him to do and then Foreman was covering his tracks."

"You have a suspicious mind," Golden said.

"It's kept me alive." Neeley leaned back in the chair, stretching out her long legs and mud-covered boots. "According to the RFS file, we started surveillance on him in Cambodia. But there was nothing unusual noted beyond the criminal activities."

"Maybe something was missed," Golden said. "I'll have to look at the file from a different perspective."

"What about the Caymans?" Neeley asked. "Was he followed there?"

"A local asset was assigned," Hannah said. "You saw the report in the Sanction folder: nothing unusual or of note reported."

"Then that report isn't a complete one," Neeley said. "Local assets are of varying capabilities."

The three women fell silent for a moment, and the only sound was the machines pumping air into the room.

"What about motivation?" Neeley finally asked. "Why would Coyne do something that he had to know would bring a Sanction? At the airport, Roland said Coyne mentioned some things just before being Sanctioned, while under the gun. People say lots of strange things in that situation if given the chance—" She paused at the look Hannah gave her and explained. "Roland isn't an assassin like I am. He's a soldier. He paused momentarily, but he did complete the job."

"What did Coyne say?" Golden asked.

"That he had powerful friends," Neeley said. "Roland said Coyne used the term 'Ratnik' when talking about these friends. Coyne said we needed to know about them."

Hannah nodded toward Golden. "I'll check into it," the psychiatrist said, adding to her growing list.

"He also mentioned what might be a name: Sin Fen."

Golden wrote it down.

"And he mentioned Operation Red Wings," Neeley said. "That's the SEAL team that got attacked in the 'Stan back in 2005. All those guys on the rescue chopper got killed. Coyne was there at the FOB, but not part of either op. Why would he bring it up?"

"Survivor guilt?" Golden suggested.

"It's all connected," Neeley said. "We just have to figure out how."

"I'll coordinate from here," Hannah said. "The Keep is updating me from New York. Both of you keep me up to speed on what you learn."

Neeley had something else on her mind. "Why did you bring Roland in on this? It was a straightforward operation. Why have a Nightstalker along? Did you suspect something wonky about the op? That I might need Nightstalker support?"

"You worked with Roland in South America," Hannah said.

Neeley leaned forward and met her old friend's, and boss's, gaze. "That wasn't authorized. It was off the books and you chewed my ass about it when I got back. And you didn't answer my question. Did you suspect something strange would happen?"

Hannah sighed. "No."

"Soooo . . ." Neeley dragged the word out. "Roland was sent along to be my babysitter."

Neither of the other women responded.

"So," Neeley repeated, accepting that judgment, "who exactly is Foreman and what is he up to? That's what we have to find out. Who or what is this Ratnik? Who or what is Sin Fen? We've got too many questions and not much time to answer them."

"And we can't count on Foreman for answers according to the Keep," Hannah said.

"So we treat this as a possible Sanction on Foreman," Neeley said. "We have to find out what Foreman knows and what he's been doing. And the best way right now for me is backtracking through Coyne."

Hannah pointed to the door. "Get going."

"Line me up the fastest thing moving to the Caymans," Neeley said.

Moms turned to the rest of the team. "We're a long way from control on this operation. We've barely got containment. That thing had to have been hiding in that cavern, probably up near the top—"

"Got to look up, people," Nada said. It was a spin-off of his famous Nada Yadas: No One Looks Up.

"Or it came through the gate," Doc said.

"We don't even know for sure it's a gate," Eagle pointed out.

"What else do you think it could be?" Scout asked. "You want to call it the-thing-we're-not-sure-is-a-gate?"

"Okay," Eagle allowed. "Let's call it a gate."

"You." Moms pointed at Edith. "That thing might have been down there with you for a couple of hours. You didn't notice anything?"

Edith shook her head. "I didn't go in the cavern. The door was shut the entire time. I stood by the guard post and waited, as I was instructed to do. That's all I remember about that place."

The Keep put down a phone and spoke. "Your support team has pulled that 'thing' out. They're working on it at the triage center as we speak. We should know who or what it is shortly."

"What else were you instructed to do?" Moms demanded of Edith. "What else do you know?"

Edith put a hand to her forehead. "My head hurts. I'm trying to remember. But I just can't. It's so strange. I know I know. But I don't know. It makes no sense."

Nada was staring at her. "This loss of memory just happen? Now?"

Edith shook her head. "I don't know. But if I worked down there, I should remember more. A lot more, right?"

"What do you know about this loss of memory?" Moms asked Foreman.

He shrugged. "Your guess is as good as mine."

"I doubt that," Moms said. "Can we go into that gate?"

The rest of the team glanced at her in surprise. They had all sensed the evil field emanating from the shrinking darkness. No one had any desire to try to go into it.

Foreman shrugged. "You can go in. Coming out is the problem. No one, as far as I know, has ever come back after going into a gate. And I've been tracking them for around seventy years."

"Let's back up," Moms said, trying to get this Gordian knot of information, or lack thereof, untangled. "What is the real threat here? That thing and others like it coming through the gate or the missing Time Patrol?"

"The missing Patrol," Foreman said.

"Why?"

Foreman opened his mouth to answer but was cut off as the Keep hung up the phone and joined them. "Someone has just landed who can help us with Ms. Frobish's memory problem."

Nada went over to one of the windows and peered out. His face tightened as he recognized the person hustling up to the large van.

The door to the command post opened and Frasier came in, his sunglasses on.

"Great," Scout muttered. "Men in Black."

Frasier looked about and settled his glasses' gaze on Edith. "Ms. Frobish?"

She nodded.

"I'm here—"

Frasier didn't get the next word out before Nada had his machete against the shrink's neck.

"What did you do to me?" Nada demanded.

Frasier didn't seem perturbed. "What had to be done." Surprisingly, he smiled, as best he could smile, which was really more a twitch. "The memory block has been done to others besides you." He nodded toward Edith. "It was done to her, tethered to the alarm. Once that went off, the block went into place. She can remember generalities but not specifics. A security Protocol. We all understand the importance of Protocols."

"My wife," Nada growled. "My child. Those are specifics, not protocols."

"Yes, they were," Frasier said. "And the memory was destroying you. You were trying to kill yourself slowly with alcohol and, at times, quickly with your guns. You were a detriment to yourself and the team. You were reckless on missions, putting not only your life in danger but the lives of others. The choice was to either have you Sanctioned or to block the memories since you were considered a valuable asset. Ms. Jones chose to block you. She saved your life. It was her decision and you should be thankful for it."

Moms reached out and placed her hand on Nada's arm. She pulled on it, removing the machete from Frasier's neck. "I don't know what you're talking about, Nada, but we'll deal with it later. Frasier must have been doing his job. We all did a lot of things upon Ms. Jones's orders. Can you do your job now?"

Nada swallowed hard, and then sheathed the machete.

"How does this block work?" Doc asked, always on the search for knowledge. "It has to be selective."

"It's complicated," Frasier said. "And you have to be preconditioned for it."

"Ah," Doc said. "So I assume we're all preconditioned for it."

"Enough." Frasier didn't waste any more time. He pulled a small device out of his pocket and stepped up to Edith. "It won't hurt," Frasier said with all the bedside charm of an axe murderer. He unreeled earbuds and told her to put them in her ears. Once she did that, he turned on the device.

Edith grimaced, disputing Frasier's statement.

It lasted ten seconds, and then Frasier had her remove the pods and he put the device back in his pocket. "The block was an implanted protection initiated by the alarm in case your facility was breached and you survived and were captured. You *couldn't* give up the details of what you know. But now you can tell us."

Edith blinked rapidly several times, and then shook her head. She took a couple of deep breaths. "All right. All right." She pressed her hands on both sides of her narrow head. "Oh my gosh. It's crazy. Too much but I can't remember everything."

Scout placed an arm around her. "Take some deep breaths."

Nada stepped forward, into Frasier's personal space. "I want my memories back. All of them. I can remember being told of my wife's and daughter's deaths. And I can see their faces. But not much more. I don't know how they died. I want the details. How? When? Where?"

Moms's mouth dropped open in shock.

Scout let go of Edith and hugged him. "I'm so sorry!"

The Keep stepped up to Nada and Scout. She shoved her arms between the two. She grabbed Nada's combat vest and looked up into his eyes, speaking in a flat, cold voice. "I am terribly sorry for your losses, team sergeant. But we have to deal with this problem. Here and now. If we don't, there won't ever be any dealing with anything else."

"Nada," Moms said, half a request, half an order, both tentative.

Nada waved his hand about, letting go of the machete handle and indicating the others in the CP. "How many other people in here have memory blocks? As Doc noted, I'm sure we're all preconditioned for them."

"That's not relevant right now," Frasier said.

"I think it's relevant," Eagle said. "Maybe you have one," he said to Frasier.

The team shrink twitched a smile. "Well, I wouldn't know if that was true, would I?"

"Funny guy," Scout muttered. "Not."

Frasier heard her, but didn't allow himself to be distracted. "Let's focus on the job at hand, shall we?" He gestured at Foreman. "We need what Ms. Frobish knows, don't we?"

Foreman nodded. "She's worked directly with the Time Patrol for a long time and can explain it much better than I can."

Edith looked at Foreman. "I remember you now. You visited occasionally. Met the Administrator."

"I did," Foreman said.

Edith took a deep breath. "All right. It's coming back to me. Strobe-like, but settling down."

Edith looked about, taking in everyone in the command post. As she did so, Roland and Mac came back in and silently joined the group. In the background they could hear a helicopter taking off and knew Kirk—Staff Sergeant Winthrop Carter—was en route to the morgue, and then would begin the long journey that would end in Parthenon, Arkansas.

In the back of each Nightstalker's mind was the knowledge that they could be making a similar journey before this was over.

When Edith began speaking, her voice was level and focused. "I'm going to explain it to you the way it was explained to me as best I can remember. It's still a little patchy but smoothing out."

"Start at the beginning," Moms said.

Edith shook her head. "What beginning? Okay. I'll start where they began explaining it to me when I first joined the Patrol. I was given the explanation simply to help me do my job and understand the importance of it." She took a deep breath and let it out.

"It's a basic truism that if time travel is ever invented then it has always existed in our history. Which means it exists now."

"Huh?" Roland muttered.

"Cool," Scout said.

"Exactly," Doc said, as if he'd thought of it himself, which he probably had, more than once.

"There are dangers to time travel, of course," Edith continued. "The most glaring is interfering with the past. By the way, we can't travel forward from our time for some reason."

"Because it doesn't exist yet," Doc said.

Edith shrugged. "I don't know. I also think it has something to do with math and physics, which isn't my area of expertise."

"Intriguing," Doc said. "How far back can one travel?"

Edith shook her head. "I have no idea. I know I've researched things from the beginning of recorded history." She shut her eyes for a moment and then opened them. "Getting beyond the clumsy paradoxes of what happens if you kill your own father, which is a non-starter because it can't happen, because it's a fundamental paradox loop, we have certain truths."

"Say that again?" Roland said.

"If we wait for Roland to understand this," Mac said, "then we're going to be here forever."

"Do *you* understand?" Roland challenged.

"Not yet," Mac admitted. "But the pretty lady has just started."

"Not now, Mac," Moms said. "Continue," she said to Edith.

"First. You have to accept that there is time travel. That's a reality that just needs to be accepted."

"When was it invented?" Eagle was unable to restrain himself. "By who?"

Edith shook her head. "I don't know. I'm not sure anyone does except maybe the techs who service the HUB or, more likely, the Administrator."

"Who is that?" the Keep asked.

Edith seemed confused by the question. "He's the Administrator. That's the only name I've ever heard him called."

The Keep turned to Foreman. "The Administrator?"

"He runs the Patrol," Foreman said. "I've met him a few times. That's the only name or title I know him by. I don't meddle in the details of how he runs things or how things operate here. He's rarely about. I'm his contact for funding and in DC."

"So ultimately the Patrol works for you?" the Keep demanded.

"The Patrol works for mankind," Foreman said.

Moms slapped one of the counters, rattling the phones lined up on it. "Stop it! We're not playing a game here. We've been called in to this for a reason, but no one's told us what it is. We're not even sure what our mission is. And we've lost a member of our team. So, Mister Foreman, with all due respect to whatever you are and whatever position you hold, stop with the obfuscation!"

"Huh?" Roland whispered.

"She means stop with the bullshit," Eagle said to him.

"Yeah," Roland said in a louder voice. "Stop obfuscationing." He stepped up right behind Moms's shoulder, a hulking presence to punctuate her statement.

Foreman held up his hands in surrender. "The Patrol *does not* work for me. It exists for its mission."

Everyone took that in for a moment.

Nada shook his head. "I'm not buying that. Someone formed the Time Patrol. Everyone works for someone."

Foreman indicated Edith. "Let the lady speak. She knows more than I do."

Everyone turned back to Edith.

"The HUB was in the center of the base, in the cavern." Her forehead furrowed as she tried to remember. "I can't remember what it looks like yet. But it drew a lot of power. There was a legend that the HUB caused the Great Northeast Blackout of 1965."

"There were power cables in the floor of the cavern," Doc said. "Connected to the grid." He turned to Edith. "When was it invented?"

"Frankly," Edith said, "*when* it was invented doesn't matter. As I said. If it's ever invented then it was always invented. The Patrol used the HUB. That's the bottom line." She sighed. "It's so much easier just to write things up in a report and turn it in. Even in just six pages."

"My head hurts," Roland said.

"This is really cool," Scout said.

"Just tell me how to kill those things," Nada muttered.

"Wait a second everyone," Doc said, weighing in on his area of expertise: science. A difficult undertaking given the Nightstalkers' propensity to shoot first and ask questions later. "We've got to understand this."

"No," the Keep interrupted. "You don't need to understand it. Because it seems even the Patrol didn't understand the HUB. They used it. We need to solve the immediate problem, the Time Patrol being missing, and fix it. Because the clock is ticking."

"But they had to get the technology somehow," Doc argued. "It had to come from somewhere and sometime. From our own future? Invented in our present? Actually that would be our past since it existed already and you insinuated it was active during the '65 blackout."

No one answered Doc's questions.

Moms stepped into the silence. "The Patrol didn't just up and decide to disappear. Someone made them disappear. Most likely that thing we killed in the cavern. And its buddies."

"Why don't we just listen." The Keep wasn't asking.

So Edith continued. "Time travel is dangerous. Both the actual mechanics of it, which, again, I am *not* familiar with, not being an agent or a scientist, and the possible effects a time traveler could have, or someone coming into our timeline and changing it could have. The latter was the focus of the Patrol's mission.

"It's not a case of stepping on a butterfly a thousand years ago and changing the course of history. The way it was explained to me is that our history, our timeline, is a powerful river churning through deep banks that it has cut through the space-time continuum." She cupped her long hands together to emphasize her point. "If a time traveler or infiltrator into our timeline changes something in the past, we call that a ripple. Like throwing a pebble into that river. Almost always it won't have any effect. The flow of history will absorb the change and the ripple sooner or later fades away into nothing.

"But if it's a major change—think Hannibal killing Scipio Africanus—that might have an effect."

"Who killed who?" Roland muttered, perking up at the hint of violence, but everyone ignored him.

Edith plowed ahead, trying to explain the unexplainable. "Note I say *might* because generally one person or one event isn't enough. People can be replaced by like-minded people. Very rarely is one person that important. And rarely is one event so important. But in such cases where they are, the Patrol has dealt with those attempts to change time and negated them."

That got everyone's attention.

"Who is making these attempts to change history?" the Keep asked.

"That's the problem," Edith said. "We don't know. We assume they are from a parallel Earth timeline. One at least."

Moms turned to Foreman. "So that's your connection to the Patrol."

"Yes," Foreman said. "Our research overlapped, but we still know so very little on either side."

"That thing down in the cavern," Scout said. "It was from another Earth timeline?"

"It's possible," Edith said.

"Maybe it might be other time travelers from our own time-line," Doc said.

"Does anyone else on the planet, our Earth," Moms asked, "have time travel capability?"

"Not that I'm aware of," Edith said.

Moms turned to Foreman. "Do you know?"

"The same—no one else as far as I know," Foreman said.

Roland was a bit behind. "Who is Skippy Africanus?"

Edith continued. "The Patrol has been a reactionary force, protecting our timeline. The agents, that's what the individual members are called, each have specific eras and locations assigned that they're responsible for."

"How many agents?" Moms asked.

"Thousands," Edith said. "But most are almost always gone. In the past. On patrol in their time. Only a few are here, were here, at any one time. Usually checking in. Making sure the flow is smooth. Doing research. The weird thing is, only a handful of the agents are from our time, each with a responsibility for a large era. The vast majority of operatives are from our past. Recruited for their expertise in their own specific eras, usually the duration of their lifetime, overlapping, of course with agents before and after. No current-era agent is allowed to go into the past unless they are matched up with an agent from that era. Those past agents are recruited and then trained by the Patrol to act as agents."

"Trained where?" Nada asked.

"I don't know," Edith said. She shook her head. "That's something that's not clear in my memory. I know I know. I just can't remember."

Nada shot Frasier a dirty look, which was a wasted effort.

"That has to be a major operation," Eagle said. "To adequately cover our entire past around the planet would require thousands and thousands of people. Think of the time and geography that needs to be covered."

"The information given agents from the past," Edith said, "is tightly controlled. They're told only what they absolutely need to know in order to deal with any ripples in their time. The Patrol works very hard to make sure they don't know their future."

"Makes sense," Doc said. "No one misses someone from the past. But someone from the present in the past could cause a problem. No matter how well trained one was, it would be impossible to completely blend in to a different era."

"*A Connecticut Yankee in King Arthur's Court*," Eagle said.

"Exactly," Edith agreed.

Roland was starting to twitch and Scout went and stood by him. "Ignore most of what they're saying," she whispered to him. "Nada will tell you who to shoot."

That soothed the big man for the moment.

"So these agents," Moms said, having had a moment to think this through, "are probably still in place, doing their jobs."

Edith nodded. "Most likely. But. We can't communicate with them without the HUB. That's the portal through which they come and go. Came and went. But there's a good chance those in their eras, which they are experts in, are indeed still in place. The problem is, when you're in an era, it will take time to realize a ripple has been enacted. By then, in that time, it's most likely too late to negate the ripple. The agent can come back to the present through the HUB, research the ripple or the shift, if it gets to that, and then go back, perhaps with a current operative, to earlier in their era, and make the correction by preventing the change.

"*And*, more importantly, we can't tell them if there's been a problem in their time if we see the ripple from our perspective looking back, but they haven't noticed it. Most ripples are noted in our present, and we go back and alert the agents of the appropriate era to take corrective action, negating even the need for them to come to our time. That's the more usual Protocol by far."

"I got a bad headache," Roland said.

"Go on," the Keep prompted.

"So a ripple is different than a shift?" Doc asked.

Edith cleared her throat. "I was told it is extraordinarily unlikely that a single ripple can cause a shift in our timeline. But a series of ripples, coordinated on a specific path, can cause what they call a shift. That's when something begins to change in our present."

"That's what we've begun to experience," Moms said. "The weird stuff that's been happening to us."

"What weird stuff?" Foreman asked, but he was ignored by the team.

"Are the changes permanent?" Doc asked. "You say the Patrol can go back and revert the timeline?"

"The Patrol can fix the shift," Edith said. "Whether that reverts ancillary changes is something I don't know."

"What?" Roland said.

"The big danger," Edith continued, "is if there are enough shifts which aren't corrected, we could get a time tsunami."

"That don't sound good," Roland muttered.

"It's never happened," Edith said. "But if twelve hours go by in the present and the shift isn't corrected, then it will be a tsunami. Our timeline will change permanently."

"Why twelve hours?" Doc asked.

Edith shrugged. "I don't know."

"Geez," Nada said. "We're flying blind here."

"That's the countdown that started," the Keep said.

"What countdown?" Moms asked.

"Upon the alarm being sounded," the Keep said. She looked at her watch. "We now have seven hours and twenty-two minutes."

"To do what exactly?" Nada demanded.

"Silence!" The Keep was surprisingly loud for such a tiny person. "I admit I'm not used to working on a team. But we need to work together. Let the woman finish. Then we'll deal with the situation."

"Hold on," Doc said. "Why has the countdown started? Has there been a change in our past? Or has it started because the Time Patrol is gone?"

"I don't know," Edith said. "We know the HUB is gone. Here's the key. The *but*, so to speak. If you follow the logic, then an agent has infinite time in the past to make a correction. But in the present, we only have the twelve hours."

"Let me see if I follow," Moms said. "If a shift is experienced now, as long as it's noted, and an agent is sent to the past to alert the agent of the era the ripple or shift started in, within twelve hours, things are good to go?"

"Yes," Edith said. "But we almost always deal with ripples. No rush on those, except we never know if they're adding up to a shift."

"So the Time Patrol disappearing," Eagle said, "is a shift."

"Right," Edith said.

"Hold on," Eagle said. "So no ripples were noticed?"

"Apparently," Edith said, "some of you have experienced ripples. But the Time Patrol disappearing; that's unprecedented."

Doc took a step forward. "That's cutting it awfully thin, twelve hours. It would be easy to miss these ripples."

Edith shook her head. "Don't you understand? That's why the Patrol stretches all the way back to the beginning of mankind. We have twelve hours in the present, but all of history, after the initiating event of a ripple, to notice it. So any agent *past* the initiating of a ripple up until the present can report it." She pointed toward the Metropolitan Museum of Art. "And that's why we're here. We have art in there from across the world. A series of ripples make it to a shift, it will show up in the art from some time and some place."

"Ingenious," Eagle said. "The backup reporting system."

Edith nodded. "Yes. The Patrol disappearing, that wipes out any agent reporting in other than through the art."

A phone rang, cutting through all the talk. The Keep picked it up, listened for a moment, and then put it down. "Support has removed the armor from the thing you killed. And they're afraid the body might be booby-trapped."

The team headed out of the van toward the Met. The Keep waited until they were all gone, and then sat down in the chair facing the encrypted audio-visual channel. She turned it on. The screen flickered for a moment as it was frequency jumped and then matched to the set on the other end.

The image of the President appeared.

"I've considered the situation as per your reports," the President said. "Your summation?"

"We can't allow a breach to occur from this location," the Keep said.

"Recommendation?"

"You authorize Furtherance for this locale. I will take personal charge. I've had some people run the numbers. It will be contained underground."

The President bit her lower lip as she considered this, a habit her aides had managed to break her of—mostly. "Are you certain?"

The Keep hesitated, Edith Frobish's words about a shift and possible tsunami echoing in her troubled thoughts. "I'd prefer to err on the side of caution on this. Containment is a priority."

The President nodded. "I'll issue the order."

THE SPACE BETWEEN

"What is this place?" Ivar asked, eyeing someone who looked suspiciously like a pirate sharpening his cutlass about fifteen feet away.

Ivar was seated in an airplane seat set into the black "sand," and since the ashtrays hadn't been sealed shut, one from before 1990. Earhart was in a similar seat facing him. The camp was a hodgepodge of not only people, but gear. Airplane seats, canvas sails for overhead cover (did it rain here? Ivar wondered), wooden chests and barrels, and even a bronze cannon, which Ivar suspected was somehow connected to the pirate, since he was sitting on it as he sharpened his cutlass.

"The Space Between," Earhart said.

"Between what?"

"Worlds," Earhart said.

"Who are these people?"

"We're the Outcasts. People who were taken from our timelines and can't go back." She leaned forward. "Listen. The world you are from. The timeline. I assume I disappeared on my round-the-world flight?"

"Yes," Ivar said.

Earhart gave a sad smile. "I think I disappeared in every time-line. Would have been nice to know I made it in one of them. That event seems to be a constant, except for those where civilization didn't survive long enough to invent the airplane." She shook her head. "A different timeline is a different world, even though it's still Earth. Has the Shadow attacked your timeline?"

"Um, I guess not," Ivar ventured. "What's the Shadow?"

"The Ones Before?" Earhart asked. "The Others?"

"No idea what you're talking about," Ivar said. "But like, shouldn't you be really old?"

"What year did you come from?" Earhart asked.

When Ivar told her, she sat back and considered him. "Interesting. Much further along than most who come through here. Your timeline must be doing well if you are not aware of the Shadow."

"We've had some things called Rifts," Ivar said. "And Fireflies came through." He then explained the Nightstalkers' experiences with those strange phenomena. When he was done, Earhart pondered it for a few moments.

"Very different from the way others have experienced the Shadow," she finally said, "but who knows? Maybe it took a different form in your timeline. What are you doing here?"

Ivar's mouth worked, trying to formulate something to say that sounded intelligent, but he couldn't. Finally he fell back to habits learned as a PhD candidate: He pled ignorance. "I don't even know where *here* is. I don't know what this Space Between is. I was at work in the Archives at Area 51, then I woke up on the beach, or whatever you call what's next to the water."

"What is Area 51?" Earhart asked.

"A supersecret government base," Ivar said, and then regretted it, because it was supposed to be secret. But then he wondered why he regretted it because this was just frakking insane.

Ivar had a hard time with change.

"I don't understand any of this," he said. "Did I get sucked through a Rift?"

"You must have come through a gate," Earhart said.

"Is a Rift a gate?"

Earhart shrugged. "I don't know what a Rift is, and it seems you don't either, so I can't tell you that. A gate goes from one timeline to another. Or to this place."

"Okay." Ivar thought about that for a moment. "So sort of Rifts. But probably different. So. Um. Who exactly are you people?"

Earhart gave a thin smile. "I told you: the Outcasts. People who got sucked in through a gate, whether on purpose or by accident."

"But you look—" Ivar paused, because even he knew, even here in this strange place, that talking about a woman's age and appearance was a subject fraught with peril.

"Not any older? I was thirty-nine when I came here," Earhart said. "I know I've been here a while. How long, I don't know. There's no sunrise or sunset in here. But it has to be a couple of years at least. It seems none of us really age in this place. Or if we do, not in a way that's noticeable. One small advantage of this purgatory." She held up her hand. "My fingernails don't grow. My hair doesn't. We all seem suspended in time." She nodded over her shoulder. "The one of us from the furthest back is a Phoenician sailor. From about one thousand years before the birth of Our Lord as near as we can tell. I ended up here in 1937."

For Ivar, like most millennials, 1937 was as distant in the past as horse-drawn buggies and no video games. Incomprehensible. "What happened to you?" Ivar asked.

Earhart sighed. "We—my navigator, Fred Noonan and I— took off from Australia and flew to New Guinea. Then we took off on a leg to Howland Island." She fell silent for a moment. "We hit a gate, although I didn't know what it was at that time. I managed to ditch and then we were attacked by terrible sea creatures. Kraken. Noonan was killed. I blacked out. And when I awoke, I was here."

"Kraken?" Ivar had visions of "Release the Kraken!"

"Like a giant squid," Earhart said, "except worse. They seem to go in and out of gates when gates open in certain places. We're lucky we haven't encountered any here." She looked about. "We currently have sixteen people. From various times and various timelines. We've learned to talk to each other.

"Since we have no night or day, we count sleep cycles, but even that is confusing. We have patches of earth soil, salvaged from various vessels. Seeds we've scavenged. We make do. Animals sometimes come through. If we can eat it, we do so." She laughed. "Once there was something I could only describe as a small dinosaur. It wandered about for a while, terrifying everyone, then went into the water. We never saw it again."

She got serious. "But those who have tried going into gates?" She shook her head. "I've seen two men try. Both went in and immediately reappeared, screaming in agony, their skin burned. Both died within an hour of their attempt. It could have been wherever they went to was in such terrible condition it caused that, or simply the traversing of the gate out of here did that to them. It was enough, though, to keep others from trying."

"Where do these gates lead?" Ivar asked.

"Other timelines. This place—" she waved her hand, indicating the surrounding environment, "is the Space Between timelines." Earhart paused, and then leaned forward once more, holding her hands out to demonstrate. "You understand engines, right?"

Ivar nodded.

Earhart continued. "Imagine that each timeline is a ball bearing. All the timelines are clumped together and spinning, touching each other but not really affecting each other, rolling smoothly, the places where they touch causing some slight friction, but not truly affecting things in the larger picture.

"But gates are pathways between adjoining spheres at those meeting points. Sometimes timelines directly adjoin each other and there can be direct travel. But otherwise you have to come here through the Space Between. For some reason, even timelines that don't adjoin each other adjoin this place. I don't know if it's because this place is all encompassing, or what special properties it has. But I believe it adjoins *all* timelines. Maybe it's the center of everything."

"This is . . . remarkable. How, how do you possibly know all this?" Ivar asked. "If you're isolated here, how can you know what's beyond this place?"

"We're not completely isolated," Earhart said. "Travelers come through. Bad, good, and evil."

Ivar sat back, a bit overwhelmed. "I'll have to think on it. The physics of it." Then he asked the question second uppermost in his concern. "Have you attempted to go back to your timeline?"

"Not only is it probably fatal, I also can't," Earhart said. "For some of us, our disappearance is an integral part of the sanctity of our home timelines. So we can't go back."

"Okay," Ivar drew the word out. "You mean, like important people?"

Earhart shrugged. "I don't know."

"Can I go back?"

"I don't know," Earhart said. "You'd have to find the gate

you came through. And we really have little idea which gate goes where. And there is the possibility you could get burnt up doing it."

"So what do you do here?" Ivar asked.

"We survive," Earhart said. "And we fight."

"*Fight*? Who are you fighting?"

"We fight the monsters. We're the ghosts in the machine."

CHAPTER 9

Seven Hours

Where the annual Met Gala had held their dinner a week previously was now a hastily converted Level Three containment facility, since no one was certain what they were dealing with in terms of the body. How the glitterati who'd attended the Gala would respond to such a transgression mattered nothing to the Nightstalkers or their support team. Heavy clear plastic barriers surrounded the large banquet table on which the creature the team had killed was displayed, while pumps worked to push filtered air into the hastily constructed facility.

The area was mostly empty except for the body splayed out on the table, an autopsy half-completed. Hovering over it were several cameras on long arms.

"It's human," was the first comment, made by, of course, Roland, who was a master at observing the obvious.

"Indeed," replied the Acme pathologist who'd been alerted to active duty to perform this task. "Homo sapiens."

Blast shields had been hastily erected and the Acme pathologist was hunkered down behind one of them, staring at a computer screen, while a bomb disposal squad from the New York Police Department waited on call.

Moms and the team were with the pathologist on the safe side of the wall. "What's the problem?"

"I was working," the Acme said, "and when I did the chest incision and separation, I found that!" His shaking finger pointed at the screen. The Acme, part of the group of varied specialists the Nightstalkers kept on call, was a young man, obviously on his first live mission.

"Mac." Moms called forward the team's demolition expert. "What is that? Something like the couriers are wired with?"

Couriers for Area 51 traversed the country, transporting dangerous cargos between research labs, the Archives, and other facilities as needed. They had a catheter inserted into their heart in order to monitor something very important: whether they were alive or not. If the "not" happened, that would lead to the Nightstalkers alerting and scrambling to find out the cause of the "not" and, more importantly, get their cargo secure.

This had happened more than once.

Mac peered at the screen.

"Similar," Mac said. "Something definitely got tripped when that thing's heart stopped beating."

"Any sign of explosives?"

"No," Mac said, "but if I were wiring the body to blow, you wouldn't see any sign. Could also be a remote to something built into the suit." He turned to the Acme. "Which is where?"

"The suit is in another part of the building and experts are gathering to examine it," the Acme said.

"I'd suggest they isolate it," Mac said, "until I can check this out."

"That thing was big in the suit," Scout observed, remembering that this was the being who'd killed Kirk. "But that guy seems pretty normal size."

"The suit arms and legs and torso were extended," the pathologist said. "Internal controls. It didn't exactly fit like a glove."

Mac glanced over at the NYPD bomb disposal unit, and then shrugged. "If it were gonna blow, it would have blown by now."

He walked around the blast barrier to the entrance to the decontamination facility.

"Wait!" the Acme called out. "You need to go through Protocol and wear a protective suit!"

Mac ignored him. "Moms, if that thing is contagious with something, I breached containment with my forty-mike-mike round that blew its arm off."

"Roger that," Moms said.

Mac unzipped the first barrier and quickly made his way through, leaving everything behind him open.

"That's not proper Protocol," the Acme complained.

"Mac had a good point," Moms said. "You put *it* in containment, but not us, which doesn't make sense."

The Acme had no response to that. Mac appeared on-screen, leaning over the body. He pulled out a Leatherman tool from his combat vest and began prodding and poking.

"Oh!" the Acme exclaimed in dismay. "He's messing with the evidence."

"Where do you work?" Moms asked him.

"City coroner."

"Don't worry," Moms said. "This isn't ever going to see the inside of a courtroom, so don't worry about the evidence. Our job is to kill things like your evidence. Obliterate them."

"Oh." This time it was said with no exclamation point.

Mac's voice came over the team net. "There's no explosives. It's similar to what we use with couriers but more sophisticated. More like a medical tracker, not just indicating whether the heart is beating, but leading into the bloodstream. I'd say it's a pretty comprehensive health status monitoring system. More advanced than what we use. Although even with the surgery, this guy doesn't look very healthy."

"Transmitter?" Moms asked.

"I don't see one, but we should do a body scan and also check the brain."

Moms looked at the coroner, who wasn't privy to both sides of the conversation. "Did you x-ray the body?"

The coroner nodded.

"Well?" Moms was getting tired of leading him by the hand. "Want to bring up the images?"

The man quickly typed into his computer.

"Doc," Moms said. "Tell me what I'm seeing."

Doc pushed his way forward as several x-rays of the thing's head appeared. "Whoa! Not good." He pointed at a dark mass at the base of the skull.

"What the frak!" Mac said, jerking back from the body. "Is this thing rigged with something in the head to blow?"

"No, no, no," Doc quickly said over the net. "Sorry about that, Mac. Something different. That's a tumor in its brain. A bad one." Doc leaned closer to the screen. "Hmm. And there is something mechanical in there, at the base of the skull. Very small."

"Mac?" Moms said.

Mac picked up a small saw and began cutting.

The pathologist made a whimpering sound, like an artist who'd just seen someone take a can of spray paint to his masterpiece.

"Yep," Mac said, holding up something small and bloody in his hands. "A transmitter."

"Come on," Moms said, walking around the blast barrier and leading the way. They all followed as Moms headed into the makeshift containment facility and they gathered around the autopsy table.

"That is indeed a human," Moms said.

"And with tattoos," Scout said, half bored already with the obvious, wanting to move to the less obvious.

"Yes," the Acme said. "Should this young lady be in here?" The Acme indicated the naked body splayed out on the table, cut open, various organs resting to the side.

"She's part of the team," Nada said in a way that brooked no argument and gained him an adoring look from Scout. "We killed this. She was with us."

The Acme shut up.

"Go ahead with the rest of your report," the Keep said.

Everyone gathered round, Scout up front along with Moms and Doc and the Keep and Foreman. The second rank was Mac, Nada, Edith Frobish, Frasier, and Eagle.

The pathologist was a typical Acme, meaning a typical scientist, focused first on impressing everyone with his presentation. He picked up a clipboard and began. "Male, Caucasian, approximately thirty-five years old."

"What's that?" Scout asked, no longer bored. She was pointing at the man's left side. The skin was rippled and red.

The Acme was once more thrown off-balance. "Burns. I'll get to it."

"Let the man finish, Scout," Moms said.

"Roger that," Scout said.

The Acme checked his clipboard. "Cause of death, multiple wounds in upper right chest as well as severing of right arm, all leading to exsanguination."

"He bled out," Mac said quickly as Roland began to open his mouth.

"There were two postmortem, ventilation wounds to the skull via the right eye," the Acme said.

"Nada's double-tap after he was dead," Mac interpreted for Roland.

"Yeah, yeah," Roland said. "We know we killed the S.O.B. Tell us something we don't know."

The Acme was flustered, but pointed at what Scout had already noted. "Those burns were caused by exposure to radiation. Checking his thyroid, where radioactive iodine concentrates, we found high levels. In his bones"—the Acme pointed at an incision along one thigh, where the skin and muscle was peeled back, exposing bone—"we found traces of strontium-90 and radium-226." The Acme looked up from the clipboard. "In essence, this man was dying."

"Mercy killing then," Nada said.

"The odd thing, though," the Acme said, "is that he's apparently been dying for a long time. Which doesn't make sense."

"Explain," the Keep said.

The Acme shook his head. "I can't explain. But from the data we've accumulated on the radiation he absorbed and the state of the body, he should have been dead long ago. I have no idea what's kept him alive this long."

"Hold on," Moms said, processing the information. "You're saying he should have been dead based on your analysis, but he was still alive. And alive enough to attack us?"

"Yes."

"Could the suit have been keeping him alive somehow?" Moms asked.

"Doubtful," the Acme said. "But here's the more interesting thing." He picked up an internal organ; which one wasn't quite clear as it was part of a mass of red goo. "He's had several transplants."

"Define several," the Keep said.

"Both lungs, heart, kidney. More than any hospital would ever do or is capable of doing. And the surgery, it's perfect. I've never seen anything like it."

"So dead guy had a good medical plan," Scout said.

"And here." The Acme pointed at the same side of the burned thigh. "See his buttock. Skin grafts. They start all the way up at the arm on that side and go down to the scar. It was as if whoever was doing this to him was working their way down his body."

"He was getting fixed," Nada said.

The Acme looked up. "What?"

Nada pointed at the body. "He was getting fixed, bit by bit. He got exposed to lethal radiation but didn't die. And part by part, he was getting fixed. Stuff replaced."

"Yes," the Acme agreed, "but medical science doesn't have that capability."

"Our medical science doesn't," the Keep said.

"What about the suit he was wearing?" Moms asked.

"Armor with some sort of gyroscopic enhancement," the Acme said. "Also, on the inside of the head part, various imaging screens. As I said, the hands and feet ended well short of the end of the suit where there were controls to be used. But that's not my area of expertise. There are others working on it right now."

"How did the thing fly?" Roland asked, cutting to the chase.

"No idea," the Acme said. "Again it's—"

"Not your expertise," Nada finished for him.

"The spear?" Roland asked, as always, focused on weaponry.

"The metal is being analyzed, but we couldn't immediately identify it."

The Keep was frustrated. "So we're not closer to figuring out who this is or where—"

"The tattoo," Scout said, coming full circle. She pointed at the symbol of an inverted triangle with the face of a roaring black bear on the inside, framed in red.

"Yes," the Acme said. "We had it imaged and it's being run."

"Spetsnaz," Nada said. "Russian Special Forces. From a while back, while the Soviet Union was still a union."

"Always lead with the headline," Scout said to the Acme.

"He's not old enough," Moms said. "The Soviet Union fell apart over a quarter century ago. The guy would have been in elementary school at best."

"That's what it is," Nada said.

Moms summarized. "So we have someone who was Spetsnaz, who was exposed to radiation and should have died but didn't, has had organ replacement and skin grafts at a level our science can't do, and armed with a weapon with metal we can't place."

"Great," Nada muttered.

"And he flies," Roland said.

"Yo," Mac said. "Anything in the database about something like this? White armor? The red—is that hair?"

"Yes, it's human hair," the Acme said. "We're trying to track its DNA, but it's not his hair. It was added on to the suit. A brief examination reveals the strands to be that of numerous types of hair, woven together, all dyed bright red."

"A trophy," Nada said. "Of its victims."

"A Valkyrie." Foreman's voice was low, but everyone heard him, and they all turned to face him.

"Valkyries," Foreman said. "There have been reports of creatures like that around gates. We've never captured or killed one before. But that's what they've been labeled."

"You never had the Nightstalkers before," Scout said, earning an appreciative nod from Roland.

"Labeled by who?" Eagle asked.

Foreman looked surprised, as if caught in a lie, but recovered quickly. "The Patrol, of course. Tell them of the legend of the Valkyries," Foreman instructed Edith.

"Valkyries," Edith Frobish said, reminding everyone she was still with them. "The handmaidens of the gods. From Norse mythology. The Valkyries are rather complex creatures in the role they play in the infrastructure of that mythology. The name means 'chooser of the slain.' In essence, the belief was that the Valkyries chose which warriors lived or died. For those who were killed while fighting bravely, the Valkyries bore them to Valhalla, the hall of the slain."

"Is that what happened to the guard's body?" Nada asked. "Carried off by these Valkyries?"

"I have no idea. Although Valkyries were technically female," Edith continued, "once someone was in that suit you couldn't exactly tell the sex. The concept arose among the Norse as a way of changing the gore of the battlefield to a place of honor and potential paradise. We have a painting here in the Met. *The Ride of the Valkyrs* by John Dollman, painted in 1909. I can show it to you."

"We've seen the real thing," Moms said.

"Mythology doesn't spring out of nothingness," Foreman said. "I believe there is truth at the core of practically every myth. And since, as you say," he nodded at Moms, "we're looking at the real thing, then others in our past have looked at the real thing. Not being able to explain it, it then evolved into myth."

"Monsters," Scout said.

Foreman nodded. "Yes. Many of the legends of monsters come from things like this. Things that came through gates into our world. I don't believe it has happened often or in great numbers and only in certain places. Thus there is little trace other than legend."

"This wasn't a creature," Scout noted. "This was a man in a superhero suit."

"A Russian man," Roland said, his way of throwing a non sequitur into a conversation, but hitting on a key point.

"That's not a monster," Nada said. "It's a guy. Who can be killed."

"That guy I sanctioned on Whidbey," Roland said. "He said something weird. He said something about the Patrol and about the Ratnik. Neeley said Ratnik might be Russian."

Doc had his phone out and was already Googling it. "Ratnik has a couple of definitions. It's the new generation of Russian military equipment: night sights, body armor, etc. That might apply here."

"The Russians fielded this?" The Keep was skeptical.

"It was also a Bulgarian right-wing movement prior to World War Two," Doc added. "Pretty much wiped out during the war."

"More likely on the first one," Moms said. "But this technology is way ahead of anything the Russians have. That anyone has."

"In *our* timeline," Foreman said.

The group stood silent, each member lost in thought, but apparently no further in those thoughts until Scout spoke up.

"Excuse me."

Everyone turned to look at the youngest person in the group.

"We're skipping something very important," she said. When no one challenged her, she continued. She turned to the Keep. "You said that your instructions were to wait for the entire team to arrive before moving forward, correct?"

The Keep nodded. She seemed about to say something about the young girl hijacking the meeting, but bit it back.

"So we wasted over four hours doing that, right?" Scout didn't wait for an answer. "Who wrote those instructions you were following?" she asked, and this time she did wait.

The Keep shook her head. "I don't know. They were in a safe in my office. A safe that could only be opened by myself and the President."

"Did you write them?" Scout asked Foreman.

"No."

"All right," Scout said. "Let's assume the Patrol wrote them. And the Patrol has managed to keep a very, very low profile all this time. Not as hard as we would think given most of its agents are not of or in this time. So we're caught in a bad loop here, but not as bad as we think it is. The Patrol wanted all of us here for a reason and must have expected some time to be used up getting us here. The Nightstalkers. Why?"

Scout waited, but there was no answer. She rolled her eyes. "This is the center of it. The first anomaly. Ripple. Shift. Whatever."

Doc jumped in. "Yes. Exactly. The HUB disappearing."

"Right," Scout said. "But it's not just the place. It's us. We're part of it." She pointed at herself, then waved her hand taking in the team. "I think we're noticing things the rest of the world isn't. I had something strange occur right before being alerted. Nada, you too, right?"

The team sergeant nodded.

"Who else?" Scout asked.

That caused a reaction as several of them started to speak at once.

Moms took charge and slapped the autopsy table. "Listen to Scout."

"I don't know why," Scout said, "since the rest of the world seems to be doing okay, but something affected *us*." She pointed. "Doc says Ivar disappeared. Roland, something happened to the Sanction you just completed, right?"

"We killed the sonofabitch," Roland said. "But then he just disappeared from the body bag." He didn't add that Neeley had kissed him, but his face flushed red at the memory.

"So that's two people disappearing," Scout said. "Ivar and the sonofabitch." She turned to Nada. "You remembered something that Frasier blocked. But Frasier didn't use his little Men in Black headphones on you to unblock you. You just started remembering, right?"

Nada nodded. "But only bits and pieces," he added with a glare at Frasier.

Scout also looked at Frasier, who'd remained inconspicuous throughout all this. "How did that happen? How did Nada start remembering what you blocked?"

"I don't know," Frasier said.

"Has something like this happened before to a block?" Scout pressed.

"No." He opened his mouth to say something else, but stopped.

"I noted that details had changed in the historical text I was reading," Eagle said.

Scout nodded and turned to Moms. "What happened to you?"

"Someone appeared in a family photo from a long time ago," Moms said. "Someone who wasn't in the original photo." She also seemed about to say something more, but halted.

Scout nodded. "My mother made bacon this morning. And sang. That's as weird as Ivar disappearing. Trust me."

"I don't understand what you're getting at," Nada said.

Scout looked at the Keep. "What happened to you?"

The Keep shook her head. "Nothing. Other than getting the alarm from here."

"Hmm," Scout said. "All right. If the Time Patrol left those instructions, and they wanted to make sure we were all here before we did anything, but they also knew we'd pretty much be clueless, then there has to be a connection between those occurrences."

"Why us?" Nada said.

"Exactly," Scout said. "So the answer is in this room. We just have to figure out what it is."

For once, Doc had an answer. Sort of. "We've all been near disturbances in space-time. Except for the Keep," he added.

"Near what?" the Keep asked.

"Rifts," Roland said, for once elated to have an answer. He knew Rifts and Fireflies well because he'd dealt with quite a few in his time. And killed quite a few Fireflies.

"Exactly," Doc said. "Maybe we're more susceptible because we've already been touched by a shift in our time-space continuum? We're closer to the edge of our timeline in some way."

"How are the Rifts associated with this?" Nada asked.

Doc shrugged. "We still don't even know what Rifts are. But we shut the last one down and got our people back from all the years they've been opening since the first one at Area 51 in 1947. As far as we know, that was the first one. And as far as we know, the one in Tennessee at the dam was the last one. Whoever's on the other side returned the people who sent over the Demon Core and opened the first Rift."

"The Can at Area 51 didn't pick up any activity here," Moms said. "We would have been Zevoned if it had. We haven't had a Zevon," she added with a glance at Nada, "since Tennessee. Whatever this is, it's different."

"But it affected us first, apparently," Scout said.

"Yo," Mac said, getting everyone's attention. "Let me ask you all this. Where the hell *is* Ivar?"

No one had an answer for that.

"We have to remember," Doc said, "that in North Carolina, Ivar went through a Rift. And he came back. He's the only one on the team who did that. So maybe he was the most susceptible of all of us. Maybe he's the only one that's traveled to another time-line and back?"

"But he didn't remember much at all," Eagle said, "about what was on the other side."

Everyone turned to Frasier. He held up his hands defensively. "I had nothing to do with Ivar or his memory."

"Wait a second!" Edith Frobish almost yelled, which meant she was barely heard. She reached out and grabbed Eagle's shoulder in her excitement. "What exactly was changed in that history you were reading?"

In reply, Eagle pulled out his phone, accessed his Kindle app, and directed it to the appropriate page. He handed it to her as he spoke to the rest of them. "The author writes that the Lateran Obelisk is still in Egypt. But it's in Rome. Has been in Rome since 357 AD."

This time Mac didn't have a smart-ass observation.

"Is it?" Scout asked.

"Frak," Moms muttered. "Kirk get me—" She paused in her order to the commo man who was no longer with them. She picked up the blood-covered comsat set and made access back to Pitr at the Ranch.

The Keep was also on her phone.

But Edith wasn't paying attention. "The Obelisk. That's it. The marker. We have to check it."

"Check what?" Doc asked.

"According to my sources," the Keep said, "it *is* still in Rome."

"But for Eagle," Edith said, "it *isn't!*"

Roland grabbed a chair and sat down in it. "Can we just shoot something?"

"We're having a divergence of realities," Doc said.

Edith was excited. "Yes. The Administrator said a ripple wouldn't be noticed, even a shift, unless it was specifically looked for by someone who also was affected by the ripple."

"I don't get it," Nada said.

Edith was vibrating, edging toward the door. "This young lady," she said, indicating Scout, "has it right. Not only is our time starting to be affected, but *we're* affected to varying degrees. Those of you who have been on the edge of a disturbance are being touched by the ripple first. Everything is normal for everyone else. Until it's too late. Because Patrol agents travel through gates, they also are more susceptible to noticing changes that others wouldn't. That I know."

The Keep got that. "That's why the Patrol ordered me to wait until all of you were here. You're the one that would see the changes if the Patrol wasn't around."

"Exactly," Edith said. "But now, let's see if we've gotten a marker or a message about what changed in the past to affect the now."

"What kind of message?" Moms asked.

"An agent sending a request for information or noting an anomaly from what the agent knows to be true history."

"The art?" Eagle asked.

"Yes," Edith said. "But there's one place I always check first. Cleopatra's Needle." Edith began to head toward the door.

"Hold on," Moms said. She pointed at the body. "We know we can kill this. Doc, take Mac and Roland and Eagle. Go down to the cavern. Send a probe into that gate. Get me more information on it. Mac, build us up a ramp so we can go into that gate if we have to. Roland, anything comes out, you kill it. Eagle, back him up and prepare for infiltration."

The nameplate read LOUISE SMITH. She had a thick gray bun, reading glasses perched on her nose, and wore a bulky sweater of some indeterminate muted color that was draped over her shapeless body.

She was the gatekeeper to the inner sanctum of the Cellar. She'd sat in this outer office for over twenty-five years for Hannah's predecessor, Nero, and she'd simply stayed in place as he passed on and Hannah took his place. If Ms. Smith had a life outside of this office, Hannah knew nothing of it. She could undoubtedly have retired years ago on a government pension, but the fact she didn't indicated she actually didn't have a life outside of this office.

She was rarely perturbed or startled, an essential trait for someone in this position. No one entered the doors behind her, leading to the hallway to Hannah's office, without her permission.

But when the doors behind her suddenly hissed open on their pneumatic arms, Ms. Smith was indeed startled. She turned with surprising alacrity for someone who sat so lumpily in her chair.

"Ma'am?" she asked, while she tried to remember the last time her boss had left her office unannounced. Had she missed something on the schedule? A meeting with some senator or congressman who needed to be threatened into silence? A briefing at the CIA? Such an oversight would be unprecedented.

"Ms. Smith," Hannah said, nodding. She further surprised her secretary by walking up to her and sitting on the corner of her desk.

Ms. Smith turned her seat to face Hannah, uncomfortable with both the action of her boss and her proximity. Ms. Smith did not enjoy people within five feet of her, and Hannah had breached that distance by six inches.

But Ms. Smith did not protest. She didn't scoot her chair back six inches. "Yes, ma'am?"

"In your time with Nero," Hannah said, "did you ever hear of a program called the Time Patrol?"

There was no hesitation in the reply. "No, ma'am."

"Certain?"

A tic of irritation, uncontrollable, registered in Ms. Smith's left cheek. "I'm certain, ma'am."

"Ever hear of a man named Foreman?"

"The Crazy Old Man?" Ms. Smith nodded. "Is he still around? It's been years."

"He's still around," Hannah assured her. "What do you know of him?"

"He visited Mister Nero several times over the years. I was never privy as to what transpired between them."

"Do you know what Foreman does?" Hannah asked. "Who he works for?"

"Foreman was early Agency," Ms. Smith said, referring to the CIA. "In it before it was even called the CIA. If he's still there, probably no one knows what he does anymore. He's outlived everyone. Including Mister Nero." She paused, as if considering what she said next was an indiscretion. "Mister Nero thought Mister Foreman was a bit bonkers."

"As good a cover as any," Hannah said. "Native Americans actually respected those who were considered crazy. Thought they had special powers and insight."

"Yes, ma'am."

"Did someone called the Administrator ever visit Nero?"

"The 'Administrator' of what, ma'am?"

"That's the point," Hannah said. "He just goes by the Administrator."

"Not that I recall."

Hannah slid off the desk. She reached under her business jacket and pulled out a pistol. She pulled the slide partly back, making sure there was a round in the chamber. "Have a helicopter ready for me."

"Yes, ma'am."

Golden felt claustrophobic in the booth as it rattled along the tracks underneath the Pentagon. She had an identification tag clipped to her jacket with the highest possible access level, but it still had taken a frustratingly long time to clear all the security checkpoints to get this far.

With a lurch, the booth came to a halt, and the double doors whisked open. Golden stepped out of the booth, the doors shutting behind her, unaware she'd just tripped the IR beam that crossed the inner doors. She took in the large, square room.

The first thing she noted was the tinfoil lining the walls. She considered that, then dismissed it as a ploy. It was too obvious for a man who'd survived inside the CIA-Pentagon–Black Budget–Covert world for so long. Of course, there was the possibility Foreman was getting Alzheimer's or some other form of dementia, but the reports from New York didn't indicate anything of the sort.

She went over to the desk and sat down. She'd always believed that literally sitting in someone's seat gave insight into their psyche. Golden had come to the attention of the Cellar because of her studies in profiling, trying to ferret out dangerous people *before* they committed any acts. She'd been using the military's extensive database to do this, and the concept of predicting behavior based on past experiences and traumas had caught Hannah's eye.

Directly across from the desk was the world map, so that must be a priority for Foreman, but Golden shifted her attention to the desk, because objects here were closer at hand. She saw the ancient coins, and that fit in with the Time Patrol. There was a black and white photo in a simple frame. Foreman, as a very young man, was in it, standing with a man on either side. In front of him were two rows of men in white lab coats, one row seated, the other kneeling. They were in a desert somewhere in front of an old army building. Golden took a picture of the picture. She pulled open the file drawer on the right-hand side. It was stuffed full of old manila folders, papers bulging out of some of them.

Golden prioritized and wasn't totally surprised to find exactly the three things she was looking for, each carefully labeled and in alphabetical order. She pulled out three thin folders: COYNE, RATNIK, SIN FEN.

She quickly opened them and photographed the scant contents.

Putting the folders back, Golden noted the world map next. She walked over. She took a couple of photos of it, and then read the notes.

Here There Be Monsters
Bermuda Triangle
Devil's Sea

She knew some of the locations by reputation, but others were new to her. She'd have to brush up on her viewing of the UFO cable channel, she reflected as she leaned over and peered at the MRI image pinned to the Shakespeare quote.

"Crap," Golden muttered as she saw the dark mass. She looked at the face of her cell phone and wasn't surprised to see she had no signal.

She looked back up at the map and frowned. The line drawn around the area labeled Bermuda Triangle wasn't exactly a triangle. It zigged and zagged in the Bermuda area but also had arms reaching out, one of them across Cuba and ending near the Caymans.

"Double crap," Golden said.

She spun about as the doors slid open. A man dressed in black fatigues with a submachine gun tight to his shoulder stepped out. He was aiming it directly at Golden.

"I have authorization!" Golden yelled, holding up the pass.

The man said nothing, edging to his right, her left, the gun remaining aimed at her. When he got halfway around the room, he gestured with the barrel toward the door.

"You want me to leave?" Golden asked.

In reply, he gave a quick jerk of the muzzle toward the exit.

Golden didn't need any further urging. She scuttled across the room and got into the booth. She breathed a sigh of relief as the doors shut behind her and she began moving. She had the photos, which was the key thing. Golden had butted heads with people inside the Pentagon throughout her career. She found the military mindset to be—

The booth jerked to a halt and the doors slid open. Two men dressed in black had their weapons trained on her, while a third stepped in, looped a zip tie over her hands before she could react, and yanked her out of the booth.

"What the—" Golden began, but one of the men hit her in the stomach with the butt of his submachine gun before she could get the third word out.

Golden doubled over, gasping for breath. The man who'd jerked her out and zip-tied her hit her across the back of the legs and she fell to her knees, her forehead coming perilously close to smashing into the floor.

One of the men stepped behind her and Golden felt the muzzle of a weapon pressed against the back of her head, in that soft spot at the top of the neck, just below the bottom of the skull. She realized she was looking at a rusty stain on the tile floor and dimly realized it was a bloodstain, so deep and so persistent it could never be washed away.

And that's when she realized her blood would join that stain.

"No!" Golden tried to cry out, but she only made a squeal.

The tableau was frozen like that for a long second, and then was broken as the doors slid open once more.

The executioners were more surprised by that than Golden, who was still trying to process the inevitability of death.

"Not today, gentlemen."

Golden felt a rush of relief hearing Hannah's voice.

One of the executioners spoke for the first time. "We have authorization."

"From a traitor," Hannah said.

Golden felt a hand around her arm, and she was lifted to her feet. Hannah looked calm and businesslike, but she held a gun in her other hand, not aimed at anyone, but more as a leveling of the playing field.

"I'm Hannah."

The three men took a step back. Glances were exchanged. "The Cellar?" one of them asked.

"The same." Hannah pointed at Golden. "She works for me. Please cut her hands free."

One of the men whipped out a knife and expertly severed the zip tie with a single slash. He slid the knife back into the sheath without missing a beat.

"Foreman is rogue," Hannah said. "Correct, Doctor Golden?"

Golden could only manage to shake her head in the affirmative.

"Have a good day, gentlemen." Hannah took Golden's elbow and led her into the booth. It was slightly crowded, but Golden didn't notice. The doors slid shut and they began moving.

"They were going to kill me," Golden finally managed to say.

"Yes."

"Why?"

"Foreman had his office rigged with an IR alert if it was

compromised. You compromised it. He had a standing order with those who rule that place to terminate anyone who made unauthorized entry."

"How did you know that?" Golden asked.

"I didn't. I'm surmising that based on the evidence."

"But then why did you come?"

"Because there's something wrong about Foreman," Hannah said. "What did you discover?"

"There is something wrong about Foreman."

"Let's go to New York," Hannah said.

"He stayed at that hotel," the Asset said, pointing out the window of the car. "He would order room service. Drink at the bar in the evenings. That was pretty much it."

The Asset was sweating, which might be due to the high temperature on Grand Cayman but more likely because of Neeley sitting in the passenger seat. She was dressed all in black: slacks and a collarless, armless shirt, which displayed the long, toned muscles in her arms. She wore wraparound sunglasses and had a daypack resting on her lap. She'd flown in on an unmarked Learjet and bypassed customs, not an unusual thing in the Caymans.

Neeley said nothing, letting the silence drag out.

"It's all in the report," the Asset insisted, as he had when Neeley met him planeside. He was an old man, face flushed red from sun and alcohol. A stringer, not a Cellar Asset. A big difference. He worked for whatever various US government agency tapped him with a request. He was well past what Gant had called ROAD: Retired on Active Duty.

"*All*?" Neeley finally said. "Every second of his time accounted for?"

"I've got a small team here," the Asset protested, which answered the question.

Coyne had not come here just to lie in his room and eat room service and drink in the bar in the evening. Gant, who'd never read Conan Doyle, had a rule that Sherlock Holmes's inventor would have loved: The obvious answer is usually the answer.

Gant had had a lot of rules. They'd kept him alive for a long time until the cancer took him. Neeley had appropriated his rules as her inheritance and she was still alive, thanks in large part to them and the training he'd imposed on her.

She felt a trickle of sweat slide down her back and get absorbed into her shirt. A long way from the rain and deep forest of Whidbey Island, but the target was the same. What had Coyne been here for?

Neeley felt it, a sensation that had occurred several times in her life. She'd first felt it on that plane in Berlin with a gift-wrapped bomb in her lap. She'd honored the feeling, getting off the plane, and that was when she first met Gant. He'd told her to always trust the instinct.

"Get out of the car," Neeley said. "Leave the keys in the ignition. Walk away and don't look back."

The Asset's mouth opened to say something, but snapped shut. He might be ROAD, but he'd been places before he'd punched out. He got out of the car and walked away.

Neeley had her finger on the trigger of the pistol, which was hidden underneath the daypack. It had been there ever since she got in the car, which is where a pistol in a car should be: in the hand in the lap, not in a holster or under the seat. If people could hold cell phones in a car, an operative could certainly hold her weapon.

She caressed the tiny sliver of metal, knowing exactly how much pressure she had to exert in order to fire the gun as the driver's door opened and a woman got in. A rather striking woman. Tall, a tad taller than Neeley, with exotic features. The woman started the engine and drove away from the hotel without saying a word.

Neeley also didn't speak.

The drive didn't take long, not that it could on such a small island. They were near the airport when the woman drove them into a warehouse.

"I don't like ambushes," Neeley said, lifting the pack up and showing the muzzle of the pistol.

"Few do," the woman said. "My people are around only for security. One across the alley on the second floor. One behind the warehouse out of sight, pulling rear security and maintaining our emergency exfiltration path. And two in the beams above us," she added as she stopped the car. "They protect you as well as me."

"From?"

"Those you seek."

"I'm tracking Carl Coyne. I need to know who he met with here and why."

"He's not here." The woman turned off the ignition.

"I know. We killed him."

"*We?*" the woman asked, but then answered her own question. "The Cellar. Very good." She looked at her watch. "You made better time than I expected."

"Who else were you expecting?" Neeley asked.

"May I get out?" the woman asked, gesturing toward a desk and a couple of chairs.

"Sure."

Neeley left the pack in the car, carrying the pistol openly, but not pointing it at anyone or anywhere particular.

The woman halted at the desk and turned to face Neeley, extending her hand. "My name is Sin Fen."

"Neeley." They shook, and Neeley spoke again as Sin Fen went around the desk and sat down. "I've heard your name. Second-hand. Coyne mentioned it just before he departed this mortal coil."

"I assume he was desperate," Sin Fen said, "facing a Cellar operative."

"He was."

Sin Fen smiled. "Did he speak well of me?"

"He just mentioned you."

"What else?"

Neeley countered. "Who exactly are you?"

"The person you seek. What else did Coyne say before he departed from this world?"

"He said he had powerful friends. He mentioned your name. Ratnik. The Patrol. Red Wings."

"You killed him," Sin Fen said. "And what did you do with the body?"

"That's part of why I'm here," Neeley said. "His body simply disappeared."

"Really?" Sin Fen considered that. "Most interesting. An aberration of the timeline. That could be good if it's a reboot."

"Right," Neeley said, for lack of anything else.

Sin Fen gestured for Neeley to sit. Sin Fen settled down behind the battered, old desk. Neeley sat down, resting the pistol in her lap.

"What is going on?" Neeley asked.

"One thing at a time," Sin Fen said. "Have the Nightstalkers been alerted?"

"Yes," Neeley said. "They're in New York City at a top secret facility that Coyne once guarded. We're assuming he gave up the location of the facility because it was compromised."

"The Time Patrol," Sin Fen said.

"Yes. Who did he give up the location to?"

"The Ratnik," Sin Fen said. "That's why he came here."

"And who or what is the Ratnik?"

"Former Russian Spetsnaz," Sin Fen said. "They call themselves that, which is ironic because you might actually consider them rats in the walls of time."

"Did they compromise the Time Patrol?" Neeley asked.

Sin Fen hesitated answering for the first time. "It's complicated."

"Uncomplicate it for me," Neeley said. "The Nightstalkers are on a clock. They've got just over six hours."

"To do what exactly?" Sin Fen asked.

"That's a good question," Neeley said. "They're working on answering it right now. My job is to learn what Coyne did. So where are these Ratnik?"

"Not here," Sin Fen said. "It's not easy to get to them, and it is very dangerous." She closed her eyes for a moment, and then opened them. "The gate to them is still open, but not for much longer."

"Can you lead me to them?" Neeley asked.

Sin Fen considered her for a long second. "I'm not sure you understand what you are asking or what is happening."

"No, I don't," Neeley agreed. "But I know I have to do my job."

"Everything from here on out," Sin Fen said, "is about choice. You do not *have* to do your job as you say. You have a choice."

"Do I?" Neeley asked. "Do any of us?"

"Let's not get philosophical," Sin Fen said. "You have a practical choice now, whether to go into danger or not."

"Then I choose to do it," Neeley said.

"Even having little idea what you're getting into except that it's dangerous and beyond your conception?"

"Yes."

Sin Fen abruptly stood. "Then let us go."

CHAPTER 10

Six Hours

The team, with additions, followed Edith out of the Met. They went along the path that wrapped around the back of the museum, through the tunnel under Central Park's East Drive, and then north to Cleopatra's Needle.

It was still there.

And so was Foreman, waiting for them. He was leaning on his cane, looking up at the towering monument. "I believe there is something up there for you, Ms. Frobish."

They gathered round the monument and peered up.

"A message!" Edith Frobish was up on her toes, peering at the west side of the obelisk.

"How do you know?" Scout asked.

"Different markings," Edith said. "About twenty feet up. Trust me, I know what this is supposed to look like."

"Wait a second," Nada said. "I don't understand this. We were just talking about how only those who have been near Rifts are being affected first. How can *you* see a change?"

"Because," Edith said, "there *is* an actual change on the Needle. An agent in the past actually changed it. This isn't a timeline distortion but a real change. We use this needle, the one in Rome and the one in Paris, as markers. And there are others. Always stone, that an agent can send a message through. It's in hieroglyphics and then in code."

"Have messages been sent on it before?" Moms asked.

"Yes," Edith replied.

"Then it must be covered with them," Moms said.

Edith shook her head. "No. We get the message, we go back and fix the problem. Then there's no need for the message to be written and it's reset."

"I'm with Roland," Nada said. "I've got a headache."

"Hieroglyphics?" Moms asked. "You can read them?"

"Oh, yes," Edith said. "I had to study the writing after joining the Patrol. There are many variations and our messaging system mixes several in a way that anyone not understanding the code can't break it."

"Right," Scout muttered.

"How are you—" Moms began, but fell silent as a truck with a cherry picker rolled up to the obelisk.

"I took the initiative," Foreman said, indicating the truck.

"How did you know to take the initiative?" Moms asked.

"I've been here before," Foreman said. "Apparently, Ms. Frobish just remembered, but the obelisk is an excellent field-expedient way for agents to communicate, and it's been used before under unusual circumstances when an agent can't travel back via the HUB. The Administrator took me here once to show me."

That bothered Nada. "You know a lot more about the Patrol than you've told us."

"I know a lot less than Ms. Frobish," Foreman said.

"I don't think she remembers everything," Moms noted.

"I don't either," Nada said.

Edith wasn't paying attention. She clambered into the bucket and was signaling to the driver to be raised up so she could examine the mark.

Below her, Foreman, Moms, Nada, Scout, and Frasier waited.

"Oh dear!" Edith cried out.

"What is it?" Moms yelled up.

Edith was signaling to be let down. The hydraulic arms on the bucket loader brought her back to the ground.

Words bubbled forth from Edith. "This totally applies to the Needle. According to the message from one of our agents, Caesarion was not executed by Octavian, but lives!"

"Who is Caesarion?" Nada asked.

"The son of Julius Caesar and Cleopatra," Edith answered. "At least that was Cleopatra's claim. And Caesar did acknowledge him as son but not heir."

"And this is bad why?" Moms asked.

Edith explained. "The agent reported from 26 BC, but that's four years *after* Caesarion was supposed to have died. He's alive and Pharaoh in Egypt, having struck a deal with Octavian. Octavian, who by 26 BC was now Augustus, Emperor of Rome."

"Okay," Nada said. "Lead with the headline. And?"

Edith stared at him in shock. "History is very different and going to get more so accordingly. Four years different when the agent etched this message. The fact there is no update to the message means that in that agent's time, things had gone off course enough that he could not access the Needle. Or perhaps he no longer lived." She barely paused to take a breath. "It could explain why, in your man Eagle's history, the Lateran Obelisk was still in Egypt, never having been brought to Rome.

"The implications are staggering if this is left unchecked." She looked at her watch. "We only have six hours to fix this. It's just the beginning. It's likely, if left unchecked, the obelisk will disappear and then . . ."

Moms held up a hand as Nada began to say something. "Six hours to fix something that's already gone wrong for four years in the past?"

"Yes, yes," Edith said. "That's the way the Patrol works. Go back to the day Caesarion was supposed to have been killed, although I believe the exact date isn't recorded. I'll have to do research." She closed her eyes in thought. "After the naval battle at Actium, when Antony was defeated by Octavian, he fled back to Egypt. Cleopatra was there with Caesarion, who she had claimed from birth was the son of Caesar and heir."

"Was he?" Moms asked.

Edith waved off the question. "When Cleopatra received word of Actium, it is said she was preparing Caesarion to rule without her. Perhaps hoping she could go into exile with Antony, much like Lepidus did, and that Octavian would acknowledge both Caesarion's legitimate claim to rule Egypt, which he indeed was as the son of Cleopatra, *and* his legitimacy as Caesar's heir. Of course, it was the latter that caused Octavian to have him killed. That was very personal to Octavian because he had been tapped by Caesar as the true heir and that had allowed him to rise up to power in the wake of Caesar's death. There's a famous line that Octavian heeded—the words of one of his advisors—who said, 'Too many Caesars is not good!' A takeoff of a line from Homer."

Edith shook her head. "But according to this report, Octavian *did not* take this advice. Caesarion rules in Egypt while Augustus, the name Octavian took as emperor, rules in Rome. Oh!" she exclaimed as something else occurred to her. "The way it was supposed to go was that when Octavian invaded Egypt in 30 BC, intent on finishing off Antony and Cleopatra, Caesarion, who was seventeen at the time, was sent by his mother to a Red Sea port, perhaps with the intention of sending him further away, maybe as far as India.

"Octavian captured Alexandria on the first of August, 30 BC, which history, our history, records as the official beginning of Egypt being part of the Roman Empire. Antony was already dead, having fallen on his sword. Cleopatra followed suit, via the asp, several days later. What followed isn't exactly known. Some say Caesarion's tutors betrayed him to Octavian. Plutarch wrote that Caesarion had made it to India but was lured back by false promises of the throne in Egypt. Some say he made it to Ethiopia and was tricked into coming back."

"So he's back and ruling," Moms summed up. "And that's bad?"

"Very bad," Edith said. "Think of what might happen. Egypt, while a vassal of Rome, is being led by a true Pharaoh, who also has claims to the throne in Rome by the direct blood of Caesar, which some might think is a greater claim than that of Augustus. At the very least, Augustus's enemies, and every Emperor has enemies, would use it as leverage. If it doesn't explode into war between Augustus and Caesarion, their own heirs, Tiberius and whoever is the progeny of Caesarion, will undoubtedly cross swords, perhaps completely changing the course of the Roman Empire.

"And think of what else is going on in the world within one generation; perhaps the most pivotal moment in our history. The birth of Jesus in Israel, which is a Roman province, but with Egypt even closer. The ramifications could be staggering. Not just a ripple, but multiple shifts leading to a tsunami that will wipe our timeline out if left unchecked!"

"I flunked history in high school," Scout lied, "and this is nice, but we have no way of going back to 30 BC and doing squat without the Patrol and the HUB."

"Scout's right," Moms said. "We have to find out what happened to the Patrol. Let's focus on the immediate problem and solve it. If we can find the Patrol, then they can do their job and fix this ripple."

"I think," Nada said, "we're going to have to go through that gate in order to do that."

"I agree," Moms said.

"I need that bigger gun," Scout said.

The helicopter was flying over southern New Jersey as Golden connected her phone to Hannah's laptop and began to bring up the images she'd taken in Foreman's office.

"The map," Golden said. "I'd say that's the key to everything. What concerns me is this." She tapped the screen. "Foreman labeled this, which is anything but a triangle, the Bermuda Triangle. And it touches near Grand Cayman, where Neeley is."

"A legend," Hannah said.

Golden pointed. "Another legend. The Devil's Sea. An area off the coast of Japan, south of Tokyo. It's reputed to be like the Bermuda Triangle: a place where ships and planes mysteriously disappear with no trace. And here, Angkor Kol Ker. An ancient Cambodian city that was completely abandoned for no apparent reason a long time ago."

"What's the connection to the Patrol?" Hannah asked.

"I don't know," Golden replied. "Not yet."

"Areas with unusual histories," Hannah said.

Golden changed the picture. "I found three files of interest in his desk. There was a lot more there, but I didn't have the chance to go through it all. The three were labeled: Sin Fen, Coyne, Ratnik."

"Coyne first," Hannah said. "That's what Neeley went to the Caymans for. And now we see a connection with something else Foreman was interested in: the Bermuda Triangle."

Golden scrolled through the photos. "Not much. Pretty much what we had, including our own surveillance reports after he was brought to our attention and the government's surveillance before that. But this is interesting. Foreman indicates he began his interest in Coyne much earlier. Back in 2005. Right after Operation Red Wings."

"That's the mission Coyne mentioned to Roland," Hannah said.

"Correct. Coyne was in Afghanistan at the time. In fact, he was at the airfield from which the recon team launched. And the ill-fated rescue mission."

Hannah considered. "But he didn't go on the rescue mission."

"He didn't. And," Golden continued, "Foreman back-channeled and got Coyne posted to the security detail for the Patrol. Via a double cut out. Of course, everyone getting posted to that highly classified assignment went through at least one cut out, because no one was supposed to know what those men were being assigned to guard."

"But Foreman knew," Hannah said.

"He did. And he made it happen."

"So he wanted him there," Hannah said. "He knew Coyne was unstable coming out of Afghanistan and because of his subsequent actions in his marriage. What else does Foreman have on Coyne?"

"The Request for Sanction originated with him."

"Before or after Coyne went to Grand Cayman?"

"Right after."

"But there was surveillance on Coyne by the government before."

"Yes," Golden said. "Requested by Foreman."

"But no RFI until after he went to the Caymans and did whatever it is Foreman wanted him to do."

"Exactly."

Hannah sat back and considered that for a moment. "All right. Ratnik?"

"One page," Golden said. "An elite, classified Spetsnaz unit of the Army of the Soviet Union. They were Spetsnaz, but detached for special duty."

"Which could mean anything."

"They were headquartered at Duga-3, also known as the Russian Woodpecker because of the intermittent signal it broadcast. Supposedly an over-the-horizon radar system developed during the Cold War to track missile launches at long distances. It had a very large metal array receiver, code-named by NATO as *Steel Yard*, located very near the Chernobyl nuclear reactor."

That got Hannah's attention. "Chernobyl? Ms. Jones came from there."

"She did," Golden said. "During her debriefs she never mentioned the Duga-3 array or a unit named Ratnik. Perhaps she knew nothing of them."

"Perhaps," Hannah agreed doubtfully. "So what was this Ratnik unit?"

Golden pointed at the screen. "Foreman knew very little. Formed in 1976. The unit disappeared around the time of the Chernobyl disaster in 1986. Which is to be expected. The array of Duga-3 is still there."

"But the Ratnik aren't," Hannah said. "Where did they go? Why would Coyne mention them three decades later? Why would there be a body in the Met of a man with a Spetsnaz tattoo?" She didn't wait for an answer as she supplied it. "The Ratnik were a Soviet Time Patrol or whatever they called it. Close by Chernobyl for the power."

"Likely," Golden agreed.

"The question is, what have the Ratnik been up to since 1986, and how did Coyne meet them?"

Golden had no answer to that.

"Sin Fen?" Hannah prompted as the chopper cleared the Jersey coast and headed for New York City over the Atlantic.

"Again," Golden said, "one page." She scrolled. "A page with just her name written on the top in what I assume is Foreman's handwriting. And just two words: *The Sight*."

"Curious," Hannah said. "A puzzle, even for Foreman."

"There's one other thing of interest," Golden said. She scrolled and brought up the image of the framed photo on Foreman's desk.

Hannah stared at it, and then sighed, as if punched in the chest. The picture was black and white, grainy. There were three men standing in the back row, then at least a dozen seated in chairs in the middle row, and another dozen kneeling on the ground in the front row. The men were in front of a Quonset-type building in what appeared to be a desert environment.

Hannah leaned forward and tapped the screen as she identified the two men she recognized. "Foreman. And my predecessor, Nero. My secretary confirmed that Nero had met with Foreman several times. But I didn't know he traveled to wherever this is."

"It's Area 51," Golden said.

"Who are the others?"

"The man with them in the back row is Colonel Thorn. First commander of what we now know as the Nightstalkers."

Hannah leaned closer to the screen. "And the ones in the chairs and kneeling? Some are Japanese."

"Yes. And the rest are German. That's the Odessa. The Nazi and Japanese physicists brought to Area 51 after the Second World War."

Hannah looked at Golden. "The men who opened the first Rift."

Doc didn't look up from his laptop as Moms led the others in. "This cavern is shielded for muonic transmissions. That's why the Can didn't go off, has never gone off, when a gate opens in here."

"Figured as much," Nada said.

"How can you shield muons?" Eagle asked. "I thought they passed through everything?"

"I'm working on figuring out how they do that," Doc said.

"Not a priority right now," Moms said.

Roland and Mac were dispersed to either side of Doc. Roland had an M60 machine gun slung over his shoulder, opting for its heavier rounds (and weight) over his favored M249 Squad Automatic Weapon. In his hands he held an MK14 Special Operations Multiple Grenade Launcher. With a stubby barrel for 40 mm, it held six grenades in a spring-loaded revolver-type magazine. Mac had an M203. Both weapons were loaded with thermobaric rounds, and both men were focused on the door. Eagle was with Doc, providing close-in security with an M203. Each man also had an AT4 rocket launcher slung over his shoulder.

A ramp had been constructed leading up to the gate, and Doc was kneeling at the top, just a few feet away. Roland had been busy also, requisitioning weapons and gear from the Rangers. He had a four-wheel ATV with an MK19 grenade launcher mounted on a center pylon ready nearby, the rear loaded with ammunition. The MK19 was a 40 mm grenade launcher that fired on automatic like a machine gun.

"What's on the other side?" Moms asked, Nada and Scout at her side.

"It ate my probe," Doc said, reaching down and holding up a severed cord. "It's eating every signal I send into it." He finally looked up. "No clue."

"Did the suit the Valkyrie was wearing have any sort of oxygen or filtration system for air?" Nada asked.

"It had a rebreather, but it was turned off," Doc said. He knew what Nada was getting at. "We can't assume the air on the other side is breathable, but it probably is."

As Moms and Nada discussed the situation with Doc, Scout tugged on Roland's sleeve.

"Yo?" Roland said, his eyes still on the door.

"Can I borrow you for a moment?" Scout asked.

Roland looked about, noted the other Nightstalkers in the cavern, all armed, and nodded. "What's up?"

"I want to ask Frasier something," Scout said, indicating the shrink who was part of and not part of the group, standing about thirty feet back from the door, by himself.

"Uh. Okay," Roland said.

"I don't think he's going to want to answer," Scout said. "I might need some help."

Roland grinned at the thought of potential violence. "Sure."

Scout walked over to Frasier.

"Hey, M.I.B.," Scout said.

Frasier turned his sunglasses toward her. "Excuse me?"

"Nada's my friend," Scout said.

"Mine too," Roland said, an imposing figure behind her right shoulder.

"And?" Frasier shook his head. "The block wasn't my decision. I'm just the tool that—"

"You're a tool all right," Scout said. "Why can't he remember it all?"

"I don't know why he remembers any of it," Frasier said.

"Who designed this block?" Scout asked.

"The scientists at Area 51," Frasier said. "If they designed it at all. There's always the possibility they reverse engineered it from something."

"What do you mean?" Scout said.

"Duh," Frasier mimicked with a pointed glance at Scout. He pointed at the door hovering over the floor of the cavern. "What do you think is going to happen to that suit that fellow wore? Where do you think it will end up? I imagine the Nightstalkers will be wearing something like it in a couple of years."

"What happened to Nada's wife and daughter?" Scout asked.

"They died," Frasier said, and despite the sunglasses and the cold demeanor, Scout could sense he was bothered by something.

"How?" Scout asked.

"Listen, kid. I know you think you're doing your friend a favor. Trust me on this. You're not. On several fronts."

"Let me be the judge of that," Scout said.

Frasier removed his sunglasses, revealing his black eyeball. "I'm a psychiatrist. I know a bit more about how the mind works than you do, with your wonderful eighteen years of knowledge. And you too, Roland," he added, shifting his off-putting gaze past Scout. "Nada doesn't want to know how they died. And he doesn't want to know his real history before the Nightstalkers. We did him a favor wiping parts of both of those."

"He needs to know," Scout said with a determination she didn't quite feel any longer.

"Pretty much everyone," Frasier said, "has some memory or memories they would like to erase. Forget about." He shifted his gaze down to Scout. "If you don't yet, you will. It's part of getting older."

"But aren't those memories often tied to good memories also?" Scout asked. "The two entwined?"

"You can't change—" Frasier began, but then he paused and looked past them at the gate. "Well, maybe the past can be changed. But not for personal reasons. It's never that simple. Not like making sure Caesarion is dead when he's supposed to be dead. That's putting history back the way it's supposed to be. Unchanging it."

Scout didn't move. Roland was at a bit of a loss, which wasn't unusual for Roland when it didn't involve shooting.

"Tell her," Roland finally said.

"I'll tell you this," Frasier finally said. "Your buddy, Nada? He was a drunk and a sonofabitch to his wife and kid. He was about to be cashiered out of the service. When they died, something broke in him. And even though we wiped the memory, he became a different man. Memories aren't emotions. Nada became a better man at a very high price. He was always a good soldier. Now he's a good man. We just removed the memory of the cost. Isn't that enough?"

Scout bit her lower lip as she considered this twist. Before she could reply, Moms called out, her voice echoing in the cavern. "Scout. Roland. Let's gear up. We're going in."

THE SPACE
BETWEEN

Ivar had told Amelia Earhart as much as he could about his timeline. He knew there was a lot he'd left out, but her questions had been pointed and targeted. Which had left no time for Ivar's questions about her, this place, or what the frak was going on. Though loaded with quite a bit of new knowledge, he still felt almost about as clueless as he'd been when he'd first arrived in the Space Between.

After describing the events of 9/11 and the aftermath, Earhart gave him a pause as she processed those strange twists of events.

"Are you certain it was terrorists from your own time?" Earhart finally asked.

"Yes."

Earhart leaned back in the airline seat and shook her head. "Sometimes I wonder if all of this is just a test by some higher power out there. When will we ever learn?"

Ivar assumed that was what Eagle would call a rhetorical question, so he didn't say anything.

Earhart leaned forward. "When—I" but she paused and canted her head to the side. "There's a disturbance."

Ivar couldn't stop himself. "In the Force?"

That one flew by Earhart by about a forty-year gap. "In the Space Between," she said. "It's a way station between many worlds. Few tarry here. Some, like us, make our homes here. But there are times when there's a disturbance . . ."

"How big is this place?" Ivar asked.

"That's the strange thing," Earhart said, head cocked as if listening, even as she spoke. "We've tried to circumnavigate the inner sea, but have never made a complete circuit. We always have to turn back, either because of lack of food or encountering forces, other Outcast groups who aren't as friendly as we are and others whom we choose not to engage in battle. But it's very large." She stood, almost sniffing as she turned about slowly. "After so much time here, I can feel the way it is and I can feel when it becomes disturbed. Something is disturbing it."

One of the Japanese samurai came over to Earhart, and she spoke to him quickly in his language.

"This is Taki," Earhart said, by way of brief introduction.

Ivar nodded and Taki nodded back, but he was focused on something else. Earhart said something more in Japanese, and he bowed ever so slightly. Taki ran back to his comrades and they took off at a trot, away from the wall, which was the only way Ivar could determine a sense of direction here.

"Come," Earhart said.

She led him to a makeshift rack on which several dozen silver spears were arrayed. Earhart grabbed one and tossed it to him. Ivar managed to avoid splitting himself on it by batting the haft away and it fell to the ground. He bent over and picked it up. It was surprisingly light.

"Take a second," Earhart said.

"I doubt I'll be much good with one," Ivar said.

"Think beyond yourself," Earhart said, so Ivar secured a second spear, having no clue what she meant by that other than to take a second spear.

"What are we doing?" Ivar asked as others came over and grabbed multiple spears.

"We're going hunting," Earhart said.

"Hunting what?"

"Monsters."

CHAPTER 11

Five Hours

"What's out here?" Neeley asked, one hand on the rail around the flying bridge of the catamaran. She was on one side of the boat's captain, Sin Fen on the other. The crew consisted of a half-dozen men. A mixture of ethnicity and age, they all had one thing in common: lots of tattoos, scars, and weapons, the predominant one being the M203, a combination of the venerable M16 with a 40 mm grenade launcher under the barrel. Near the bow, one man was standing behind a pylon on which an M2 .50 caliber machine gun was mounted. The men also sported a variety of axes, machetes, and knives.

The surface of the water was strangely calm, not a wave in sight. Neeley could feel a slight swell as the boat cut through the water, but the water seemed thick. The air was thick, almost humid, but different, with the heavy stillness that comes just before a terrible storm.

"Your answers," Sin Fen said. She was peering straight ahead as if she could actually see over the horizon.

Neeley looked in that direction and noted a whitish gray smudge far in the distance. A smudge they were heading directly toward.

"What is that?"

"A gate," Sin Fen said.

"Is this where Coyne went?"

"Yes."

"How did he know to get here?" Neeley asked.

Sin Fen nodded as if Neeley had finally asked the right question. "Foreman gave him directions."

"Foreman is playing both sides," Neeley said. "Why?"

"He has goals," Sin Fen said vaguely.

"What?" Neeley said. "Personal enlightenment? Self-actualization?"

Sin Fen didn't descend to the sarcasm. "His motives are good, although one might judge his methods differently. He trusts no one, so he often uses deception in his methods."

"So he lies," Neeley said. "Does he trust you?"

"No. He doesn't trust anyone."

"This gate." Neeley pointed ahead. "How come we've never heard of it? Satellite imagery? Remote sensing?"

Sin Fen gave a slight smile. "You have heard of it. The Bermuda Triangle. The reason it hasn't been studied is because it is rarely open."

"How did you know it's open now?"

Sin Fen glanced at Neeley. "I know. It's my gift, or perhaps a curse; a part of what I am." She reached down and picked up an M203. She extended it to Neeley. "You need something more than your pistol. There are rounds in both chambers."

Neeley accepted the weapon. Sin Fen also passed over a bandolier of grenades and 5.56 magazines. The strange patch of mist was now about two kilometers away, and they were closing on it quickly.

Neeley took a moment to check her cell phone.

"It won't work," Sin Fen said. "Gates interfere with electronics."

"Contact two o'clock right," one of the crew yelled, his forehead pressed into a sonar display. "Sixteen hundred meters."

"Just one?" Sin Fen asked.

"Multiple," the man replied.

"I don't see anything out there," Neeley said, looking off the starboard front.

"They're underwater," Sin Fen said. She put her firearm into a rack and secured it, and then picked up a long axe. "Blade weapons are best for what's coming."

Neeley put the M203 into the rack on the console and grabbed a long-handled axe. "What's coming?"

"Kraken," Sin Fen said. "They live near gates, usually staying deep, only rising when a gate opens. Which is why they've so rarely been recorded in history. Ships that encounter them either are destroyed by the kraken or sucked through the gate."

"Kraken," Neeley said. "All right."

"You wanted to do this," Sin Fen reminded her.

"I'm always open to a new adventure," Neeley said.

Sin Fen gave her a hard stare. "There is darkness in you. A certain fatalism."

"Perhaps," Neeley acknowledged.

"Eight hundred meters," the man on the scope announced.

"Quarter us to port," Sin Fen ordered.

The boat canted, angling away from the contact, but still toward the mist, although at an angle.

Neeley could feel the tension and fear coming off the crew. She'd gone into combat numerous times, but she'd never felt a fear quite like the one the crew was emanating. It was primal.

Sin Fen startled her. "You have some of the sense."

"What sense?" Neeley asked.

"Six hundred meters."

"Of knowing things beyond the five senses," Sin Fen said. "It is an ancient thing. From the first days."

"Five hundred meters to contacts. Nine hundred meters to objective."

"Back to this kraken thing. What exactly is a kraken?"

"Unfortunately," Sin Fen said, "you might shortly see. Aim for the eyes if you can. Beware the end of their tentacles. They have mouths there. Sharp teeth."

"Great," Neeley muttered as she hefted the axe to get its balance.

"Three hundred meters to contacts. Four hundred to objective."

"Although," Sin Fen said, looking ahead to the mist, "we might make it."

The scope man put an end to that optimism by suddenly shouting: "Deep rising! Directly below. Contact!"

A long red tentacle lashed out of the sea and grabbed him. He slashed away with a machete as Sin Fen and Neeley leapt to his defense. Five more tentacles appeared around the edge of the catamaran, waving about wildly. A six-inch-wide mouth on the tip of the tentacle that was wrapped around the scope man displayed razor-sharp teeth as it opened wide, and then it snapped shut on the man's shoulder.

He screamed in agony.

Neeley and Sin Fen swung in concert, severing the tentacle. The man, the piece still wrapped around him snapping, fell to the deck.

The .50 caliber machine gun was pounding away, bullets tearing through the tentacles as the gunner did a sweep. Sin Fen grabbed a grenade, pulled the pin, and then tossed it overboard.

Neeley went to her knees, grabbing the severed tentacle, keeping the still snapping teeth from taking a second bite out of the man. Prying it loose, she tossed it overboard, just as the grenade went off.

Water and pieces of kraken showered the deck.

Through all this, the helmsman was holding them steady on course, full speed for the mist, which was now taking on a darker hue.

"Protect the con!" Sin Fen yelled as a new set of tentacles reared up into the air on the starboard rear. "We have to make it through the gate!"

Swinging around, the .50 gunner let loose a long burst, keeping the muzzle suppressed so far that some of the rounds tore pieces from the edge of the deck as they churned into the dark water from which the tentacles came. Neeley could see that kraken now, the body thirty feet long, seven wide, two large saucer eyes, larger than full-sized pizzas staring up.

That is until the half-inch-diameter slugs from the .50 hit them.

The creature, and its tentacles, abruptly sank down into the depths.

"We've got five more coming!" Sin Fen yelled in a calm voice.

And then the bow of the catamaran touched the mist. It slid in, enveloped, as if going into something more tangible than just air and mist. Neeley shivered, not from cold, as the boat was completely engulfed.

"Follow me," Moms said, her voice transmitted via a microphone in her mask, and the Nightstalkers did just that. Nada was half a step behind her, on her right shoulder. Each was armed with M203s.

Behind the team leader and team sergeant came the rest: Eagle driving the ATV, Mac standing behind him, manning the MK19 grenade launcher, Roland on the flank with his MK14 in hand and M60 slung over his shoulder.

And in the rear was Scout, holding Nada's venerable MP5 submachine gun and a pistol holstered in the oversized ballistic vest Nada had insisted she wear. After seeing what had happened to Kirk, she wasn't sure of its practicality, but Nada had made the point that they weren't sure what they would encounter on the other side of the door.

If they survived going to the other side of the door was the unsaid issue no one voiced.

Every member of the team had a mask on and was breathing via a rebreather slung on top of all the other gear they wore. They looked anything but human, they were so encumbered with gear.

Scout glanced over her shoulder at Foreman, the Keep, Edith, and Frasier, all gathered in a little clump at the base of the ramp.

"Don't want to join in the fun?" Scout pulled aside her mask and asked, looking at Foreman, then Frasier.

In front of her, Moms and Nada snapped out of existence into the door.

"Not my job," Frasier said. "I spent my time in the trenches."

"I'll come," Edith said, taking a step forward, but Foreman put a hand on her forearm, just as the ATV was gone.

"Not today, dear. Let the experts handle this."

"Experts," Scout muttered, thinking about her limited training. "Right." She put the mask back in place. She took a deep breath, knowing it was stupid as she did have the rebreather, just before she hit the utter black of the gate.

Not so stupid as she fell fifteen feet and hit water, going under, the weight of her body armor, weapons, and assorted other gear incumbent upon a Nightstalker taking her down, the mask ripping off.

Scout fought to jettison the gear, fingers fumbling in the pitch black to unbuckle, unsnap, discard. The water was pressing in on her and she was disoriented, uncertain which way was up even if she got the gear off. As she shed the combat vest of the body armor, she couldn't keep her breath anymore. She had to breathe.

She opened her mouth.

Darkness fell.

CHAPTER 12

Four Hours

"They're gone," Foreman said. He looked at his watch. "Missed them by about ten minutes."

Hannah stared at the old man. "What are you doing?" She was with Golden, standing on the rock floor of the cavern, facing Foreman. Edith and Frasier were flanking the old man, but not with him. The Keep had disappeared back to the elevator the second the team went through.

"Please be more specific," Foreman said. "At the moment, I'm standing here, awaiting the return of the Nightstalkers."

"The Bermuda Triangle, Devil's Sea, Angkor Kol Ker, and the other locations outlined on the map in your office," Hannah said. "What's special about them?"

"You went into my office?" Foreman asked.

"I did," Doctor Golden said.

"And you're here," Foreman said. "Very good to have survived that."

"Is everything a game to you?" Hannah demanded.

"Wasn't everything a game to your predecessor, Nero?"

Foreman challenged. "Didn't he put you and Neeley through the ringer, so to speak, in order to determine what you're made of? He taught me well." He jerked a thumb at the door hovering at the top of the ramp. "I can assure you, this is no game, Ms. Hannah. The fate of our planet rests on understanding these gates and what lies beyond. We are under assault, both in time and space. It's only been by the effort of the agents of the Patrol and the members of the Nightstalkers and other organizations that we have survived. I assure you, other timelines have not fared as well."

Hannah wasn't distracted. "Why are you focused on those locations?"

"Because they're vulnerable spots in the space-time continuum on our planet," Foreman answered. "There is a reason locations become the center of myths and legends. Area 51 is a modern myth, is it not?" He didn't wait for an answer. "But it *is* real as we all know, and hides things most people couldn't imagine. Why should we not think the same of the Bermuda Triangle? Or the Devil's Sea?"

"Is my agent Neeley in danger being near the Bermuda Triangle?" Hannah asked. "Tracking Carl Coyne's movements?"

Foreman smiled. "Neeley is in excellent hands. And she most likely is not in the Bermuda Triangle anymore."

"Sin Fen," Hannah said, finally starting to sort out the moves on this chessboard.

"Yes."

"Where *is* Neeley?"

Foreman nodded toward the gate. "Most likely heading to the same place the Nightstalkers just went."

"You set Coyne into play," Hannah said. "Why?"

"Coyne was racked by guilt for not getting on that rescue helicopter in 2005," Foreman said. "Survivor's guilt plays out in different ways. He came back, was abusive to his wife, and became a dangerous man. Such men are also useful men because their guilt can be leveraged. As you know," he added pointedly to Hannah.

"You got him assigned here as security," Hannah said. "Were you planning on having him give up the location? Why would you do that? You're threatening the very thing you say you're protecting."

Foreman hesitated. "It's not that simple."

"It never is," Hannah replied. "The Ratnik. Spetsnaz stationed near Chernobyl. Were they Russian time travelers? Their Patrol? Just as they have their own version of the Nightstalkers?"

Foreman didn't hesitate on this question. "Yes."

"What happened to them?"

"They got stupid and careless," Foreman said.

Frasier took a step forward, turning toward Foreman. "Ms. Jones. Did she know about the Ratnik?"

"Not exactly," Foreman said. "She knew what happened at Chernobyl wasn't the result of mistakes by the engineers as history has recorded it. The Ratnik were the Soviet Patrol and they, like our Patrol, were battling incursions into our timeline. They experienced, shall we say, a particularly aggressive incursion. In the course of stopping that incursion, Chernobyl went critical."

"And the Ratnik?" Hannah pressed.

Foreman shrugged. "They were lost."

"Apparently not," Hannah said.

"Apparently not," Foreman agreed. "But we assumed so at the time."

"Where have they been?" Hannah asked.

"Traveling in time, one assumes," Foreman said.

"To what end?" Hannah asked.

A new voice spoke up. "To heal themselves," Frasier said. "All the surgeries. The transplants the coroner talked about. It makes sense. That body. The Acme said the surgery on it was beyond our capabilities. And that the man should have been long dead. They've been in there"—he pointed at the door—"fighting to stay alive. Traveling to different timelines for help. Different times."

"Most likely," Foreman said. "We know they've been dealing in antiquities, stolen during time travel. To get funding for whatever they need funding for." He turned toward the door. "All we can do now is wait."

They all turned as the Keep came back. And she wasn't alone. Six heavily armed men accompanied her along with two men rolling a trolley. A cylindrical object rested on it.

"What are you doing?" Hannah demanded.

"I have Presidential authority to implement Furtherance in order to keep this place secure," the Keep said.

"What does that mean?" Edith Frobish asked.

The Keep ignored her and turned to the trolley, which they parked at the entrance of the cavern. She checked her watch, and then opened a panel on the object. "I am coordinating execution of Furtherance on my command and on a timer for two hours from now."

"What does execution of Furtherance mean?" Edith asked.

"It means," Hannah said, "that the nuclear weapon, which she is arming right now, will go off when she decides or in two hours. Whichever comes first."

THE SPACE BETWEEN

Scout opened her eyes to the vision of Nada's face barely inches from her own. She coughed, sputtered, and then he rolled her to her side as she vomited. Her head was throbbing, as if a band of pain had wrapped around, squeezing her brain.

"Everyone in scuba school drowns at least once," Nada said. "It's a rite of passage."

Scout finished losing everything that had been in her stomach, and, it felt, part of her stomach. She struggled to a sitting position. "I would never volunteer to go to scuba school," she managed to say. "Especially if it involved drowning."

"It's easier the second time around," Nada assured her.

"Where are we?" She looked around. The other members of the team were scattered about in varying degrees of disarray. Roland was chest deep in black water, disappearing every so often as he dove. He was right next to the base of a six-foot-in-diameter black column that ascended overhead into a misty distance. Scout could spot other black columns of varying diameters in the distance, some quite massive. There were various vessels stranded on the beach, but Scout couldn't focus yet to make them out.

"The other side of the gate," Nada said. He gestured about. "We lost most of our gear. The ATV is down there somewhere."

Moms was issuing orders. Mac and Eagle spread out, their pistols, the only weapons they had left, in their hands. They moved about forty feet along the black beach and took up security. No one had their harnesses or body armor on, ripped off in an effort to get back to the surface and then the shoreline. They were down to their black fatigues and the pistols that had been in their thigh holsters, along with their knives.

"This ain't good," Scout said. The pain in her head had receded slightly, but was still a steady throb.

"Yo!" Roland yelled in excitement as he surfaced, holding an MK19 in his hand, a bandolier of ammunition attached to it.

"That's a start," Nada said. He helped Scout to her feet and they went over to Moms. Doc had his handheld out, but his equipment case was somewhere under that slimy-looking black water.

"Well?" Moms asked.

Doc shrugged. "No clue. I'm getting nothing. As if electronics don't work here."

"We might be able to scavenge weapons from the ships and planes," Nada said. He pointed at some military planes, obviously American with white stars on their wings, but old, propeller driven.

"Flight Nineteen," Moms said, recognizing it from the briefing book of strange events she'd reviewed when she'd first been recruited into the Nightstalkers.

"Oh crap," Nada said.

"We've gone down the rabbit hole," Moms said.

"I take it that ain't good?" Scout asked.

"Doc," Moms said, "can you recognize any of these other craft?"

Before Doc could answer, Roland popped up, sputtering. "I

can't find anything else. There's a steep drop-off and I think most of our gear went down deep. I can—"

"Come ashore," Moms ordered. "You did good enough."

Roland, as always, flushed at the praise, and he waded ashore.

"That ship there," Doc was pointing, "is the *Cyclops*."

"Eagle," Moms called out. "That ship is the *Cyclops*. What can you tell us? Weaponry?"

Eagle came over. "A collier, resupply ship in the US Navy. She disappeared in the area known as the Bermuda Triangle in 1918. Probably small arms in a locker on board. I think it had some larger-caliber guns on deck for basic defense."

"Great," Scout muttered.

"Over three hundred crew," Eagle continued, "it's still the largest loss of life for the US Navy that didn't occur in combat. There is speculation she was sunk by a German U-boat—"

"Not," Scout said.

"—or buckled in a storm, as vessels of that class were believed to have issues with I beams running the length—"

"Not," Scout repeated.

"—of the ship not being sufficient to handle stress, especially with a full load. At the time of its disappearance, it was coming from South America with a load of manganese ore and believed to be overloaded, which led to its foundering. The ultimate determination was that she sunk during an unexpected storm."

"Not," Scout said. "It got sucked into the Bermuda Triangle just like those planes and just like us. And the real question," Scout added, "is where did those three hundred–plus sailors go?"

The Nightstalkers looked about, the black landscape and flat water eerily still. And not a good still.

Moms pointed at the black column. "The first question is, can we go back through that? Doc?"

"Uh, well," Doc began, but it was obvious without his gear, his guess was as good as anyone else's. "No idea."

"We need to find these Valkyries," Nada said. "They know something about the Patrol. Heck, maybe the Patrol is in here somewhere."

"But where?" Mac asked.

Nada and Moms exchanged glances. Moms pointed to the left. "I say we do a sweep in that direction for an hour—"

"My watch isn't working," Scout said.

Everyone checked their timepieces. They were all dead.

"We go that way for five kilometers," Moms finally said. "Using pace count," she added quickly as Scout seemed about to say something.

"Roland," Nada said, "you've got the grenade launcher. And point."

That suited the big man just fine. He opened the breach on the launcher, checked the rounds, locked it shut, and began to move.

"Whoa!" Scout called out, pointing toward the water.

A catamaran appeared out of the mist, moving slowly toward them. There was no sound of an engine and the sails hung limp. It seemed to be relying purely on momentum.

"Neeley!" Roland yelled as he spotted the figures on the bridge of the boat.

———

Ivar saw a golden glow ahead, a distinct contrast to the drabness of the Space Between. "What's that?" he asked Earhart.

"Shh," Earhart said. "Keep your voice down. We're in enemy territory."

"What enemy?" Ivar asked in a lower voice.

"Everyone's."

The outer wall came into view and it was clear the glow was coming from the base of it. Earhart signaled and everyone stopped and dropped to their bellies. Gesturing, she indicated for Ivar and Taki to accompany her to the forward edge of the dune right in front of them.

"Geez," Ivar hissed as he took in the tableau before them.

A cavern had been cut into the outer wall, with columns of stone spaced haphazardly about. Several dozen upright metal tables were set in rows. On each of four tables, a person was strapped down.

Ivar's gaze flashed from body to body, but one thing was clear: these people were literally being disassembled while still alive. Limbs had been amputated in some cases; skin peeled off and replaced with a clear wrapping that showed the organs underneath. There were other bodies, obviously dead, slumped down against their restraints, decay setting in.

"It's hell," Ivar whispered.

"A form of hell, yes," Earhart agreed.

Ivar stiffened as a figure in white with flowing red hair and just red bulbs for eyes floated into view, hovering a few inches above the black sand.

"What the frak is that?" Ivar harshly whispered.

Earhart pointed to the right. Two men were standing in front of one of the tables, apparently arguing. They were dressed in camouflage fatigues and their voices were faint in the distance, but Ivar could recognize they were speaking Russian. The body they were standing in front of was missing a leg, most of the skin from the torso, and both eyes, gaping sockets where they had been.

"The Russians are doing this?" Ivar asked.

"That is a Valkyrie," Earhart said, pointing at the white thing, which floated over and joined the two men. One of the men gestured at the chest of the victim. The other man apparently agreed. The Valkyrie raised an arm, claws snapping into place. It cut into the chest with quick, decisive movements. Seconds later, it had a lung cradled in its claw. It turned and disappeared further into the cavern, the two men following.

The victim was bleeding, blood pouring down into the sand. There was a gag in the mouth so that the screams were muted. The body spasmed for several seconds and then went limp.

Earhart rolled on her back and began talking to Taki in Japanese as she wrote a note in a small pad. He nodded in assent, took the note, and slid down the dune. He collected another samurai, and they headed off. The other two samurai came up the dune and settled down into overwatch positions.

Earhart gestured for Ivar to follow, and they both retreated back down the dune to the main party.

"Is this what you sensed?" Ivar asked.

Earhart nodded her head. "This has been going on for a while. We first spotted them a long time ago. Many sleep cycles. Years in your time. But we didn't have the strength to defeat them. Also, there are several groups like that in here. We're not the only Outcasts." She smiled. "And most are not as nice as we are."

"Then what—"

"Others are coming," Earhart said. "I've sent Taki to meet them."

Scout focused on Sin Fen as the catamaran scraped onto the beach, using up the last of its momentum. And Sin Fen was ignoring everyone but Scout. She jumped over the side and splashed through the water until she was in front of the young woman.

"You have the sight," Sin Fen said.

"I can see *you*," Scout replied, taken aback.

Sin Fen smiled. "Good. Very good." She turned to Moms. "You are in command?"

"I am."

Sin Fen looked over the Nightstalkers. Roland had edged close to Neeley, blushing bright red, but saying nothing. If he were a dog, his tail would be wagging.

"Your weapon is useless here," Sin Fen told Roland.

Roland looked at Moms, eyebrows and barbed wire tattoo raised in question.

"Go ahead," Sin Fen said. "Test fire it."

Moms nodded.

Roland aimed the MK14 out toward the water and pulled the trigger. The firing pin struck home with an audible click, but nothing happened. Roland rotated to a new cartridge and tried again. And again. And again. And again. And again.

"What does work?" Moms asked. "We fought one of those Valkyrie things, and it took a lot to kill it."

Sin Fen looked past Moms. "I believe the answer has just arrived."

Everyone turned and stared at the two samurai who had just crested the closest dune.

"Cool," Scout said.

"Awesome," Roland said.

"Ancient," was Eagle's take.

"This is getting weirder by the minute," Nada muttered.

"It will get stranger," Sin Fen said.

One of the samurai jogged down the hill and extended a note to Sin Fen. She indicated it should be given to Moms, as if she already knew the contents.

Moms unfolded the paper:

Please Come With Taki.

Amelia Earhart.

Without comment, Moms passed the note to Nada, who passed it to Scout.

"Double cool!"

CHAPTER 13

Three Hours

"Our people will come back," Hannah said to the Keep. "There's no need for Furtherance."

"The President, and I, think differently," the Keep said, stepping away from the tactical nuclear weapon. The six men flanked her, weapons at the half ready. That they would be vaporized when the weapon detonated didn't seem to bother them in the slightest.

"If you destroy this place," Hannah argued, "there's no way the Patrol can fix our timeline."

"That's a theory," the Keep said. "And I agree, most likely true. But this gate is a reality. We've gotten a glimpse of what can arrive. According to Mister Foreman, worse things can come through, correct? An invasion perhaps? And we also know about Rifts and Fireflies. The President feels we have to terminate this problem as best we can." She gestured at the nuke. "This is the best we can do if your people are not successful. Besides, you have your FPF flying overhead with two live nukes on it. I think this would be a much better solution with an underground detonation, the explosion and fallout contained by six hundred feet of granite above us. The yield is not that large, but more than enough to do the job here. And," she added, "if push comes to shove, we can literally shove this bomb through that gate to whatever is on the other side."

Foreman snorted. "We sent a damn atomic pile through to someone's timeline with the first Rift back in '47. That just irritated them."

"It wasn't a bomb," the Keep said.

"If we'd sent through a bomb," Foreman said, "maybe they'd have sent a few back at us over the years."

"You don't even know who was on the other side of the Rifts," the Keep said. "This is all too dangerous with too little knowledge."

"So just hit with a sledgehammer?" Foreman asked.

The Keep didn't reply.

Hannah shook her head, realizing the implacability of the Keep. She would implement Furtherance because she'd been ordered to. That was that.

Hannah turned to Foreman. "I saw the photo you had on your desk. You were standing with Colonel Thorn and Nero. And the members of Odessa at Area 51. That was 1947, wasn't it?"

"Yes, I was there in 1947."

"Were you there when they opened the first Rift?" Hannah asked.

"If I had been, there's a good chance I'd be dead," Foreman said. "That photo was taken about a month before that event. A lot of people died, and the rest disappeared when Odessa opened that Rift."

"And you were the one behind it," Hannah said.

"In a way," Foreman replied. "But don't give me too much credit."

Between the team being gone and the nuclear weapon counting down, Hannah's frustration was growing. "Stop hedging. What happened back then? How did anyone even know about the possibilities of Rifts?"

"It was 1945," Foreman said. "Trinity. *'As west and east / in all flat maps / and I am one / are one / So death doth touch the Resurrection.'*

"I'm sure Eagle would know what that's all about," Hannah said.

Foreman deciphered it for her. "Oppenheimer was the one who gave the first nuclear test its code name: Trinity. He said it came from a poem by John Donne. Near as I could ever figure out, that was the poem. Oppenheimer was a strange man. He helped invent nuclear weapons, then spent the rest of his life trying to rein in the beast he'd help create. Sort of like giving birth to a wolf, then trying to hold on to its ears as it grew, trying to control it."

"Yes," Frasier said. "Moms loves to quote Oppenheimer, *'the destroyer of worlds.'* She also believes that Trinity was the real moment the Nightstalkers came into being, not 1947."

"She's correct in theory," Foreman said. He glanced over his shoulder at the door, but there was no activity. "All rather ironic, talking about Oppenheimer, considering our present predicament," he added, with a nod toward the Keep and her bomb. "We touched something far beyond our knowledge at Trinity and have been scrambling to catch up for decades and still haven't." He turned toward the Keep. "So yes, we are touching the void, but you must be aware that sooner or later, the void will be reaching for us. It might have already."

"I don't know what you're talking about," the Keep said.

"And that is the problem," Foreman said.

Golden checked her watch. "We're down to under three hours." She was spending half her time checking out the nuke, as if her glances could make it go away.

Foreman shrugged. "We're doing all we can." He smiled grimly. "And the Keep has our fallback position. Perhaps extreme, but sometimes extreme is called for."

Hannah shook her head. "No." She pointed at the gate. "*They're* doing all they can. We're just waiting."

"Be that as it may," Foreman said, "you said you wanted to know, so it's best you know, because from this moment forward, if we survive this, the Cellar and the Nightstalkers will no longer be as they were.

"After the war, and detonating three atomic weapons, Oppenheimer moved east to Princeton. Publicly he was working on a lot of theory. Secretly he was working on applying those theories via Area 51."

"Via Odessa," Hannah said.

"He didn't know who comprised Odessa," Foreman said. "If he had, he surely would have never participated in working with the Nazis. It was one of his great regrets that they didn't finish the bomb soon enough to use on Germany before it surrendered. After the war, Oppenheimer, and others like him, wanted to see beyond what they had done. To understand the elemental forces they had tapped into. They studied quantum physics and focused on elementary particles."

Foreman waved his hands in dismissal. "It's a lot of scientific jargon which Doc, when he makes it back, can take a look at. But they did discover the two types of meson particles: pions and muons."

"We use muons," Frasier said to Hannah, Edith, and Golden, "to alert us when a Rift opens."

"Yes," Foreman said. "And Odessa used the Demon Core to open a Rift at Area 51 in 1947, with disastrous results. In a way, we opened up Pandora's box. While our timeline had been penetrated many times over the course of history, it was always from the outside, never from our world out. It might well be the Sentinel concept, where we'd advanced to the point where our technology was a threat to others, and they finally took notice of us."

"Sentinel?" Golden asked.

"Arthur C. Clarke's story," Foreman said. "On which the movie *2001* was based. There are lines our civilization can cross that indicate we've advanced enough to be a threat."

"It didn't help sending the Nazis on Odessa through along with the Demon Core," Hannah pointed out.

"That wasn't the plan," Foreman said. "I'm not really sure the scientists who did that had a plan. I think they were fumbling around in the dark, experimenting."

"And how were you involved in all this?" Hannah asked.

"I wasn't at first. I was investigating what I thought were natural phenomena: places on the planet where people, ships, and planes disappeared, such as the Bermuda Triangle and the Devil's Sea. I'd lost comrades to those places. When Odessa opened the first Rift, I saw the classified report, because I was on the committee that helped form Majestic-12. We were, still are, like children, trying to understand things far beyond us."

"What do you understand now?" Hannah asked.

"Above all," Foreman said, "we have to protect our timeline. Everything else is secondary to that. You understand that. Bodyguard of lies, etc."

"So you've been lying." Hannah didn't say it as a question.

Foreman turned to Frasier. "Unblock the rest of Ms. Frobish's memory if you will."

Edith's jaw dropped. She stared at Foreman. "You, you—" She couldn't phrase the proper profanities, being a person unused to such.

"Wait." The Keep finally spoke up. "There's more?"

"Are you sure?" Frasier asked.

Foreman held up his hand, indicating his watch. "I think it's time we learn more about the Patrol. Things seem to be reaching a crisis point."

Frasier pulled out the device and handed the earbuds to Edith. "You know the drill."

"The heck with you!" Edith exclaimed, slapping his hands away.

Frasier shrugged. "Just doing as ordered. You want it all back or not?"

Golden put a hand on Edith's shoulder. "Just do it. We'll sort all this out later."

Edith reluctantly put the earbuds in and Frasier activated the device. Edith squinched her eyes shut, grimaced, and it was over just as quickly.

Edith ripped the earbuds out and looked up at the gate. "We need the HUB to align it correctly."

"Yes, we do," Foreman agreed.

THE SPACE
BETWEEN

"Ivar!" Scout said, hugging the short, lost Nightstalker.

"Guess you didn't go AWOL," Nada allowed as their small group linked up with the band led by Amelia Earhart.

Moms approached the legend with more deference than she usually showed. "Ma'am."

"Call me Amelia," the other woman responded. She held up a hand, getting everyone's attention. "Gather in close. There's no time for explanation or discussion," Earhart told the combined groups. She pointed at Sin Fen. "We've met before, and we trust each other. The rest of you are going to have to decide whether to trust or not." She turned to Moms. "You're here for the Ratnik?"

"Yes. But our priority is to locate our Time Patrol."

Earhart frowned. "If you lost contact with this Patrol of yours, it must be because of the Ratnik, since they are from your time-line." Earhart pointed toward the dune, where two samurai lay in watch. "The Ratnik are on the other side of that. There are about twenty of them. We've never been able to get an accurate count. The good news is, they all aren't in the Valkyrie suits all the time.

We've been watching, and we've only seen two suited up. We have to assume there are more, as their camp is beyond the tables past the columns in the cavern."

"What tables?" Nada asked.

"They're reaping," Earhart said.

As the Nightstalkers and Neeley exchanged confused glances, Ivar quickly explained the people secured to the tables.

"Vivisection?" Eagle said when Ivar was done.

"Huh?" Roland said.

"The Ratnik are reaping what they need from their victims," Earhart explained. "They're not the only ones here in the Space Between, and in other timelines, who do it. But they're the ones going into *your* timeline and reaping your people."

"It's how the Ratnik are still alive," Doc realized.

"Yes," Earhart said. "Others die so they may live."

"But we're not here because of this reaping, are we?" Scout said.

Earhart focused on her for a moment, and then looked at Sin Fen. "She has the sight?"

Sin Fen nodded. "A touch of it."

"That's good," Earhart said.

"What sight?" Scout asked. When neither woman answered, she plowed on. "We're here because a unit called the Time Patrol disappeared from our timeline. And we've got problems in our past that need to be fixed or else our timeline changes. Which will be bad."

Nada nodded at Scout's summary. It would have gone over very well in the Ranger Battalion, leading with the headline.

Scout wasn't done. "But Kirk is dead. And these people are people, whether they're *our* people or from some other timeline. We *should* be here to stop the reaping."

Earhart and Sin Fen exchanged glances. Earhart faced Scout and gave a quarter bow at the waist. "I defer to your sense of decency and humanity. Let us destroy these Ratnik together."

"How?" Moms asked. "We lost most of our weapons and the ones we have"—she slapped the pistol in the holster against her thigh—"don't work here. Those Valkyrie suits are hard to take down."

"These work on the suits," Earhart said, holding up her spear. "We have extras."

"What's special about these?" Nada asked.

"They're Atlantean," Earhart said.

"What?" Moms said, surprised.

"I can feel it," Scout said, hands wrapped around the one she'd been handed. "Ancient."

"Yes," Sin Fen said.

"Wait a second," Eagle said. "Atlantean? You mean from Atlantis?"

"Yes," Sin Fen repeated.

Eagle shook his head. "That's just a legend. A minor plotline from Plato in the *Timaeus and Critias* dialogues."

"We can discuss legend and reality later," Sin Fen said. "For now, trust that these spears will cut through Valkyrie armor."

Her people passed out the rest of the spears until everyone in the amalgamated group was armed with one. Roland spent a few moments twirling his, getting the feel. He had a big grin on his face, a warrior going elemental. He had a spear in his hands. He had Neeley nearby. It was a good day to fight.

When Roland stopped playing with his new toy, Nada spoke. "Who's going to be in command?"

Earhart gave a half bow. "I am in charge of our small group, but I defer military decisions to Taki." She indicated one of the samurai. He said something in Japanese and Earhart nodded. "Since he has not quite mastered English, and your group is organized and military, he defers to you."

Everyone turned to Moms. She stepped forward. "We want at least one prisoner to interrogate. For the rest, kill them all." She turned for the dune. "Follow me."

CHAPTER 14

Two-Plus Hours

"What are you talking about?" the Keep demanded.

Edith glared at Frasier for a moment, and then turned to the others. "This chamber held the gate to the Time Patrol headquarters, not the headquarters itself." She shook her head in frustration. "I should have known. I *did* know. It would be foolish to put the Patrol in any time where its sheer presence could affect things."

"What are you talking about?" the Keep asked.

"This chamber held the HUB, which propagates a gate to the Time Patrol headquarters," Edith said.

"Where are the headquarters?"

"Not now," Edith said, which confused everyone for a moment except Foreman.

"The past?" Hannah asked.

"Of course," Edith said.

"When in the past?" Hannah asked.

Foreman spoke up. "That is classified."

"Nobody has a higher classification than I do," the Keep said.

Foreman laughed. "You think a lot of yourself. There's a level of classification you aren't even aware of. Our problem right now is hoping our people find out who changed the alignment of this gate and get back here with the HUB so we can realign it and make contact with the Patrol."

The Keep looked at the countdown on her bomb. "They don't have much time."

"No, *we* don't have much time," Foreman said.

THE SPACE BETWEEN

The group crested the dune and started down toward the Ratnik cavern at a trot, Moms in the lead, Nada at her right shoulder, Amelia Earhart at her left, Sin Fen directly behind them with Neeley. Everyone else fanned out from them.

The opening to the cavern was a hundred yards wide. The ceiling at the front was about twenty feet high, slowly tapering down. Columns of stone stood every few yards, holding up the ceiling. It was impossible to see very far into the cavern as the team descended the dune toward it.

They reached the first table on which a person was strapped. Scout was sickened to see that the woman was alive, her one intact eye tracking them. Her chest cavity had been cut open, encased in some clear material, and one lung was struggling for air. A strip of the clear material was across her mouth.

Carefully, very carefully, Scout used the spear to cut the material away from her mouth.

"Kill me," the woman managed to rasp.

"We'll get you to safety," Scout promised.

The woman shook her head. "Too far gone. Kill me."

"We'll—" Scout began but Taki stepped by her and slid his spear right into the woman's heart.

He looked at Scout. "It is mercy." And then he turned to hurry after the others.

Scout pressed a hand against her own forehead. The pain was growing stronger with every step she took into the cavern. She forced herself to move, to follow the others.

And then contact was made. With a flurry of edged weapons, Moms's Nightstalkers and Earhart's Outcasts attacked the surprised Ratnik.

Three of the Ratnik were geared up in Valkyrie suits. The others ran toward a row of suits that were split open along the sides.

"Stop them!" Moms yelled, pointing with her spear, and then she was engaged with the lead Valkyrie, ducking underneath a swipe of long claws. The thing didn't have a chance for a second swipe as Roland impaled it with his spear. Muscles straining, Roland lifted the Valkyrie over his head, twisting the spear as he did so. He slammed the creature into the ground and put all his weight behind the haft of the spear, sliding it out the back of the thing's armor into the sand, pinning it in place with his weight.

Three of Earhart's Outcasts came up and slammed their spears home into the Valkyrie, finishing it off.

Taki and one of his samurai took on one of the other Valkyries. Mac, Eagle, and Doc were facing off with the other, while everyone else intercepted the Ratnik, keeping them from the other suits. A battle of sword, spear, and other edged weapons broke out.

Taki's partner managed to jab his spear into the Valkyrie's neck but at the cost of taking a set of claws in the chest, which killed him instantly. Taki didn't waste the effort, also jamming his spear into the neck joint and twisting.

The Valkyrie's head popped off and tumbled to the ground, coming to rest in a cradle of red hair.

The Valkyrie surrounded by the Nightstalkers chose a different course of action. It rose up into the air, out of range of spears, and accelerated away.

"Follow it!" Moms ordered. "Take it alive if you can."

Mac and Eagle raced after it.

Nada was in the midst of the melee near the suits. A Russian was jabbing at him, a commando knife in each hand. Nada had his machete in one hand, the spear in the other. He dropped the spear, since the Valkyrie threat seemed over, and focused on using the machete.

As the Russian made a vicious attack, both blades flashing, Nada took a step back, bumping into the pirate who was using his cutlass against another assailant. Without saying a word, Nada and the pirate both pivoted, reversing positions and attack angles. Nada severed the new Russian's hand, and then, as the man staggered back in shock, the Nightstalker finished him off by slamming his machete down into the man's neck, slashing his carotid.

As that Russian bled out, Nada turned back in time to see the pirate finish off the dual-knife-wielding attacker.

Nada took a deep breath and got oriented.

The fighting was over. Over a dozen Russian men, and two Valkyrie, had been slain. Two of Earhart's people had been killed.

"Where's Mac and Eagle?" Nada yelled to Moms.

She pointed. "Chasing a Valkyrie."

"Oh frak," Nada muttered, and then he took off in that direction, grabbing a spear, still seeing the footprints from the Nightstalkers in the distance even as the black sand slowly settled back into place. He became aware someone was next to him and glanced over. Scout was keeping pace, a spear in her hand. A few steps behind them, and gaining, was Neeley, also carrying a spear, and next to her, Sin Fen.

"Stay with the rest, Scout," Nada ordered.

"Nope."

"Frak," Nada muttered as Neeley and Sin Fen caught up. The four sprinted across the black sand, stride for stride.

Back at the Ratnik camp, Taki mercied the last two people who'd been reaped. They were beyond saving. He also finished off three Ratnik who'd been getting the parts from the reaped. The Russians were on horizontal tables further in the cavern, hooked up to machines.

Doc was standing next to those machines, mesmerized. "These are amazing! I believe they do the transplants and other operations automatically. We have robotic surgery but nothing like this. We have to—"

Moms interrupted him. "The HUB, Doc. Find the HUB."

Doc shook himself and shifted his attention. "It would help if we knew what it was."

The Ratnik camp looked very much like a rat's nest. Debris scattered all about, pilfered from ships and craft in the Space Between, but also taken from various moments in the Nightstalkers' timeline. Piles of cash and jewelry seemed pathetic given the surrounding environment. There was even a cluster of ancient Cambodian artifacts.

Hoarders of time, surrounded by their own craziness.

Eagle was standing in front of one of the bodies strapped on a table, and Moms joined him.

"The guard from the Met," Eagle said, pointing at the pile of gear at the base of the table. He reached into the pile and pulled out dog tags, slipping them into a pocket.

"Snatching bodies is how the Valkyries began their myth," Moms said. "No one knew how real the myth was and what the purpose was."

Amelia Earhart walked up, a blood smear on one cheek.

"Are you hurt?" Moms asked.

Earhart shook her head. "It's not mine. I lost some people."

"Several of mine are chasing the last Valkyrie," Moms said. "Do you know what the HUB looks like?"

"I don't even know what a HUB is," Earhart said. She sighed, looking down at the dead Ratnik member. "They were evil, but they were also tired. Tired of this existence, living off of other people."

Mac and Eagle had their spears at the ready. The Valkyrie was hovering over the shoreline, about five feet up, facing them, claws extended. There were several columns in the water behind it, but for some reason, upon reaching the waterline next to the Spanish galleon, it had halted and turned.

Both men glanced over their shoulders at the sound of others approaching and were relieved to see Nada, Neeley, Sin Fen, and Scout.

"It's just holding in place," Eagle reported.

"They fought," Nada said, "but not like Spetsnaz."

"Judging from the body we autopsied back home," Eagle said, "they're not in very good shape."

The Valkyrie was in place, slowly turning left and right about thirty degrees, enough to take all of them in. Then, surprisingly, it descended until it touched the sand.

"Ready," Nada said, lowering his spear.

With a slight hiss, the white suit split open along one side. A man stepped out of the oversized suit. At least what remained of a man, the figure seeming to be mostly bones and desiccated flesh. His camouflage uniform was mended many times over and threadbare.

He took a step onto the sand, staggered, regained his balance. "I am Major Alexie Serge, originally of Alfa of the Seventh Administratorate and then on special assignment to the Vympel Group of Duga."

"Sergeant Major Edward Moreno," Nada said, lowering his spear. "United States Army Special Forces."

"You must be Delta Force," Serge said, "to have fought so well."

Scout was staring at Nada, processing his real name. "You don't look like an Edward."

"Hush," Nada said.

"Are my men dead?" Serge asked.

"Yes."

"They did not want to take orders anymore," Serge said. "I could not blame them. We just wanted to stay alive." He recognized one of them. "Sin Fen. You have followed me."

"I told you this was over."

"You were correct. I am glad I did not allow my men to kill you as they wanted."

"It wouldn't have made any difference," Sin Fen said.

"I believe it would have to you," Serge said.

Eagle spoke up. "Did you keep Caesarion from being assassinated?"

"I have no idea of what you speak," Serge said.

"Do you have the HUB?" Scout asked.

Serge sighed. He nodded toward the galleon. "It's in there. We took it because the Patrol was after us. We thought we could stop them. Their machine is better than ours was, but that was back in 1986. I'm sure improvements have been made."

"You were the Soviet Time Patrol," Nada said, not a question. He gestured, and Mac and Eagle went over to the galleon and began climbing a long ramp set against the side.

"Yes." Serge began coughing and he covered his mouth with his hand. When he pulled it away, it was stained with bright red blood. "It is almost over for me."

"What happened at Chernobyl?" Nada asked.

Serge wearily shook his head. "Too long of a story." He coughed again, with the same result. "We were trapped here, and it took us a very long time before we found your Patrol and managed to get its, what do you call it, hube?"

"HUB."

"We called ours by a different name. It was destroyed on our last mission."

Nada glanced to the side. Eagle and Mac were carrying something down the plank. It was an obsidian, three-foot-high, triangular column. They placed it down on the sand.

"How does it work?" Nada asked.

"I didn't know where to go," Serge said, ignoring the question and indicating the columns behind him. "I am exhausted. Down to my very bones. I have never known such weariness." He cocked his head. "They're coming. I thought you were them, but you're not."

"Who is coming?" Nada asked.

"The Patrol." Serge coughed, so deeply and hard, he bent over double, and then he went to his knees.

"Eagle, Mac," Nada ordered. "Keep an—"

He halted as the smoothness of the water was disturbed and a vessel broke the surface. It looked like a plane with stubby wings. The front part was curved, but solid, no glass for a cockpit.

Neeley went to Serge's side, checking his condition as Nada focused on the incoming craft, Scout at his side and Eagle and Mac behind him. The craft hit the sand about ten feet from shore with a grating sound.

All remained still for a moment, and then a hatch on top was thrown open. A man appeared, hoisting himself out and onto the top of the vessel. "Sin Fen!" He was of medium height, with thick black hair sprinkled with gray. He had a stubble of beard, mostly white, that appeared more from lack of time to shave rather than a look.

"Dane," Sin Fen called out. "You are a bit late."

"I'm never late," Dane said with a slight smile. He climbed down off the front of the craft and splashed down into knee-deep water. He walked up onto the sand. He glanced at the Russian. "They went too far."

"They almost caused a lot of trouble," Sin Fen said.

Dane nodded. "We've had problems in other timelines. I couldn't spare any resources until now."

He looked over the group. "This is it?" he asked Sin Fen.

"There are others at the Ratnik camp. Along with Amelia's Outcasts. They should be along shortly."

Nada stepped forward. "I'm the team sergeant for the Night-stalkers. Nada."

"Yes. The Nightstalkers." The man offered his hand. "Eric Dane. Formerly of Recon Team Kansas, MACV-SOG, a long time ago. Well, a long time ago for you." He was referring to the Military Assistance Command Vietnam–Studies and Observations Group, a rather innocuous name for an elite counter-insurgency group of Special Forces during the Vietnam War.

"But now," Dane said, "I'm the Administrator."

"Of what?" Nada asked.

Dane nodded. "That's a good question."

"Where's the Patrol?" Nada asked. "We have an emergency that"—he looked at his watch, and then remembered it wasn't working—"that time is running out on."

Dane held up a hand. "Relax. Time is different in here than back in your timeline. You're talking about the Caesarion anomaly?"

"Yes," Scout said.

Dane looked at her and his focus zeroed in, ignoring the others. "You have the sight."

"Everyone keeps telling me that," Scout said, "but no one has told me what it means."

"You're young," Dane said, "yet you are with these people." He indicated the members of the Nightstalkers and Neeley. "Why did they choose you?"

"Because I knew my way around a gated community?" Scout said with much less than certainty, going back to her first encounter with the Nightstalkers in North Carolina.

"You were in the right place and time," Dane said, "and it turned out to be more than that. Things that look like chance often aren't when you begin to see the big picture of the universe."

"What big picture?" Neeley asked.

Dane looked at her. "You have some of it too, but there is much sadness in you." He looked past as Moms arrived with Amelia Earhart and the rest of the Nightstalkers and Outcasts.

"Amelia," Dane said, holding up a hand in greeting.

"Dane." Amelia Earhart walked through everyone and gave him a hug. "It's been a while."

"It has." He looked around. "So these are the Nightstalkers?"

"We lost a man," Moms said. "Back in our timeline."

"I wouldn't be so sure of that," Dane said. "This is"—he paused, searching for the right words—"the moment of choices before we reboot."

"Reboot?" Doc asked. "What do you mean?"

Dane pointed at Serge lying in the sand, Neeley pressing a wet rag on his forehead, about the only comfort she could give. "The Ratnik were a problem, certainly. Your timeline's problem, so your timeline was allowed to solve it. Given some help," he added with a nod to Amelia Earhart.

"Doc," Moms said, pointing at Serge. Doc headed over to do what he could. Taki was twitching, looking like he was ready to take Serge's head off.

"Who are you?" Moms demanded.

"I'm the Administrator of the Time Patrol," Dane said. "I'm not from your timeline, although there is, or was, an Eric Dane in your time. He might have died in Vietnam. He might still be alive. I don't know and I don't want to know. He might even end up on your team, because he might have the sight like I do."

"What *is* this sight?" Scout demanded.

"It is what it is," Dane said. "I can't explain it, but you know it when you have it, and you can see it in others. To see beyond what is right in front of you." He tapped the side of his head. "The mind is so much more than what we have used. Even your scientists will tell you that. Those with the sight simply use more of what is already there."

"Right," Scout said, but without doubt or sarcasm for once.

"Regardless," Dane said, "we have come to the moment of choices. For each of you."

"We're on the clock," Moms said. "Your Patrol needs to fix a problem in our past. There are only a couple of hours before this ripple turns into a shift or whatever the frak you people call it."

Dane smiled again, but it was a tired one. "Edith? She's a great actress. Plus there is the memory block. You know that works the other way? It can impart information. Information, mind you, is not intelligence. Big difference. But to ease your minds, the Caesarion anomaly isn't a real problem. It was part of the test."

While the team absorbed this news, Earhart stepped forward. "I'm sorry. But I need to get back to my camp with my people. We've taken what we can from the Ratnik base. There will be others, scavengers, coming. It's best if we're not around when they get here."

Dane nodded. "Once more, thank you, Amelia."

She walked up to him and gave him a hug. "One day we'll all be free of this."

"That is the goal," Dane said, but they could all tell he wasn't putting much faith in his words.

Earhart said farewell to the rest of the Nightstalkers, and then headed off with the rest of the Outcasts, disappearing over a dune.

"This is just weird," Ivar said, a bit too loud.

"It is," Dane agreed. "But your timeline invited this when it began to punch holes in the space-time continuum. Of course, you'd already had visitors from other timelines over the millennia via the naturally occurring gates. Places like the Bermuda Triangle. By the way, is Foreman still alive?"

"He is," Nada said.

"Good. We need the funding he gets us for the Patrol." Dane continued. "Your Ratnik were the first to abuse the capability. They had to be eliminated."

"So you used us," Nada said.

"Tested you is more like it," Dane said. "You've been tested before, haven't you? Various training courses. Colonel Orlando and his little plays. And you've all passed thus far, in order to become Nightstalkers. This is just another step along the way."

"A test?" Nada stepped forward. "People have died. The guard for the Patrol was killed."

Dane shook his head. "All that was real. Foreman just saw an opportunity and took it. You'll understand shortly. The clock will start over after you reboot."

"What do you mean 'reboot'?" Doc demanded.

"You'll see," Dane said.

"So where is *our* part of the Patrol?" Moms asked.

Dane frowned. "You wouldn't understand. Let's just say they're not available right now."

"Try us," Doc said.

"No, really," Dane said. "It's not worth the time to try to explain that. The Patrol is multiversal. We work in a number of timelines, but never allow members to cross timelines. That is where danger begins. The analogy I can come up with is we're like the United Nations of timelines. We try to help each timeline preserve its integrity."

"The UN doesn't do that great a job," Roland said.

"True," Dane said. "Because most countries put themselves first, and it is underfunded, undermanned, and not a priority. Unfortunately, the same is true of the Patrol. Some timelines fully support us. Others, not so much. With others, like yours, we have to act in secrecy. Your Mister Foreman gets us the funding for your timeline, and it is rather inadequate, but we make do. And that's where you Nightstalkers come in. We need agents from your present to help the agents already in place in your past."

Moms stepped forward, in front of her team. "What now?"

Dane walked over to the HUB. "This is when each of you gets to make a choice." He gestured. "Sin Fen?"

IN THE MOMENT OF CHOICES

"In the course of a timeline," Sin Fen said, standing behind the HUB, "there are billions and billions of lives. It is not a bad thing to say that, for history, and the overall timeline, few of those individual lives make an impact. That's not to say in their personal lives, for their family, their friends, even their enemies, all those people aren't important. But if any of those people ceased to exist, blinked out of existence, the course of history would not change."

"What about their descendants?" Eagle asked.

"Even then," Sin Fen said, "it is almost always the same."

"So we don't matter?" Scout asked.

"It is not a value judgment or a weighing of your life in itself," Sin Fen said. "I am simply speaking of the larger picture. And remember, the scales of that are balanced. An impactful life can as easily be negative as positive. Sometimes both."

"I got a headache," Roland said.

"Even those who seem to make a large difference by a specific action," Sin Fen continued, "say, John Wilkes Booth shooting Lincoln, are usually not important, because if Booth disappeared or were stopped, someone else could easily take his place and produce the same result." It sounded as if she were talking about something that had actually happened, not theory.

"Why are you telling us this?" Moms asked.

"Because each of you has to make a choice," Sin Fen said. "As Dane has said, it is the moment of choices. You make it now, before you go back to your timeline."

Dane spoke up. "What is needed to be a member of the Time Patrol is that you are a person who will never, ever, use the HUB and go back and change something for personal reasons. Every one of us has something in our past, some point, where we wish we had chosen differently. Many points probably. But you can't ever use time travel for personal reasons." He stepped back to let Sin Fen continue.

"Because of that, each of you will make a decision now to take one of three paths.

"One is to do nothing, to walk away, go back to being a Nightstalker. Frasier will wipe your memory of this once you get back to New York. Your life will go on as if none of this ever happened.

"Two is to see the key moment in your past and go back and change that moment."

"How do you know these key moments?" Nada asked.

"I know," Sin Fen simply said. "If you believe I'm wrong once I show you, please tell me."

It was obvious she was quite confident no one would tell her she was wrong.

Sin Fen continued. "If you choose to go back, and it doesn't affect the timeline, and it most likely won't, you *will* be allowed to go back. But that will be the end of you as a Nightstalker, as a member of the Patrol, as a member of this timeline. And if you begin to interfere in the point you go back to by knowing the future, you will receive a visit from one of Hannah's, or Nero's, operatives at that time and be Sanctioned."

Doc spoke up. "Won't we run into ourselves if we go back?"

"You supplant your old self if you travel back," Sin Fen said.

"What?" Roland asked.

"It won't screw things up," Mac said.

"Okay," Roland said, but he sounded, as he often did, confused.

Sin Fen continued. "Three is to know your past and accept it. Fully. Completely. Accept who you are now, where you are now. All that has happened to shape you into who you are. And choose to be part of the Time Patrol."

She paused and looked over the group. "Do you understand?" Everyone nodded.

"Then let me give you each your choice," Sin Fen said. "I ask that you give us some space." The Nightstalkers, with Neeley, backed up about forty feet.

"This is frakked," Mac said.

"It makes sense," Doc said. He gestured toward Serge. "He's not going to last a few more minutes."

"Guess he made his choice," Mac said.

"Wonder what my moment is?" Scout said.

Moms and Nada didn't say anything, which was as significant as if they had. Eagle looked thoughtful, and Neeley looked tired. Roland. Was Roland.

Sin Fen called out. "Eagle. Come here, please."

Eagle left the team behind and went over to Sin Fen.

"I thought it was tough when Ms. Jones asked if I wanted to be a Nightstalker," Mac said. "I never thought something like this would come up."

"What do you think your choice is gonna be?" Roland asked him.

Mac's face tightened. "I know the moment."

"And?" Roland asked.

"Sometimes you talk too much," Mac said.

"Easy," Moms said, putting a hand on Mac's shoulder. "This is hard on everyone. Let's not speculate, people," she said in a louder voice. "And make your choice freely and without reservation. No one will think anything different of you regardless of which path you take. You have all served honorably as Nightstalkers. That was all that was ever asked of you. I want—" She paused as the HUB projected a gate about ten feet in front of it. Without a word, Eagle walked into the gate and disappeared.

"Mac," Sin Fen called out.

—

"The night your brother died," Sin Fen said without preamble.

Mac nodded. "I figured as much. But you know, I might save his life, but it wouldn't change anything else. And I'm guessing, since you're giving me this choice, that his life didn't amount to a hill of beans one way or the other. Nor mine. But at least I've contributed to something bigger than me. With the Nightstalkers."

"Your parents would treat you differently," Sin Fen said.

Mac laughed. "Listen, lady. I am what I am. You know what this whole clusterfrak has shown me? To be what I am. I've hidden it. Tried to bury it in the Army. Volunteering for every dumb and dangerous assignment out there. Prove my manhood. Chasing skirts. Well, I'm a man. And I'm going to volunteer for this dumb and dangerous assignment too. But I'm going into it being what I am openly."

Sin Fen spread her hands in acceptance. "You've made your choice."

Mac walked into the gate.

"Doc!"

***

"Geez," Scout said as they heard Doc cry out. "Did she tell him he didn't get all his PhDs?"

Her attempt at humor fell flat and she knew it, but everyone was antsy. This wasn't playing out the way any of them expected. Saving the world had devolved into something so much more personal. It wasn't the way a Nightstalker mission usually went.

And then Doc was gone, through the gate.

"Neeley."

"Good luck," Roland said. "I—" He ran out of words, after three, which wasn't unusual.

Neeley walked over to the big man and shocked everyone by leaning in, looking up, and grabbing his head. She pulled it down and gave him a kiss. It was a surprisingly tender gesture and then it was over as she headed to Sin Fen and her choice.

***

"Anthony Gant," Sin Fen said.

"I couldn't save him even if I went back," Neeley said. "Cancer got him. Ate him down to nothing. Can't do anything about it."

"Ah," Sin Fen said. "That is what you saw and that is what he wanted you to believe. But how do you know his cancer wasn't treatable? Did you ever go to a doctor with him?"

Neeley opened her mouth to respond, but then realized the impact of those words. She'd just accepted Gant's prognosis. Terminal. No treatment possible.

"He lied to me?"

"He covered for you to the end of his life," Sin Fen said.

"And if I go back?" Neeley asked. "Is his cancer treatable? Will he live?"

"That I can't tell you."

Neeley hung her head and thought. Hard. Then she looked up at the other woman. "He didn't die in combat, which is what he would have wanted."

"He died in your arms," Sin Fen said. "Isn't that what he truly wanted?"

Neeley swallowed hard. "All right. I've made my choice."

Neeley disappeared into the gate.

"Roland."

The big man walked across the sand. "I'll go where she went," he said, before Sin Fen could even give him a choice.

Sin Fen stared at him. "You've never questioned your past, have you?"

"Nope."

"Do you worry about your future?"

"I didn't," Roland said. "But now, maybe."

Sin Fen smiled. "Go. To where she went."

And then Roland was gone.

"Scout."

Moms and Nada were the only ones left as Sin Fen talked to Scout.

"What the frak does she have to feel bad about?" Nada muttered, gesturing at Scout.

"What makes you so sure it's something you feel bad about?" Moms asked.

"Would you change something good?" Nada asked.

Moms had no answer to that.

Scout walked toward the gate, waved at both of them, and then was gone.

"Moms."

"The note," Sin Fen said.

"What note?" Moms was confused. "I thought this would be about the man. The man my mother was supposed to marry."

"It is," Sin Fen said, "but only tangentially."

"What note?" Moms repeated.

"The one your mother left when she hung herself."

"How do you know all this?" Moms demanded, buying time.

Sin Fen touched the HUB. "We can time travel. We can see. This is why you have to make a decision now. A decision you will take with you the rest of your life."

"What was on the note?"

"First," Sin Fen said, "you need to understand that the man who was engaged to your mother left because he read the note. He left because he hadn't protected her and he believed there was nothing more he could do. And he was angry. He lived with that guilt the rest of his life. Guilt is a terrible, terrible thing to live with. It was so powerful, it led him to actions that actually saved a lot of his soldiers' lives in Iraq. He died, but many lived. And he left you his allotment from guilt."

"So I don't change that," Moms said. "I don't make him stay and marry her?"

"That's not the choice," Sin Fen said. "The note."

"Tell me what was on the note."

Nada was alone, except for Dane, who was standing by the water, watching it all play out.

"This was all a test?" Nada asked.

Dane sighed. "Mostly. Joining the Time Patrol would be a bit overwhelming if someone just sat across a desk from you and tried to explain it. And you still really have no idea what it entails. This is just a taste of what's going on."

Nada nodded. "Scout's a good person."

"She has the sight," Dane said.

"I don't care about the frakking sight," Nada said. "She's a good person. That's pretty rare in my experience. Remember that."

And then Nada was summoned as Moms disappeared. He walked across the sand, each step heavier than the next.

"My wife and daughter," Nada said. "Can I save them?"

"Yes. But it will be painful for you to remember it all."

He ignored that warning. "What about the team?" Nada asked. "Scout?"

"You've already lived that," Sin Fen said. "And so have they. They'll be fine. You'll be gone from this moment forward to them." She reached forward and touched his forehead. The memories came in a torrent. Of pain.

Nada cried out, went to his knees, head bowed. He remained like that for almost a minute. Then he got to his feet.

"I'll go back."

"Good." Sin Fen nodded. "Because you are the one who reboots all of this."

IN THE TIME BETWEEN: 28 JUNE 2005

Nada found Carl Coyne behind the ammunition bunker. The SEAL was leaning back against the bulkhead, eyes tightly closed, lips moving either in prayer or silent exhortation. Nada paused for a second, staring at the man, recognizing the paralysis that overcame men, even the best, but more often with the worst, when faced with the prospect of combat.

Nada grabbed Coyne's combat vest, startling the man. "They need every man they can get on the rescue bird!"

"Who the—" Coyne began, but Nada wasn't listening, literally pulling the SEAL around the shipping container toward the landing strip. Blades were turning and two Apache gunships, two Black Hawks, and two Special Operations Chinooks were powering up.

Nada had no sympathy for Coyne as he pulled him toward one of the Chinooks, checking the tail number to make sure he got the right one. It wasn't like this was an immediate response and Coyne hadn't had a chance to consider it. After getting a report about the four-man recon team getting attacked, it had taken precious hours to receive permission from higher head-quarters for a rescue force to be launched. Coyne had had plenty of time to get over his paralysis.

He'd made a decision not to go.

Which Nada knew from the future.

A possible future.

As they got closer to the rear ramp of the helicopter, swirling dirt and debris filled the air. Coyne shrugged off Nada's hand, straightening up and moving forward. He ran up the ramp, Nada right behind. Coyne's fellow SEALs welcomed him on board.

They ignored Nada.

Which was what he counted on.

Nada's uniform was unmarked, but his gear was top of the line, and he'd configured it exactly the way he remembered from his time in Afghanistan with an elite unit that had no designation. They'd worked directly for the in-country commander and carried out the dirty missions for which no trace could be left behind. The SEALs had seen his like before and ignoring was as much policy as reality. People like Nada went where they wanted and did whatever it is they did. No one got in their way.

The SEALs were simply glad to have an extra weapon on board.

The Chinook lifted. Nada settled onto the red web seats along the port side of the cargo bay. Manned by the correctly designated Nightstalkers of Task Force 160, the Army's elite helicopter unit, the chopper banked hard and headed toward the last known location of the four-man SEAL team.

Nada reached into a pocket and pulled out a worn photograph, unfolding it carefully along the crease to maintain its integrity.

He smiled grimly: There was no need to worry about that.

He stared at the images of his wife and daughter, posed in front of *The Mad Hatter's Tea Party*, feeling them in his heart. Joy blossomed because they were images of people who were living, not long dead. He'd kept them in his heart so long, buried so deep, the feeling caused him to sit back against the bulkhead of the chopper gasping for breath.

As he got his breathing under control, he looked across the cargo bay.

Coyne was sitting there, staring at him.

Nada met Coyne's eyes and nodded, giving him the thumbs-up. Coyne had a puzzled look on his face, then the SEAL also nodded and returned the thumbs-up.

Everything's going to be all right now, Nada thought.

He tried to do that math: How old was Scout now in 2005? Was she living in the gated community in North Carolina?

One of the crew members was shouting something, a time warning to the objective. The SEALs were locking and loading their weapons, pulses quickening. Fast ropes were readied near the ramp in case they were needed for a quick exit.

Nada did nothing except hold the picture.

Everything's going to be all right now.

A Navy Lieutenant Commander, the man in charge of the SEAL element, staggered down the cargo bay and leaned over Nada, yelling to be heard over the double turbine engines above their heads and the roar coming in the open ramp in the rear. "My men go in first. I don't know why you're here, but stay out of our way. We're getting our people out."

Nada nodded. "Roger that," he yelled.

The LCDR looked at him oddly for a moment, and then headed for the ramp, to be the first off.

A good leader.

Nada twisted in his seat and looked out the small round window. They were flying low, up a valley, high ground on either side.

Nada saw the puff of smoke from the backblast of an RPG—rocket-propelled grenade—firing on the hillside.

Everything is just right.

Nada tracked the rocket as it sped toward the chopper and then disappeared above. There was the roar of explosion, the shudder of the aircraft. Pieces of shrapnel from both the grenade and the destroyed turbine engine ripped through the cargo bay. Wounded men screamed, others were shouting commands.

Everything is just right.

Nada was an island of calm amidst turmoil as the helicopter dropped like a stone without engine power, the blades ripping off from the sudden stoppage.

Nada saw Carl Coyne cross the bay. Nada smiled at him.

The ground came rushing up.

Everything is just right.

WHEN IT CHANGED BACK

The Keep was sweating, beads collecting on her forehead, rolling down her face.

"How much time?" Foreman asked.

"Two minutes," the Keep answered.

"You can turn it off," Hannah said.

"We have to contain—" the Keep began, but then the gate snapped out of existence, leaving the HUB sitting in its place on the top of the ramp.

"I'd turn the bomb off, if I were you," Foreman said.

"Where are the people?" Hannah asked. "Neeley? The Night-stalkers?"

"They've rebooted," Foreman said. "I hope."

—————

When it changed back, Mac hung from the wall of the mineshaft by one hand. "Where the frak is Kirk? They said we'd reboot!"

Eagle looked up. "It doesn't work that way."

"Frak that!" Mac said. He leapt off the wall and grabbed the rope, sliding down as fast as he could. "She told me Kirk would be okay."

"She told me that too," Eagle said. He put a hand on Mac's shoulder. "Let's go. We take care of our own."

When it changed back, Doc and Ivar were in the massive Archives at Area 51 arguing, which wasn't unusual. Doc was sitting on the bottom stair of the large rolling steps and Ivar was in front of him, pacing back and forth on the concrete floor.

A box was on the floor, one they'd just managed to find, buried deep on a top row, shoved well to the rear.

They didn't understand how they'd found it, but they accepted it was part of things changing back. They'd begun going through the material and immediately launched into an argument over what they were reading: Odessa's last notes.

"Everything is the same, but it isn't the same," Doc said. "Things must be self-consistent in the universe. There are rules to physics."

"I know there are," Ivar said. "But there are rules we haven't even begun to realize exist. Conservation of mass and energy might not be what we think it is. We've rebooted, so where is Kirk?"

"If a single person represents a measure of order in the universe," Doc said, "then there has to be some sort of balance. If Kirk is gone, something must be taking his place. We've seen some weird stuff, but there are rules!"

"Not the time to go into higher theory," Ivar said.

"There have to be rules to this," Doc insisted.

Ivar laughed. He was a long way from the university.

"You know, of course, it's entirely possible that twenty penguins all farted at the same time and that brought the universe into existence and time travel along with it."

"Why can't you take anything seriously?" Doc demanded.

"I can," Ivar said. "But my question again to you, oh genius, is where is Kirk if we rebooted? That means he didn't die, right? So where is he?"

Doc's phone rang. He answered, listened, and then put it away. "Let's go. Eagle has the same question, and he thinks he knows the answer."

When it changed back, Moms was driving down a two-lane road in Kansas with the faded yellow lines and raggedy asphalt that's a testament to a road way less traveled and even more forgotten. If a road could be homeless and pushing a grocery cart full of worthless, tattered treasures, it would be this road. She'd been on it so many times, from trips in the bed of a pickup to a schoolbus to her last visit, that she remembered every pathetic inch.

Moms could see to the horizon in all directions and wondered, not for the first time, how any place could be so flat; and more importantly, why anyone would have stopped here on their way across the country to put down roots. Had they come from some place east that was worse? Had they not heard of the sunshine and beauty of California, which lay ahead?

Seriously.

The dark circle of a gopher hole to the right stuck out as much as one of those flailing balloon men in front of car dealerships because it shattered the monotony. As she drove on, she thought of all the places she'd been in this part of her life. The mountains of Afghanistan. The deserts of the Middle East. The high plains of South America along with its lower jungles. The cities of Europe. The job, however, had always been similar. She wondered what it said about her to come from this flat land, this place which is such a nothing. Nothing to see, nothing to amaze, and certainly nothing to inspire.

She paused at the battered mailbox, the victim of too many bored boys swinging a bat at the only thing vertical near the road. The numbers had been faded in her childhood, and now they were gone. As she started up the long drive, her tires crunched on the remnants of gravel and her stomach lurched. "Car Wheels on a Gravel Road" was a poignant song to Moms. Nada might have his Zevon, but she had her Lucinda Williams. But it didn't grab her heart. It gave her a dull ache in her forehead, a reminder of how your head can get so sad and lonely that a sound can make your hair feel like crying.

The house was in view. People round here said it was on a hill. "You live in that house on the hill," they would say. Now, she wondered what could be under that house to raise it the mere couple of feet so that anyone in Kansas would happily call it a hill.

A door to hell, perhaps?

Moms had just been through a gate that was close to that, where monsters, and men worse than monsters, abided. But this place wasn't even high enough for a gate, or a Rift, and Moms found some dark humor in that as she stopped the car.

She didn't get out. Not yet.

Moms knew what was beneath it. A root cellar with a dirt floor and wood beams and rotting ropes to hold the bags of onions, and whatever else was grown during the nauseating hot summer, to tide them through the brutal cold of winter. Everything here was extremes.

Moms got out of the car, but she didn't start for the house. Not yet.

Everywhere else a bag of onions is a bag of onions, but under this house it was a ghost in burlap creaking as the drafts blew through the gaps in the crumbling rock and mortar foundation. Everything about this was a nightmare when she left, and not one thing had improved in the decades since. The paint that was once peeling was now completely stripped. The porch where no one had ever drunk iced tea and rocked and tried to make small talk about the weather was half collapsed, taking part of the overhang with it.

But the half-finished wooden dollhouse was still there.

All Moms's life it was an old, neglected house that reflected the small and neglected family that it housed.

Moms was startled to realize she'd never called it home. It was never a home. She felt tears on her cheeks, sliding down. Because if you can't say *home* then you never had one. She'd run away so fast and so far, she'd forgotten that. But standing in the drive, feeling the heat coming off the car engine, she began to remember.

Moms walked around and hit the little button. The trunk popped open.

She retrieved the shovel and one of the jugs of water and ignored the other contents. She walked to the porch, and then did an about-face. Army training. She paced off twenty steps and began to dig.

She dug for hours, stopping only to drink some water or pour it over her head. Before long she had to get another jug. But she was prepared; Nada had taught her well. As she got the next jug, she looked into the well-stocked trunk and thought of how much more she brought back with her now than she'd taken with her when she left.

She hadn't brought gloves. She'd known Nada would have chided her for not purchasing a pair when she got the shovel. Her hands were calloused from her work, but the incessant shoveling began to dig through the rough skin, tearing through and bringing forth first blisters, then blood.

Moms relished the pain.

She kept digging, arcing the cleared space around to the side of the house. She paused for a moment to wipe blood off her hands and the shovel handle, and noted the broken glass in the window that was over the sink in the kitchen. The room where her mother spent all of Moms's life sitting there in the same old kitchen chair, hair lank and gray far too early, her face weathered by alcohol and cigarettes, and carved into permanent creases of brittle disappointment.

Moms resumed shoveling, a mindless activity that allowed her mind to roam. Every day she'd come home from school and the only things that had moved were the pile of cigarette butts and the cracked teacup that had once been part of a glittering tea service for someone else. The cup, like the woman who held it, had long ago slipped down the ladder of life and found itself here, alone and bruised and lacking even its saucer. Her mother had been empty for all of Moms's childhood.

Once a teacher had been kind and told Moms that when her mother was a senior in the same high school, she was the prettiest girl in her class. Always dancing and always smiling.

Moms kept digging until she turned the corner, out of the gaze of the empty socket of the window into the kitchen. She felt a bit better. But then she remembered she'd felt bad hearing her teacher's words, such a contrast to what she knew of her mother. Now it made her almost happy to know there had once been a girl inside the faded housedress and cuffed loafers.

Her mother had always worn the loafers. They'd made a clicking sound when she did move, and Moms had liked that—the fact that she never snuck up on anyone.

Moms kept digging until it was too dark to see. Nada would have told her to bring night vision goggles, but then Nada had had his own issues with memories and how to deal with them.

Moms didn't want to sleep in the car, so she threw a poncho liner on the ground and lay on it. She stared up at the moon, feeling the pain radiating from her hands, up her arms, and numbly into her brain. She remembered the creaking bags of onions, the sound etched into her brain so deep, she doubted Frasier and his machine could extricate it.

Because one day it wasn't the onions.

Her brothers never checked back. They left and never looked back; Moms supposed men could do that. But even on the other side of the world, Moms would check in once in a while. And then one day at Area 51, she'd called and there was no answer and she knew, she just knew it was bad.

She'd come back. That day the stale butt pile hadn't grown. The teacup rested on the table, but the chair was gone. The root cellar door was open, amplifying the sound of the creaking rope, but even then, Moms had immediately known it was too loud, the house too still.

She knew everything before she took the first step down into the cellar. And she stopped when she saw the loafers turning idly in the air, one half off, the other determinedly in place. She saw the piece of paper on the dirt floor and forced herself to walk back out without seeing too much or taking the note.

She'd violated a Nada Yada before she even knew what they were.

She didn't look up.

She didn't want to see.

Moms had called the police, because this had to be done right. Let them take the note, cut the body down.

She didn't want to know, because the note could be about her.

Who knew?

Some of the others might have wanted to change some one thing in their lives, something in their past. This she understood, especially Nada's choice. But Moms had finally understood that nothing needed changing for her.

Nothing changed in her past would make her now better.

But now she was fixing something for the future.

She was the result of this and there was a reason for it; she'd suspected it, but now she was certain of it.

She began digging before the sun came up and didn't finish the circle until nearly dark. She didn't stop to admire her handiwork. She went to the car and dragged out the heavy body of Mr. Calloway. He'd gone to school with her mother, and he used to be a deputy. He'd been the one who'd responded first, and she hadn't picked up a clue in her grief. She'd remembered him, too old for a deputy to ever make sheriff.

How Sin Fen knew what was on the note, Moms had no idea. When she'd finally asked about it, she'd been told it had been lost in the sheriff's files, destroyed in a flood.

But now she knew the real story.

Moms only had to break two of Calloway's fingers before he

told her what he'd done to her mother when she was the prettiest, happiest girl in her senior class. Moms didn't believe in torture, not really, but she had to know. And she found out there were more, one as recent as six months ago. So she'd simply broken his neck.

Now she dragged him down the stairs and into the root cellar and rolled him into the hole she'd dug under that one rope. She buried him quickly, finally feeling anxious to be done with all this. She went back outside and examined her work in progress: the cleared trench around the house, the man under the house, and finally something under that hill of significance. And the house itself.

It was her house now and she could do with it as she chose.

She took the wedding album with the cut-out pictures and postcards and placed it in the half-assembled dollhouse.

Then she spread the accelerant Mac had taught her how to make in one of his arcane classes about destruction.

Mac had done a good job because the house was consumed quickly. The cleared trench kept the fire from spreading to the dry grass. Moms was killing the house, but she had no intention of hurting anything but the man who'd crushed her mother and the house that was never a home because of that.

Moms was three miles down the highway before she heard the first siren.

She didn't look back. She steered with one hand. In the other she held a teacup covered in tiny painted roses.

It was enough.

When it changed back, Roland was driving a pickup truck while Neeley was in the passenger seat. Roland was totally focused on the here and now, negotiating the dirt trail in the Green Mountains, because Roland was a man who could live and flourish in the here and now.

That's a rare, and valuable, trait.

One Neeley was beginning to truly understand. She wasn't focused on the road or Roland's driving. She was focused on him at the moment. She'd decided a little while ago that the biggest difference between Roland and Gant was that Roland talked when Gant would have known to be quiet. Roland was rambling on right now about having done some Winter Warfare training years ago in the Green Mountains, and whether she responded or not didn't seem to matter to him.

The drive to the closest town, South Lincoln, had started bringing back huge swaths of memory, and she wanted to be still with them and the emotions that came from remembering each tree and rock and turn. They'd left the paved road behind and the memories had grown stronger along the overgrown dirt trail up the west side of Mount Ellen, as she recalled all the times she and Gant had made this drive down to town for supplies, or to go further, on a mission, and then returned.

She'd been short one return, which she was now making.

As they got closer to where the cabin was, or should be—she reminded herself, she felt a deep pain from the last time on this road, when she'd driven away after she buried Gant, promising herself never to return. Either in fact or in memory. But now she was doing both, and Roland wouldn't shut the hell up! Not only was he talking, he was asking her questions.

"I learned to ski in the Army," Roland was reminiscing. "I

still don't like it. It's cold. Can you ski? Maybe we can go skiing sometime."

And then she suddenly realized he was talking because he was nervous. Roland had barely said three words before the Sanction on Whidbey Island. He hadn't been nervous lying in wait to kill someone, but traveling back into her past with Gant, he was nervous and that made her smile, to think her own past could make this big man nervous and chatty.

Roland was the first man since Gant she could close both eyes with. She felt safe with him. Not just physically safe, although Roland was as fierce a protection as one could get in human form.

Neeley had been alert for years, and she was exhausted. The closer they got to the cabin, the more she feared it would be gone, and then there would be no way to orient herself or know where Gant's body lay, all alone, in these acres of meadows and wild flowers gently blowing in the mid-morning breeze.

She'd often thought of him over the years, lying in the cold, cold earth, all alone, with no one coming to visit. It would strike at the oddest times, spurred by the strangest things.

As they went higher up the mountain, Neeley thought what a sacrilege it would be to forget where the grave was that Gant had dug himself, once he knew his time was coming to an end. At the time, she'd felt nothing but his courage and remarkable loving strength that he'd saved her the task. Not because it would have been too much physically—she was stronger than him by then—but he'd sensed how much pain each shovelful of dirt would have caused her.

It had been hard enough to put him in the hole, fill it in, and then leave—leaving him behind forever because she could have never managed coming back to this place where joy and love had twisted into loss and grief. So much so that so many years later, she could feel as though no time had passed at all.

And to come back with someone else, another man, that had never occurred to her as a possibility. Neeley had kept herself very busy for so long, working for Hannah and the Cellar, and shoving all that pain into a deep pit where healing couldn't reach, trying to keep it forgotten but occasionally remembering, with the pain so fresh and raw and savage that she feared it would rip her apart.

She'd forgotten Gant because she had to. She'd forgotten all of this place and all of the memories and just started living a different life. She must have done a good job, she knew, because someone like Frasier had never shown up to wipe away her memories of Gant, like they had wiped poor Nada's wife and child away into the darkness.

That didn't mean she was psychologically healthy, Neeley knew. Doctor Golden was like a puppy on a leash these last years, begging Hannah to get a crack at Neeley's damaged psyche. What Golden didn't understand, though, was that Neeley had been damaged goods long before Gant.

Without thinking, Neeley reached for Roland's hand and he let go of the steering wheel, wrapping hers in his big paw.

"We should be here," he said, with a glance at the GPS. "I don't see anything."

"Stop," Neeley said. She looked all around. "It's gone," she whispered and began to cry. She looked around the huge meadow with a franticness that she had never felt before. There were native wildflowers blooming everywhere and she couldn't spot anything to give her a bearing on where the cabin had been.

"Nero," she finally said with a deep bitterness. "He sent his man Bailey here. I knew he would. He burned it down." She fumbled with the door and stumbled out of the truck. Roland hopped out in a hurry, scurrying, as best a man that big could scurry, around the front of the truck to join her.

Neeley walked forward, trying to remember, looking up at the top of the mountain, remembering the mornings watching the sun come over it, lying in Gant's arms. "It was near here."

Roland was at her side, pointing. "There. Rocks. Probably the chimney."

Neeley walked over, Roland hovering at her side.

He was right. The crumbling remains of the stone chimney marked the cabin's site. Pieces of charred wood were buried underneath the plant life that had grown over the site.

Roland tried to hug her, but she shoved him away. "You don't understand! No one is truly dead until no one remembers their name."

Roland reached out and gently took her face between his two calloused hands, tilting her head so she looked into his eyes. "You remember his name. And now I remember his name. Gant."

"But what does it mean if I can't even remember his grave?" She pulled away and kicked through the grass. "Here somewhere. But where exactly?"

Roland turned to look over the site. "What's that?"

"What?"

"Over there." He pointed and then Neeley saw it too.

A large swatch of blue, solid blue, in the midst of an ocean of white and green and yellow and pink. A rectangle of pure blue.

Neeley began to run, and she stumbled over rocks and chunks of wood, but she didn't care, going faster and faster until she got to the blue. A perfect rectangle of low-growing beautiful blue blooms. Within that rectangle she knew she'd found him.

She fell onto her knees, and Roland caught up to her and stood right next to her.

"Wow," he whispered. "Those are really pretty."

And his words were so true.

Neeley wrapped an arm around his firm and safe thigh, resting her head against the hard muscle. He was like a rock. Her rock. And Gant *was* here because not only had he dug the hole, he'd planted his seeds in the dirt that would go above him to bloom with the warm sun every year. To make the cold, cold earth just a little bit warmer above him.

He'd known she'd come back, even though he had warned her never to.

Perhaps he had hoped she would come back. A hope he'd never been able to say.

There was something to be said for talking.

Neeley could feel the rough fabric of Roland's trousers grow damp against her face, soaked by her tears.

And he spoke, at a time Gant would have remained silent, but she realized who she was now, that she needed the words.

"This was a righteous dude," Roland said. "You were lucky to have him while you did. These flowers are nice. Do you know what they are?"

"They're forget-me-nots," she whispered. She realized he hadn't heard and said it again, pulling her face away from his pants leg. "They're called forget-me-nots."

And Roland only said, "I have to go to the truck."

And he left her there, right when she did need to be left alone. Neeley edged forward on her knees, into the center of the blue. She lay down on her back, exactly in the middle of the grave and stared up at the blue sky and remembered the good times.

When it changed back for Scout, she was dreaming, with no sound of her mother singing downstairs intruding, nor the smell of bacon. A dream so real, she could smell the grass in the cemetery. It had been freshly mown, but the stone markers would always stand in their solemn rows. In perfect, final formation.

She knew Nada would have approved.

She was aware she was asleep, but she knew she needed to stay asleep. Not to fight it like a nightmare, but to let it glide over her like the gentle breeze that caressed the shoulders of the stone markers. They were stones for departed soldiers, the dates affirming that any decade seems to require the blood and life of young men and women, as if that greased the progress of time and history, but this part of Arlington, Section 60, had its own time, the Global War on Terror.

Gathered around some of the markers were families and friends and comrades in arms.

She paused and saw a woman standing, staring at a stone. The inscription summed up a life:

CARL COYNE

OPERATION RED WINGS

28 JUNE 2005

PURPLE HEART

BRONZE STAR

US NAVY SEAL

The woman was crying and Scout wanted to tell her not to. That fate had intervened, in more ways than the woman could imagine, for the better.

But that wasn't allowed.

Scout glided past them. Near the end of one row was a girl. A pretty young girl, her hair long and twisted into a braid so thick that Scout both admired her and envied her at the same time. Scout glided toward her and halted. She didn't have to read the marker, because she finally knew the name engraved there: Edward Moreno. And now she knew the date, one most Americans had forgotten; but it was all clear to Scout what had changed for some and then changed back and not changed for everyone.

She looked at the girl and saw her father in those eyes and the way her smile tilted.

Isabella, I knew your father. He was a great soldier and man.

The girl was startled and looked about, as if the wind had disturbed her without ruffling the flowers on the grave.

Scout moved on, not wanting to intrude anymore, but she knew Nada had made a choice. He had chosen that the stone bear his name over the alternative of standing in front of a different marker bearing his daughter's name and her mother's name. And as much as Scout would miss him, she also felt a smidge of happiness that Nada had been allowed to make this choice. That he'd been allowed to remember, both the wonderful and the terrible and then choose.

She would always miss him, as would all the other Nightstalkers, but the man they missed, they did so because he was the man who would make this choice.

And then the dream faded and Scout knew it was time to face reality. It passed like the early morning fog over the river outside her house. She was in bed and her mother wasn't singing and there was no smell of bacon permeating the air.

No mother cooking for a beloved daughter. Just the thud, thud of Mother's feet meeting the rolling trail of the treadmill.

Scout lay there and listened to the rhythmic stride of her mother's surprisingly loud tread for such skinny legs and pulled the covers over her head.

And maybe she drifted off to sleep, but maybe it was the sight, because in the noise she could hear some words.

Thud, thud.

Hey, Scout.

Thud, thud.

Nada!

Thud, thud.

I'll miss you, kid.

Thud, thud.

Everything is just right.

Thud, thud.

Keep me in your heart.

And then the treadmill stopped.

Scout got up. She grabbed her deployment bag from under her bed.

She had places to be and things to do.

The four Nightstalkers from Area 51 were gathered in the treeline watching as Winthrop Carter, the man who would now never be known as Kirk, chopped firewood, his lean body leaning into every swing of the axe.

Eagle had Googled the Department of Defense database and they knew the scant details. Carter had some pockmarks on his side, shrapnel wounds from his tour in Afghanistan with the

Infantry. After getting booted out of Ranger School for cheating, he'd gotten out of the army and come back to Parthenon, Arkansas, zip code 72666.

Carter—it was hard for the Nightstalkers to think of him as that, as he would always be Kirk to them—slammed the axe home into a log and turned as a young girl called out from the door of the old house.

"That's Pads," Eagle said. "His younger sister."

"She must be important," Doc said.

"Or not," Ivar argued, "if Sin Fen allowed him to come back here to take care of her."

Carter-Kirk walked with the girl hand in hand down the rutted dirt road to a pitted single-lane asphalt road. They stood at the intersection, chatting, while the Nightstalkers watched, not quite sure why they had been drawn here.

A schoolbus came rattling down the road and Carter-Kirk gave Pads a hug. Then she got on the bus. It began to move away.

The four Nightstalkers froze as Carter-Kirk looked up, as if sensing their presence. Everything was still for a moment, and then Carter-Kirk shrugged and headed to his axe.

Cleopatra's Needle was bathed in sunlight and Edith Frobish took the extra moment to circumnavigate it, checking all four sides with more than the usual perusal. It was as it always had been.

For now, Edith thought as she turned for the Met with a bounce in her step. For now. Who knew? Some day Caesarion might just turn out to be alive and ruling in Egypt. She was pretty sure Dane had gotten that little wrinkle from some other timeline for Foreman to play.

With extra vigor, Edith shoved open the blank metal door.

"Hello, Burt. Beautiful day outside." She held up her badge, but the guard didn't even look at it.

"Hey, Edith. It sure is."

She walked down the hallway, turned right, past the CLOSED FOR CONSTRUCTION sign, and got on the elevator.

She rode down patiently.

The doors opened and Edith walked out. She came to the guard post and the heavily armed man did his checks, without a greeting or how-do-you-do. But Edith looked at him differently now, recognizing his real job. So she paused, graced him with a smile and a "Have a wonderful day," and then breezed down to the next steel door.

She stepped in and waited for that door to shut behind her. Passed the DNA test. Then opened the next door.

A spotlight was focused on the HUB.

The gate was where it should be.

And standing by it were Moms, Eagle, Mac, Roland, Ivar, Doc, and Scout.

The Nightstalkers. And now also the Time Patrol.

Edith Frobish walked across the cavern floor to the gate and joined them. She paused, as she always paused. "Are you ready?"

An unfair question, Edith knew, because they still really didn't know what they needed to be ready for.

They stepped up next to her.

And then they all stepped through.

ABOUT THE AUTHOR

Photo © 2004 Bob Mayer

Bob Mayer is a *New York Times* bestselling author, graduate of West Point, former Green Beret (including commanding an A-Team), and the feeder of two yellow labs, most famously Cool Gus. He's had over 60 books published, including three #1 series: Area 51, Atlantis, and The Green Berets. Born in the Bronx, having traveled the world (usually not tourist spots), he now lives peacefully with his wife, and said labs, at Write on the River, Tennessee.

MORE WORLDS TO EXPLORE!

If you enjoyed this world, you can check out another timeline with Dane, Sin Fen, Foreman, Amelia Earhart, the Bermuda Triangle, the Ones Before, The Others, etc., via the six-book Atlantis series where an Earth timeline confronts the Shadow as it launches an all-out assault against *their* Earth. Terry Brooks lauded this series: "Spell-binding! Will keep you on the edge of your seat. Call it techno-thriller, call it science fiction, call it just terrific story-telling."

If you're interested in Hannah and Neeley and Doctor Golden and how they became the Cellar via Nero, you can check out *Bodyguard of Lies* and *Lost Girls*.

ALSO BY BOB MAYER

32953012012821